ANOMALY

ANOMALY

TONYA KUPER

Entangled Publishing, LLC
2614 South Timberline Road
Suite 109
Fort Collins, CO 80525

Entangled Teen is an imprint of Entangled Publishing, LLC.

Visit our website at www.entangledpublishing.com.

Edited by Liz Pelletier
Cover design by Liz Pelletier
Interior design by Jeremy Howland

Print ISBN 978-1-62266-405-4
Ebook ISBN 978-1-62266-406-1

Manufactured in the United States of America

First Edition November 2014

10 9 8 7 6 5 4 3 2 1

For Chaz, my Han,
&
Nicole, my personal reality Pusher

1.

JOSIE

"**H**ey, did you hear me?" my boyfriend, Tate, asked. His chestnut hair didn't even budge in the quick breeze sifting through the school's outdoor cafeteria. It wasn't his best feature. "I'm ready to move forward in our relationship, to take it to the next level, but…I don't think you are."

My gut knotted.

This ass with his action-figure hair was breaking up with me—on my birthday! I folded my clammy hands. I'd seen public breakups, but this was my first as an active participant. I side-eyed my two friends Charles and Lauren across the table. Lauren had stopped mid-chew of her hummus-dipped carrot. Charles paused with his sandwich halfway to his open mouth.

I felt like I was wearing Princess Leia's buns at a *Star Trek* convention.

Tate shuffled his feet in front of our bench. Waiting.

Pulling in a long sigh, I took a moment to think about my response. I knew name-calling wouldn't do much good, so I settled on calling him out. "You mean I won't put out, so you're moving on to the next girl who will?" Tate's face flamed red. Did I have to say it that way? No. But come on. He was dumping me on my birthday. Total jerk move.

Tate stood, his thumbs tucked into his pockets, and his face returned to its normal tan hue. "It's not just the physical stuff. You're...different, Josie. Distant. It's for the best, for both of us."

Seriously? Wow.

"Um, friends?" he finally asked.

Friends? Um, no. His tongue had been down my throat a few nights ago, and I didn't let just anyone do that.

"Whatever, Tate."

He walked past me, and that was it. My first real relationship over. Surprisingly, I felt like I could breathe easier, because I wouldn't have that pressure of being a girlfriend anymore. But I had managed to defy the high school social ladder. At least for a few months, I, Josie Harper, had succeeded at being a science-loving, Trekkie-dork-to-the-core girlfriend to a popular guy who literally didn't know the difference between *Lord of the Rings* and *Lord of the Flies*. And *they* didn't think it could be done.

Lauren and Charles leaned toward me, both of them waiting for details. Lauren still hadn't resumed crunching. Well, I didn't have the energy to dish, so I turned away from the table. The relationship was over and it was *still* exhausting. Leave it to Tate to make this as painful as possible. I watched him stroll off like he didn't have a care in the world. No one spoke. But really, what was there to say?

"Happy birthday to you!" My best friend Hannah's soprano voice and dark curls bounced on the balmy Florida air, cutting into the awkward silence. She skipped among the tables toward me, carrying a familiar teal box.

I glanced back across the table to our usual lunch mates, who had just witnessed my humiliation. Charles and Lauren made the "cut it" motion across their throats.

"I agree with those two. Please don't," I moaned at Hannah. "It's been a crap day."

Hannah's hazel eyes scrunched up in confusion as she positioned the box in front of me. Cupcakes. I welcomed whatever sugar euphoria they could provide me, but I didn't think they would improve my mood. They were a bittersweet reminder of the day's significance.

"How is your birthday bad already? It's only noon." She sat next to me, facing the street, and I turned so both our backs were to the school. Conversations resumed among our friends behind us.

"Thank you for that keen observation, *Wesley Crusher.*" I forced my voice to lilt up with enthusiasm, but the pathetic *Star Trek* jab hung in the air.

I peeked at my phone. "The exact time of my birth was technically three minutes ago, so maybe the rest of the day will be better."

"Josie," she whispered. "Seriously. What's wrong? Is it your dad?"

Hannah and I had latched onto each other the first day of sophomore year when we were both new to Naples and Oceanside High. We hadn't let go since. We basically knew everything about each other's pasts—like, she knew I hadn't seen my dad in more than a month and that my family was fragile.

Hannah drew a breath next to me. I wasn't about to make eye contact with her—she could read me like nobody else. She'd asked what was wrong. Well, where to begin… "You want the rundown?"

She nudged me with her shoulder. "Yeah."

"Okay," I continued, despite the hollow feeling filling my stomach. "One: my dad hasn't called, and I doubt he's coming home. Nice, thanks a lot, Dad. Way to be there. Two: the lab assistant job I landed for the summer? Fell through. They left me a message during second block."

Hannah groaned. I had been looking forward to that job—I *needed* that internship. It would've been perfect for college applications, *and* to let me escape this town. Because, for the love of Khan, I needed some space. I'd been on a tight leash since the day I was born, and an acceptance to an out-of-state university was my ticket to freedom. Case in point, the National Physics Honors Award. That was a biggie—and I wasn't complaining about that. The flippin' vice president of the country—yes, it was *that* big—would be hand-delivering my award in less than a week. Heck, that alone should've nabbed me this internship. Damn it.

I side-glanced at Hannah. I didn't think she would fully support me on anything college-related. Any conversation of where we were going for school, well, Hannah was not a fan. Because of my brainy ways, there was no way we would end up at the same place.

Swallowing a lump in the back of my throat, I tried to change the subject. "And three: Tate just broke up with me."

"He *what*?" Hannah screeched and jumped up from the cement bench, whirling to face me head-on. Her cheer skirt gave the guys behind her a one-second show. "I thought things were going well. And he knew it was your birthday!" She paced in front of me, muttering and swearing. The interesting ways in which she vowed to eff up Tate's face made me smile despite the tears that continued to push at the backs of my eyes.

After a particularly colorful threat that involved Tate and "his beloved man parts," Hannah sat back down and tore into the box. She pushed a cupcake toward me. "So no boyfriend, no dad, no job. Well, look at it this way—now you have even more reason to make a wish." She ripped into a package of candles and shoved one into a cupcake frosted in the image of Sheldon Cooper. "Plus, now you're back on the market for the party tonight." She passed the cupcakes around the table. "Let's turn this birthday around!" She was a cheerleader on the field and off, an eternal optimist, sometimes annoyingly so.

Lauren whooped in agreement. Charles slid a lighter toward the box, and Hannah's enthusiasm ignited poor Sheldon's whole face.

It must have killed her to walk into Cake, Pie, and Chai café and order cupcakes decorated with the entire cast of *The Big Bang Theory*. She caught me smiling and winked.

True. Best. Friend.

"Thanks, guys."

The yellow flame flickered. Hannah whispered, "Make a wish."

My friends watched me, so I didn't want to scoff at the

silly birthday tradition. Wishes? Puh-lease. Wishes were right up there with Rudolph and Santa doing a sleigh drive-by. Or the Easter bunny delivering eggs. And no, it wasn't my statistical analysis or scientific surety that told me so. Oh, I'd made wishes. Thousands upon thousands of them. But none brought back my brother.

When Hannah had asked about my craptastic day, I hadn't brought up missing Nick. But I did miss him. I wished my brother were here with me now. With him by my side, I wouldn't feel out of place, so different.

"Josie, if you don't make that wish soon, Sheldon Cooper is going to melt like the wicked witch from Oz."

No, there was no point in "wishing." If I wanted results, I'd have to achieve them for myself.

I wish for…choice.

Choice was attainable. Well, maybe. With all the rules and restrictions from my mom, I was pretty limited in the whole "choosing" department. But this seventeenth birthday marked me one day closer to independence. To college. To being who I wanted to be without reservation.

If nothing else, when my eighteenth b-day rolled around, this would be in my grasp. I smothered my own smile. See? A wish *could* come true, with the proper parameters.

The flame disappeared with barely a blow. My friends clapped, and I was already starting to feel better. They were sweet for trying to make my day special.

Everyone dove into the iced deliciousness, Charles, of course, grabbing for the Penny cupcake and making a gross tongue swipe across her frosted face. *Pig.* I broke off a corner of mine, savored the equal parts of vanilla cake and smooth, sugary frosting.

A rumble yanked our attention to the street as a motorcycle pulled up directly in front of us, the April sun reflecting off the red lacquer.

Our crew, along with every other student in the courtyard, stared at the biker's broad chest encased in a blue tee, tan arms bunching as he throttled the bike down. "Yummy," Hannah said. "And I don't mean the cupcake."

Another bike rolled up between the red one and the curb. A black crotch rocket. Black helmet and black tee on a whole lotta muscle. *Whoa.*

"Maybe my birthday won't be so bad after all," I murmured.

I glanced down at my MAY THE MASS TIMES ACCELERATION BE WITH YOU tank top. As I straightened the words across my chest, I licked my lips, checking for leftover frosting. In case the motorcycle guy looked my way, I needed to at least be presentable.

Hannah gasped and hit my hand. "You didn't happen to wish for a hot dude, did you?"

Both riders cut their engines, kicked down the stands, and shifted to take off their helmets. I watched the guy on the black bike. I definitely had an image of what the perfect guy under that helmet would look like to make my every birthday wish come true. I wanted him to have longish hair. Like a dark-haired young Thor, not old-school, trying-too-hard Jonas-brother long. Light blue eyes. Some scruff, not thick. More scruff meant too old. And a tattoo.

Pain shot through my eyes and magma must've taken the place of my brain. Nausea swept through me from head to toe, leaving a cold sweat on my forehead. It all happened in a matter of seconds. *What the—?*

As soon as I recognized that I might actually yak in front of the entire student body—and the hot biker guy!—the urge was gone. No more migraine. I felt fine.

I wiped my forehead and refocused on the guy in black. His arm flexed as he pulled off his helmet, and the sleeve of his T-shirt tightened over his sculpted biceps. Dark wavy locks fell into the guy's face. The rest of his hair skimmed his broad shoulders. *Holy hotness.*

He tucked his helmet under his arm, ran his hand over his face, then leaned down to look into his side-view mirror. "Are you shitting me?" he yelled.

The other rider, who'd already pulled off his helmet, almost fell from his bike, laughing.

Mr. Hottie scanned the courtyard. Who was he looking for? He swung his leg over his seat and continued to survey each table of students. Until he got to us.

The guy stared. At me. Shit, he must've caught me checking him out. His eyes locked on mine, and he strode forward to imaginary music that played in my head. Each of his steps matched the beat of the song. Each step held confidence as he moved with the purpose and grace of a uniformed marine.

When he was about twelve feet from me, I noticed the edge of a tattoo peeking out from under his sleeve in the same place as Nick's had been.

The stranger drew closer. Black lashes outlined his brilliant blue eyes. The contrast between his lashes and irises was startling. Stunning. But there was something behind the eyes. A familiarity. The lingering frosting turned sweeter in my mouth. I swallowed. I didn't know him…did I?

Four steps away. His beautiful eyes widened as something flickered across his face. He halted abruptly, furrowed brow and narrowed eyes. He stared me down. "Son of a bitch," he said slowly.

Was he talking to me? I checked out my table, thinking maybe one of my friends was doing something that had earned the hot guy's curse. Nope. They all just gawked at the dynamic duo like they were Batman and Robin.

"Come on," the sidekick said as he nudged the hot guy. The dude broke eye contact with me, and they sauntered past our table.

I rubbed my temples, trying to ease the dull headache building. The guy had cursed when he saw me. What did I do? And who the hell was he?

Reid

We'd traveled halfway across the country to this chick, and she turned me into some dude on the front of a romance novel. I'd just buzzed my head last week. Good thing she didn't want me in pigtails. Who was she hoping was under the helmet, anyway?

Santos elbowed me as we passed the last of the lunch tables. "Man, you look good in long hair. Add a couple dreads and eye makeup and you'd make one helluva Captain Jack Sparrow."

"Shut it."

Santos gave me a shove, and we moved closer to the entrance of the school.

She had to be able to see me in order to change my appearance, so I had naturally looked around for her. But a hot girl had caught my attention first. And then I'd realized the hot girl and Josie were one and the same.

Josie still had the strawberry-blond hair and green eyes like she did when I had a crush on her a couple years ago, but she'd definitely grown up since we'd last seen each other. Cheekbones and curves. Boots and a Star Wars tank. Alluring in every way imaginable. *Damn.*

I'd made sure she wouldn't recognize me. It was easier that way—for now.

Well, seeing as how she'd Pushed my new appearance, I guess that answered the question of whether she possessed abilities or not. And from the way she'd grabbed her head as I passed by, she likely wasn't a stranger to the sickening eye pain and wicked headache that came with the talent. I needed to talk to her in private, preferably before she thought she was going nuts or accidentally hurt someone. Or someone hurt her on purpose.

Most of us knew who her family was and what had happened, but I'd had an inside look. It wasn't pretty. The worst part was that Josie had been kept in the dark. She didn't know about…anything.

Her safe little world had to be disrupted, and I was the one chosen to drag her into hell. It was my responsibility to keep her alive and in check. *Her life depends on me.* My throat felt dry. She didn't deserve this, but she also didn't have a choice. She was exactly where Nick had been two years ago—and look how well that had turned out. Sweat beaded on my brow at the thought. Josie's brother's death had destroyed a lot of lives.

I shook her and Nick's faces out of my head as we entered the second set of doors into the building and approached the security guard. The lack of windows coupled with two stories of concrete resembled a jail more than a high school. The sterile cleaning-supply smell didn't help the illusion.

"What's your business, gentlemen?" the security guard asked, holding a metal detector wand at his side. "Arms out." Add the guard, and it felt kind of like a prison, too.

The knife I carried in my boot and the cool metal of the M9 Beretta pressing against the small of my back disappeared. Not a big deal. I could Push one of the weapons into my hand, if need be. I lifted my arms out to my sides, my helmet hanging from one hand. "Checking in at the office, sir. Registering as new students."

The wand made an outline of my body in the air. Without words, the guard waved me on, and then Santos stepped into my spot and cocked his head toward me. Santos couldn't Retract, so I made his HK45C, the Navy Seal–inspired pistol, vanish. Like me, he could Push a weapon if and when he wanted to. The wand waved around his body. The guard gave a nod and said, "Welcome to Oceanside."

Santos tucked his helmet under his arm. "Thanks."

"I'll do the talking. You have the paperwork, right?" I said once out of earshot of security.

"Yep. Sorry you have to do high school again. Sucks. But on the plus side…" Santos nodded to a girl passing us. "Hey," Santos said. The girl giggled.

"Hopefully this is a short-term stint. Besides, I'm not worried about my grades this time around. "

Santos smiled widely. "You graduated a year early. I don't think you had to worry about grades the first time."

"It was easy; I didn't have any of those distractions." I nodded my head toward the giggly girl walking down the hall. Santos took another few seconds to admire her again.

"While you were cheering the home team and chasing girls on the playground, I got to run with knives," I said.

"Sounds like a badass school."

Santos hadn't gone to school in the Denver Hub like I did. It was a different experience. "There were no football games or dances. It was nothing like a public school or private school—unless it was Xavier's School for Gifted Youngsters." I laughed at the thought of having Wolverine's hair. Good thing Josie wasn't envisioning Hugh Jackman when I pulled up.

I hadn't been in "school" for more than two years. It's not like we'd be here, sticking it out, till the end of the semester. Extractions rarely took long. And I'd single-handedly managed a dozen of them. The protocol was the same. Approach the target. Determine if he/she possessed Oculi abilities. Establish trust. Assess if the target was Resistance material. If they weren't...Yeah, that's where this job got interesting. I didn't want to think about what would happen to Josie if she didn't agree to come along peacefully.

"Yo," Santos said. He lobbed his helmet over a streamer hanging from the ceiling like he was shooting a two-pointer. "You do realize this girl is going to hate you, right?" He hustled to catch his substitute basketball and jump-shot it over the next streamer.

"Yep." She would despise me, and I didn't like it, but I had to put any feelings aside, because there were more important things at stake.

Santos caught his helmet and faked it to me, then tossed it up again. I'd known Santos about two years. He'd had my back on several occasions and vice versa. He was, *is*, one of my few friends. But even now, he didn't know the details of how I knew the Harper family.

We passed a bank of glass surrounding the library. All computers, few books. I caught a glimpse of myself in the glass. Santos was right—hello, Jack Sparrow. A new day, a new face, it felt like.

Santos was one of the few people alive who knew what I'd looked like before the incident two years ago. My change in appearance was the Resistance's form of a witness protection program. Appearance changes didn't happen unless it was absolutely necessary due to paperwork and identity shit. I didn't mind looking different, though. It was all in an effort to keep me safe. And being alive was always a nice perk.

Even with different looks, I was still in danger, and the same held true for Santos. Such was the life of a trainer for the Resistance. Until my trainee was ready for the Hub or life in general, I was also his or her protector. Always on the lookout. Never off duty. Potential death was just another occupational hazard.

I'd already killed more people than I'd ever be okay with. And their friends would be coming after Josie. Soon.

2.

JOSIE

The sweet smell of something baked hung in the air, and seconds before I walked through the back door, I could hear Mom shushing my little brother. *Here it comes…*

"Surprise!" Mom and Eli jumped out from behind the kitchen counter.

"Ahhh!" I faked a scream. Even though I'd known what they were up to, excitement rose in my throat when I saw the cake in the middle of the kitchen table, candles poking out of the top. I stepped closer and saw that my mom had scrawled basic physics equations around the border. Cute.

The cake was as lopsided as an obtuse triangle, and from the pile of measuring cups and bowls stacked in the sink, I knew her attempt at a homemade cake had likely taken her all day. Mom had many talents—but cooking wasn't among them. Still, when she set out to do something, she'd master it. So while the cake wasn't much of a looker, I had no doubt it'd be delicious.

"It's chocolate," Mom said.

"Aw. Thank you!"

Mom hugged me longer than usual. Maybe she was hugging me from two parents today.

Then Eli tackle-hugged me from behind, practically taking us all out, including the cake. Eli started snorting, and I couldn't help but laugh. I almost stopped when I heard my mom next to me. She had her hand in part of the cake. $P=Wt$ was smooshed. Eli looked very pleased with himself.

Mom laughing wasn't as common as it used to be, so when she did laugh, it made me all warm inside like one of those chocolate lava cakes with the gooey centers. Comforting.

Mom's laughter tapered off. She pushed back from me but kept her hands on my shoulders, staring into my face. It was like looking in a mirror. Reddish-blond waves, porcelain skin, green irises. I saw something in her eyes, a sadness maybe. "Mom?" She never showed emotion. She'd hid her feelings about everything since my brother's death.

"You're a young woman, your own person."

I thought maybe something was wrong, but no. She was only being sentimental. Or sentimental for her, anyway. Thank Thor it wasn't something bad. I couldn't handle another tragedy now; none of us could. I tried to get another laugh out of her. "It's not like I'm moving into a retirement home."

Her lips parted into a sad smile. Good enough.

Everything had fallen on her lately—kind of like she was a single parent.

I loved my dad, but there was no way I'd put up with my husband being gone for months at a time. I had no idea how my parents were still together. Dad would leave for "work" for weeks, but he'd taken the workaholic routine to a whole new level in the last two years, ever since Nick died in a car accident. And once Nick was gone, for all intents and purposes, so was my dad.

Mom slid her hands off my shoulders. A little icing dotted her cheekbone, and I noticed she had bags forming under her eyes. The woman stayed up until all hours of the night. I didn't know much about her research, only that she specialized in reversing neurological degeneration and basically survived on caffeine. She turned her back to Eli and leaned closer to me, her signature scent surrounded me—equal parts coffee and perfume. "Your dad can't video chat today." Her breath barely carried the sentence to the end.

"Oh, um. Okay, no biggie." I straightened against the counter, not wanting her to see any defeat in my posture. She didn't want Eli to hear, I got that. But what was with the long hugs? I kind of expected not to video chat with Dad today. I hadn't seen him in person for seven weeks, hadn't talked to him on the phone or on a video chat for a good three. At this point, I figured he'd left for good, and one of them would eventually tell us why. The thought was like a metric ton of osmium, twice the density of lead, settling on my chest, making it hard to breathe.

Don't go there. Not today. Glancing over my shoulder, I caught Eli playing in the cake frosting. Glad to see he was acting normal, even though I knew he was just as confused as I was about our family.

I turned back around, and Mom had slapped on her usual face, her Mom mask, happy but vacant. I knew what to expect from this Mom, the Mom who pretended everything was fine. Not that this was better, though. I'd prefer real Mom, who I never got to see anymore, who might actually answer some of my questions.

"So how was your day?" she asked. Her cane slapped against the kitchen tiles, the *tap, tap, swoosh*, of her good leg stepping forward followed by the drag of her right. She had a disability, but it didn't slow her down.

I shrugged and ran through today's events. *Total crap, sad, and kind of scary.* "It was okay." Talking about Nick wasn't something we did, so I didn't bring up the fact that he was on my mind.

"How's Hannah?"

"Fine."

Hannah was the first best friend I'd ever had. I hadn't made many friends in the years prior—it was too hard to say good-bye every time we moved. A defense mechanism of sorts, I guess. My family moved so often for my dad's job that I lost count, and my parents had homeschooled us until Nick died. The only reason they'd let me attend a public school the last two years was because it had an accelerated program and a hotshot Advanced Physics teacher.

I believe I also said something like, "I'm starving for social interaction." Apparently my endless pleading broke them down. My parents thought it'd be a good distraction for me. They even encouraged me to join activities that met during school hours. Of course I joined Science and Physics Club first thing. But despite the absolute bitch-fit I threw to go to public school, when offered the chance, I didn't sign up for every club or try out for every sport. Acclimating to so many people and personalities had turned out to be more difficult than I had expected.

Mom cleared her throat. "I was thinking dinner, movie, cake. Sound good?"

"Since it's my birthday, I was hoping to go to a party tonight at Marisa's house. Tons of people from school will be there." *Overprotective* was a serious understatement for my mom. With Nick's death and her solo parenting act, I kind of understood. My thoughts flickered to the wish I'd made today. *Choice.* Would she allow me to make this choice now than I was seventeen?

Mom knew how much finally having friends meant to me. "Mom?"

She *hmm*ed as if still in thought. Usually I could tell what would come after her *hmm*s, but this one sounded different.

We always celebrated birthdays but never with friends. This would be my first, which my friends thought was odd, and I agreed. I didn't dare say anything about the party being parentless.

Mom continued busying herself at the kitchen sink, pre-washing dishes for the dishwasher, her back toward me.

I joined Eli, now playing his newest hand-held gadget, at the table. I nabbed a finger full of frosting and shoved it into my mouth. Eli saw, gave a mischievous grin, and copied me.

She cleared her throat again. "How do you feel today? Are you okay?"

That came out of nowhere. I almost asked her the same question back because she was the one acting shady.

Her hands stilled over the sink.

"Fine," I lied. I wouldn't say anything about Tate breaking

up with me because she didn't like the idea of my having a boyfriend in the first place. She didn't even know I'd applied for the internship, so it wasn't worth mentioning, either. It wasn't that I wanted to keep the internship from her; it was just that I knew she'd find an excuse for it not to happen. And I wasn't going to mention the weird headache. Besides, Mom had plenty to worry about; she didn't need me adding to it. I looked at my birthday cake; it must have taken hours. "I feel perfectly fine."

Leaning over Eli's lap, I snuck a peek at his game. "Whatcha doing, little man?"

"I'm trying to destroy my opponent's Thunder Worm. He got me pretty good, but since I have a dark sprite, she restores my health. I should be able to take him down and be promoted to Level Twenty-six Dragon Slayer." Eli's eyes didn't leave the screen as he talked, and I was glad, because I couldn't help smiling at his explanation. Coolest nine-year-old on the planet. I ruffled his sandy hair, which he hated, and his hand shot out and squeezed my side, my most ticklish spot. He had a great sense of humor and more compassion than anyone I'd met. And we shared a common bond; he was the only person who fully understood our screwed-up family life. We got each other.

Mom let out a long sigh like she was a punctured balloon. "I don't think tonight is the best night."

Heat flooded my cheeks. Looking to the table for a reason to not look Mom in the face, I slowly gathered Eli's trash from his after-school snack. I wanted to make sure I didn't cry like a little girl when I was trying to show her I was mature.

I felt bad for the position my mom was in and the fact

that she'd lost a kid, but keeping me on a chain wouldn't solve anything. I turned and placed Eli's trash and plate on the counter.

"Mom." I didn't use an upset tone—I knew better. She wouldn't turn to face me, and I could feel the invisible barrier now up between us. "It's my seventeenth birthday. I'm not having a party with friends, and my dad isn't coming home any time soon."

Eli's eyes pulled up from his game. *Stupid. I shouldn't have said it that way.* Little dude didn't deserve the reminder. He looked back down at his dragons, but I could tell he wasn't playing anymore.

I knew I was guilt-tripping her. It wasn't like I wanted to, but it was the only way to get out of my nightly sentencing of watching a PG movie and playing a board game. I'd surely retire to my bedroom by nine, then petrify while reading about the Higgs Boson validity. I liked spending time with my brother, but not tonight. Tonight I needed to do something for me. For once, I wanted the same choices as every other person my age.

"Eli," she snapped. "Have you done your forms?"

He groaned.

"Pyongwon, Cheongwon, and Keumgang. Put down that video game and begin them now."

I know I pissed her off, but I hated seeing my brother suffer for it. "Come on, bud," I said. "We'll do them together."

He followed me into the open area beside the kitchen, and we settled into the positions for tae kwon do. I was still furious—seriously, my mom needed to dial back on this overbearing parenting style, 'cause *come on*, in a year

I'd be out of this house and on my own anyway—but I kept my temper in check and moved through the motions with my brother. There was a simplicity to the choreographed routines. It required balance and coordination and focus, but even though it was a dance of "combat," it helped to settle me.

We didn't delve into the formal "belt testing" like most kids did who practiced martial arts. This was just another of Mom's regiments. I'd been doing them since I was a kid. Unlike her schedule of yoga, study sessions, and specific reading assignments—yes, I was required to read and study beyond the school curriculum—I actually enjoyed this part.

Outside middle block. Low block. Front snap kick. Middle punch. Spin.

When Eli finished, he snatched his game from the kitchen table, shouted, "All done!" and bolted up the stairs to his bedroom to play his Xbox in peace. Smart little bugger.

Me, I wasn't as bright.

"You still haven't answered me, Mom." And I'd wait for her to. I loved my mother, but at times, I wanted to hold up a mirror and record her voice to play it back, just so she could see and hear how absurd her decrees could be.

I stared at the back of Mom's jeans and crisp T-shirt, but she said nothing. She didn't answer, and I knew that meant I wasn't going. I let the realization hit me: I was stuck in my own little prison, not just on my birthday but every day. I was trapped in a glass cage, seeing what life looked like, but I wasn't allowed to live it. It was one big tease. If I had an explanation, maybe it wouldn't feel this way, but the explanation never came, even when I asked.

I wanted to scream, but it wouldn't do any good. I turned my body away from my mom as I fought back tears. My vision blurred and came back into focus on a picture of our family in the adjoining living room. Our one family photo before Nick died. The glass frame had fallen in our last move and was left with a deep crack across our faces. I imagined Eli and I had matching cracks inside of us.

My mom had grown more protective these last couple weeks. I couldn't even walk five minutes to rent a movie at the Walgreen's Redbox without her as my chaperone. I knew it had everything to do with my dad not being around. But instead, my mom pretended everything was hunky-dory. Didn't my parents know what this was doing to Eli and me?

The photo was like a mocking metaphor. *It's already cracked. Just break already.*

White heat snapped behind my eyes. My mouth flooded with saliva. Cold sweat sent my body into shivers. I clutched my palms to my eyes as the pain grew beyond intense.

Bam.

Clatter.

I jerked, and the pain vanished. I pulled my hands away from my face. The picture I'd been staring at had fallen off the shelf. It lay shattered on the tile floor.

Mom was already headed to the family room. Her cane clattered to the floor as she slumped on the ground. She carefully cradled a chunk of the frame, her hands shaking, the photo bent and dangling.

Mom's face whipped to mine, her eyes wide and intense. I couldn't read her expression. Fear? Guilt?

If she were to ask me how I felt now, I'd be hard-pressed

to lie. It had to be what it felt like to be zapped by Loki's scepter. Water still pooled in the back of my mouth, and that piercing, crazy-sharp pain in my head lingered. She looked down at the family picture. "You may go tonight. But we'll have dinner first. And you'll need to text me every hour."

She agreed? Immediately it felt easier to breathe, and giddy teenage adrenaline quickly replaced my anxiety.

My first real party on my seventeenth birthday, newly single. This was going to be a night to remember.

Reid

We plunked our bags down in the old warehouse. Home sweet home…this month.

I inhaled and coughed. The air in here actually had a flavor. Mustiness laced with a tinge of fish. Most of the windows had been blacked out. A few broken panes let shafts of late-afternoon sunlight scatter across the floor like golden coins. Moving through the dank grime was like hiking through a swamp. Great, we'd moved to Dagobah. I wouldn't have been surprised if Yoda hobbled around the corner and told me to use The Force to walk above the nasty floor. The thought reminded me of Josie, of the tight *Star Wars*–inspired shirt she'd worn to school.

I flipped the line of switches inside the door. The warehouse was in bad shape. Luckily, we could have the place in working order in a short amount of time. It was the right price, too. The building was stripped and old, leaving only the bones of what used to be a functional industrial space.

"Dibs on the back bedroom!" Santos ran ahead, and an old hoop appeared on the wall by him. He took a shot with a ball that hadn't been in his hands the second before, but I Retracted it, making it vanish. "Hey!" he yelled. I followed Santos back to the bedrooms the young realtor had shown us just a couple hours prior. My ID said twenty-five and she'd bought it. They were desperate to rent the place, and she seemed to enjoy my flirting.

"So. Josie," Santos said.

I eyed him. His dark hair was messy from his helmet. His white shirt was half tucked in. A little disheveled, but that fit the jokester. "What about her?"

"You gonna tap dat?" he asked with a straight face.

I buckled over, laughing. "Hell no! And you're not, either, Lil Jon. Who says 'tap dat'? Really? And the only thing that would let you *tap* it is a maple tree…if you're lucky."

No way would I let Santos hit on her, let alone sleep with her. I wouldn't let anyone touch her. She was too important.

He did have good taste, though.

As I was about to flick the backlight on, the switch moved from the off position to on without my doing. Santos beat me to it. "Maple tree?" he asked. "That's just lame. Let me be the funny guy. Besides, she's not my type." He lumbered toward the back of the building. "So…how are you going to tell Josie?"

"That you aren't her type?" I snorted. That got me a basketball to the chest. I Pushed three balls, lobbing one and rocketing two more his way. "I need to gain her trust. Maybe reveal a little at a time. By now, she has to know something is up. I just need to convince her I'm not a wack job." We went into our separate bedrooms.

The square room held nothing but empty space. It reminded me of every other warehouse I'd lived in over the last year. The road was a lonely place to be. I could hear Santos shuffling around his room and crunch-squishing something very displeasing to him. "Awww, sick. Hey man, wanna trade rooms?"

At least I had one constant. Santos.

I was used to staying in dumps for training, but this time would be different. This warehouse, no matter how briefly we were here, would be where I trained Josie Harper. It was already more special than any other I'd lived in.

It would also be nice to be around a girl for a change. I wasn't a perv; I was only hoping for something different than the usual testosterone and egos that came with training mostly males.

I blinked, and a chest of drawers appeared in front of me. I loaded the dresser with the contents of my small duffel and Pushed a bed, along with bedding.

After investigating, I decided the decrepit, industrial kitchen was not so much gross as just old. The bathroom was the same. Mildew crept from behind several layers of caulking. Santos and I could fix it the traditional way—elbow grease and TLC—or we could make it whatever we wanted it to be with a little concentration. The possibilities were endless.

Would it raise questions if we decked out the place? Maybe. But no one would be in the warehouse except for training, which meant Santos, myself, and Josie.

"Hey, man. You up for some redecorating?"

Santos jogged out from his bedroom, wiping his shoe on the threshold. "Let's do it." He spun around in the center of the warehouse, taking in the dilapidated structure.

If Santos were doing this by himself, he'd have to snap a few pics to see how to Push it back to its natural state when we were done, but since I could Push *and* Retract, I could simply undo the improvements we were about to make. The Retraction worked like an eraser.

We agreed on a few points and worked in tandem. The floors, the windows, the bathroom—the cleaning, we did together. We decided the corner would be the living area. I focused there. Black leather couches. Sixty-inch LCD perched on the wall, cable and all. Stainless-steel industrial tables, lighting. Boom. Man cave.

I turned around to see Santos concentrating on the kitchen. It was a replica of something I'd seen in a Pottery Barn catalog. "You're totally killing the dude vibe here, Martha Stewart."

"What? Look who's talking. Want some guy-liner for those baby blues? Yo ho, yo ho, a pirate's life for me."

I picked up my phone and searched the web. Santos attempted to steal a look at my phone. "What're you doing?"

"I'm about to give myself a haircut." Googling one of the television shows all the chicks were addicted to, I found a guy with similar features, and I Pushed the new hairstyle. Not many could Push reality without observing it—most would have to look in the mirror, but I was one of the lucky ones. I stuck my head in the bathroom to check my new cut. Better. Why pay when I could do it myself?

Santos jogged to the middle of the warehouse and

shouted, "I'll Push the soundproofing, haus."

He was helping take the Pushing responsibility off of me, which was appreciated. I'd be Pushing quite a bit in the coming week. And the soundproofing, yeah, that would definitely come in handy with what we had in store. "Thanks, man."

Living quarters. Check. Haircut. Check. Make this girl trust me, drop a bomb on her life, and get her to use her body and mind as a weapon. On deck.

JOSIE

Hannah and I trotted up to Marisa's front door. Most of our friends would be at her party. And since Hannah gave me a pep talk and Mom surprised me by giving my leash some slack, I was determined to end my birthday on a good note. I even made my eye makeup more dramatic than usual and used lip color rather than my subtle gloss to make the night feel more special.

We weaved through the labyrinth of hot bodies. The sweltering house was enough to drive me back outdoors, but we needed to at least see who was there. I was hoping to maybe watch Ian, a super-cute guy, from afar. Not that I was a stalker.

We rounded the corner into the kitchen. Since it was the only room in the house with lights at full strength, I was almost blinded. Averting my eyes from the bright overhead CFLs, I swiveled my head to the breakfast nook. Tate, my one and only ex-boyfriend, pressed a girl against the wall, their lips locked.

Oh. No. You. Didn't. The slap of shock was quickly followed by my wounded ego getting further wounded. I didn't want to see this.

Make out in the dark like everyone else, dickhead.

The lights went out. The darkness squeezed me like a rancor with its prey. I was almost brought to my knees by the shooting pain in my head and the pukey feeling rolling through me. Mom had asked how I was feeling, and I'd lied. Maybe I should've mentioned the crazy headache. Maybe I was about to have an aneurism or a stroke. More than 140,000 people died from strokes annually in the United States, and teens contributed to that statistic.

Several people let out screams, including Hannah, who now clutched my arm. The room tilted and swayed as I tried to push myself upright. Bracing my hands on my knees, I pressed against the dark and nausea to stand. I grabbed Hannah's hand off my arm and headed out the way we came, following the slow strobe light into the next room. The bodies moved in stop-motion animation, and I couldn't predict where body parts would land next. Dodging the pulsing bodies was impossible, and the room was closing in on me. I needed to get out of this house. Something didn't feel right.

I made a shot for the front door, but Hannah yanked me backward. She'd stopped to talk to two girls from her cheer squad. I tried to listen to their yells above the music but couldn't concentrate when the room pulsated between black and flashes of contorted limbs. "I'll find you guys in a few minutes. I need some fresh air," I yelled.

Letting go of Hannah's hand, I rushed toward the door. The people on the front porch were a blur as I ran down the steps to the empty front yard. I sucked in air, gulped it like I couldn't get enough. The sweat dried cool on my skin. As my breathing calmed, I examined my shadow on the grass cast in multiple directions from the streetlights lining both sides of the avenue.

Man, Nick would've kicked Tate's ass. That thought made me smile. I paced in the grass, mentally recapping my birthday and focusing on my breathing. I pictured my ex licking the girl's tonsils.

Just one of these events from today—Dad not home, losing the internship, Tate—wouldn't be so bad, but everything at once made for an unbelievably sucktacular birthday.

Hannah's arm laced through mine, and she guided me to the steps. I didn't fight her when we sat on the top stoop. "Harsh day. Wanna talk about it?"

Hello, repeat of lunch. But bitching about things wouldn't change them, so what was the point?

"It's not about Tate," I said. And the truth of that reflexive denial brought us both to an awkward silence. I wasn't really good with people. I struggled with crowds. I could follow Hannah's lead and fake my way through social situations, but the truth was that I wasn't all that comfortable. Part of me would always be on the fringe, observing, keeping a distance, analyzing.

I was just wired to be weird, it seemed. But that wouldn't stop me from wanting to be like Hannah, from wanting to fit in. Hannah, bless her cheer-captain heart, seemed to know this.

The sound of engines pulled everyone's attention to the street. Two crotch rockets gunned around the corner and rolled up Marisa's circular drive, stopping in front of the stairs.

I recognized the bike. It was the hot weirdo from school.

"Seriously? What does Fate have against me?"

Hannah laughed.

They pulled off their helmets and dismounted their bikes. Hannah bumped my arm. "Mmm mmm," she hummed. I couldn't disagree.

The hot cursing weirdo had cut his hair. He was one of those guys who didn't try to be hot, he just *was*. He looked like a badass.

I wanted to glance away. I wanted him to know I wasn't going to fall for his bad-boy image. I wanted him to know I was different. I wasn't going to swoon over him like every other girl here...and probably everywhere he went. But I couldn't. I couldn't peel my eyes away—mostly because his startling irises didn't leave my face.

My rib cage rattled as if my heart was demonstrating Newton's Law of Inertia.

He and his friend climbed the stairs and hesitated two steps down from us. His friend was shorter. Good-looking, close-cropped hair, warm skin, and checking Hannah out big time. I didn't blame him. I guess if I were a guy, I'd check out my friend, too. Hannah had mocha skin, ebony hair, hazel-green eyes. Exotic. The exact opposite of me.

The hot weirdo guy still stared at me. "Take a ride with me? I swear I'm not a mass murderer."

Adrenaline spiked in my veins. I didn't want him to have that effect on me. I interlaced my shaky hands and spoke through a fake smile. "Yeah, because that doesn't make you sound like a creeper."

He moved toward me, took one more step, and then

leaned down so his face was level with mine. "Just a quick ride. That's all I'm asking for."

I couldn't believe he'd ask me for anything. "Dude, you cursed at me today." Some nerve. He had a rockin' bod and a gorgeous face, but I wasn't stupid. "Why would I go anywhere with you?"

The guy combed his fingers through his hair, bringing my attention to the curves in his arm. "I wasn't cursing *at* you. Look, I have an idea." He pulled his wallet out of his pocket. "I'll leave this with your friend…"

"Hannah," Hannah said, a bit too enthusiastically.

The guy gave Hannah a flirty smile and continued. "Okay. I'll leave this here with *Hannah* to assure that I bring you back."

"Not enough."

He held his hand out to his friend. "Keys." The friend shoved keys into Mr. Hottie's hand. "I'm Reid Wentworth, and this is Santos. I'll take his keys. He'll also be stranded here with Hannah until I get back with you."

Holding up a finger for the guys to wait, Hannah tugged my arm and dragged me a couple of feet away.

"Why are you hesitating?" she whispered.

"I want to be safe. Stranger danger, ya know? This doesn't seem like a logical—"

"Okay, Spock. He's given great collateral. Besides, it is your birthday and your mom let you out of the house. Live a little. Do something crazy for once."

"Nope."

Hannah pulled me around to face the guys. "She's going with you."

"I. Am. Not." I threw Hannah a death stare.

The friend, Santos, cleared his throat and pulled his hand out of his jeans pocket. "Heads you go, tails you don't."

"This isn't up for debate. Or chance."

Instead of listening to me, Santos flipped the coin up in the air. Fifty-fifty chance. I didn't like those odds.

He caught it and slapped it on the back of his opposite hand. "Heads."

"No," I said.

The guy pushed both hands behind his neck and blew his cheeks up with air. His shirt stretched taut across his chest. The breath he'd held in his mouth rushed out as he pulled his hands forward, raking over his scruffy jawline. His sleeve jerked up, revealing the tattoo on his arm I'd only seen the edge of earlier—and my lungs froze in mid-breath.

Holy shitballs.

His tattoo was exactly like my dead brother's design.

My brother's tattoo was an original, or so I'd thought. It was no coincidence this guy had one just like it. He had to have known Nick if they had identical ink. And I needed answers. Now.

I pushed my finger into the center of the stranger's chest. Rock hard. "If we're not back in a half an hour, Hannah's calling the cops."

A mischievous smile parted his perfect lips. "Fair enough."

Hannah's body shook against mine. Yeah, she was loving every second of this. I elbowed her and said, "Phone." She handed over her phone and I snapped a pic of Mr. Hottie's license plate. I slapped her phone into her hand and she winked at me. "Have fun, kids."

What the hell am I getting myself into?

3.

Reid

Some idiot had rolled his cheap-ass ride next to mine and was about to compare engines, three friends around him. I guessed football teammates. He obviously didn't know squat, because otherwise he would've known his bike wasn't in the same league.

I had to say something to make them tuck tail and buzz off, or I wouldn't ever get time alone with Josie.

"Can I help ya with something, buddy?" I asked.

"Checkin' out your bike, man."

Josie stepped between the douche and my bike. "Hey, Derek, we're heading out for a bit. If you're wondering, though, judging by the engine size and exhaust, his probably has more torque and power. Can you talk to him later?"

The idiot eyed me, then pulled his chin up at her, giving her a silent confirmation. He walked away, and his cronies followed. She held some kind of cred if all four athletes listened to her.

"Classmate?"

"I tutored him last fall."

I saddled up and held the helmet in my lap. Josie stood beside my bike, watching me, playing with a stack of bracelets. A tee, jeans, short boots. Damn.

"Are you having second thoughts?" I made sure not to have a mocking tone to my voice. I needed her to trust me. "I'll be careful."

She stared at the helmet and then looked up at me. "I haven't been on a motorcycle before."

I patted the seat behind me. "One leg on each side, and the rest is up to me." She swung a leg over and straddled the seat. I turned to hand her the helmet. "You oughta wear this. And don't worry." I watched her over my shoulder and tried not to smile, but I couldn't help it. "It's your first time," I whispered. "I'll be gentle."

She shoved the helmet over her head, her cheeks red. I struck the kickstand and started it. My bike thundered to life under us. I reached behind me, found one of her hands, and pulled it around my waist. She probably didn't have to hold on to me, but I wanted her to. Not only because she was hot, but because she was important.

I saluted Santos and Hannah. Hannah raised her watch in the air and tapped it. We started moving, and Josie's other hand circled my waist while her thighs hugged me.

"You know," she yelled in my ear. "Driving without a helmet or your license is not a smart move. You're just asking for trouble." She didn't know that I'd memorized my license and could Push a new one in a matter of seconds if I wanted to. I could also get a new helmet, but I wasn't about to make one materialize out of nowhere and have her faint on me.

We whizzed by strip malls and grocery stores closing down for the night. Headlights flashed across our faces. Ordinary people out doing ordinary things, like heading home to bed.

I was going to show Josie a few things tonight, none of them ordinary.

Josie leaned forward, pressing into my back. "Statistically, one out of five bikers who don't wear helmets ends up in an accident."

She sounded like a freaking insurance commercial. I hoped she wasn't this way about everything.

Josie yelled into my ear, "If you're going sixty miles per hour, considering your weight of approximately a hundred and ninety pounds, if your bike crashes into a standing object, you will fly through the air with fifty-seven hundred pounds of force. I'd hate to see what happens when you land. With or without a helmet, what's left can't be pretty."

What the hell? I kept my eyes on the road and yelled back at her, "I won't let us crash." I meant it. I wouldn't let anything happen to her or me. Regardless, my fingers tightened around the grips.

We turned into the park. I'd found it earlier in the day—a place remote enough we'd have privacy, but not so far from civilization that she'd wig out. Trails and trees, but no water. Water meant a possibility of gators, and I didn't do reptiles.

Instead of parking in one of the marked stalls, I popped the curb and drove up onto the sidewalk. Josie leaned forward again, and her hold around my waist tightened. "I don't think we're supposed to drive on here," she said into my ear.

I ignored her. She was going to fry my nerves if she didn't stop with the Goody Two-shoes act. Crawling along the concrete, I stopped when the trail wound through cypress and oak trees, hiding us. One lamppost illuminated the pathway, but even that was dim. Insects sang, and the smell of cedar hung in the air.

I turned the key, kicked the stand, and her fingertips slid across my obliques. Once her hands were no longer on me, she was quick to hop to the ground and pull off her helmet. I followed. Without her wrapped behind me, it instantly felt as if something was missing and the breeze seemed cooler. I grabbed the helmet from her hands, placing it on the seat.

Josie stood, one hip pushed out, arms crossed. "Okay, you have me hidden in dark trees. If you're not a creeper, what the hell do you want?" I noticed she pulled the bigger of her bracelets off, slipped her hand through, and gripped it in her fist like brass knuckles.

She was smart and cautious. Good. She needed to be.

"I didn't hide you. I hid *us* and what I need to show you." I made each of my movements intentional. I couldn't chance scaring her. We needed her.

Josie held up a finger, a warning, and said, "If you go anywhere near your zipper, I'm out of here. And screaming bloody murder as I go."

I smiled and raised my hands out to my sides. "No zipper action. Swear. Until you say you want zipper action, and then…" She shot me a nasty look. "Totally kidding."

I could smell her on my shirt. Gardenias. I didn't know a daisy from a dandelion, but I knew the smell of gardenias. I took in one last breath and clapped my hands to bring myself back to the park. The unveiling. The girl.

Showtime—bring her up to speed. The best way to do that? Give her proof without frightening her to death. "What would you like right now, more than anything?"

She cocked her head, her face serious. "Besides a Taser gun, you mean?"

Laughter spilled out of me. Her sarcasm was thick but appreciated. She made me laugh.

Josie didn't crack a smile. "I want to know where and when you acquired that tattoo. Who were you with?" She leaned over, trying to peek at my new ink.

I knew what she wanted to hear. But I hadn't had any cool bonding moment with Nick Harper where we got matching tats. I couldn't and wouldn't lie to her. "You gave it to me this morning."

Josie stepped closer, and confusion twisted her stunning features. "Are you on crack? I think I'd remember tattooing someone."

Man, I didn't want to be the one to have to do this. This was going to crush her. I could see the hope in her eyes—the possibility of a connection to her brother. "I'm sorry, but I didn't have a tattoo before this morning. You gave me the ink when you saw me pull up in front of the school."

Josie shoved her hands into her pockets. She snorted. "Right."

"For real. You and me. We are called Oculi. We, Oculi, have the unique ability to make what we observe a reality. We think; give a mental Push; and, through the act of observation, we manifest our thought into reality."

"Yes. That's such a logical explanation. And at midnight,

my ball gown will turn to rags," she said, rolling her eyes.

Right, nobody believed it when I told them. "Let's simplify this," I said. "What do you want to eat?"

She stared at me. A deep crease formed between her squinted eyes. "What?" Josie's voice raged with frustration.

I was going to lose her if I didn't do something drastic.

Screw it. Without giving it another thought, I stepped beside her and pointed to my bike. "Keep your eyes on my bike. Popcorn sounds good to me." I blinked, and the movie theater treat sat on my seat. I loped to my bike and picked up the box.

"You're kidding me. You dragged me out here to show me a childish magic trick?" Her voice lowered, cold and pointed.

"Wait. You think this is an illusion? This is real." I plunged my fingers into the red-and-white-striped box and shoveled popcorn into my mouth. "Here." I offered it to her.

Josie crossed her arms again. "I don't doubt the products are real. I just think a magic trick is a little pathetic as a pickup attempt."

She thought this was an attempt to hit on her? No, no, no. "You'd know if I were trying to hit on you. There'd be no question. And I'm not."

Josie's eyes bulged. "Wow. Okay." Her voice cracked. "Can you take me back now? I've had the worst birthday ever." She tipped her head back and bit her quivering lip.

Shit. She was on the verge of tears. "That's not what I meant. I'd totally hit on you; I just don't have time right now."

Josie turned in an about-face, but I caught her elbow, pulling her back to me. "You call it. What do you want to eat?"

"Fine," she huffed, jerking herself out of my grasp. "Ice cream."

I Pushed and blinked while staring at my bike. And it appeared in the next millisecond—a brand-new tub of peanut butter fudge ice cream.

Josie yanked her arm out of my hand and lurched for the dessert. Picking it up, she examined it and my bike. She opened the container, setting the lid on the seat, and stuck her index finger into the ice cream. Her head snapped up. "It's cold."

"Because it's *real*."

Hesitantly, she licked her finger. "It is real. And it's my favorite." I knew it was her favorite, or it had been a few years ago.

Plunging the same finger back into the divot from the first try, she examined the ice cream container and then her finger from above, then from the side. This time her finger was covered when she pulled it out, and she spooned it into her mouth. Her eyes closed and she moaned around her finger. She was hot, and she didn't even know it. I rubbed my mouth to hide the smile I couldn't keep off my face.

Josie pulled her finger out of her mouth. "How about black flip-flops?" She looked at me expectantly, her brows raised. I nodded toward my bike where the cheap sandals already sat.

She placed the tub of ice cream down to inspect the flip-flops. "If this is real, then wouldn't you be able to make them dis—"

I thought, blinked, and they were gone. What Josie held in her hand seemingly vanished into thin air. She whirled around. The ice cream had disappeared, too, as well as the popcorn. She twisted back to me.

"This is what I looked like this morning." I Pushed.

Josie let out a screech so loud it would've woken zombies. Fear, astonishment, and confusion took her face hostage. I couldn't imagine what was going through her mind, and I felt terrible having to break it to her this way. "It's okay. It's okay," I promised, holding my hands up as if calming a startled horse.

I wanted to somehow make this better, but I knew there wasn't anything I could do to comfort her right now. All I could do was appeal to her intellect, give her validation and evidence. I needed to find a way for her to trust me.

I ran a hand over my buzzed head and my clean-shaven jaw. "It's still me. Look. No tattoo." I pulled up my sleeve.

Josie's wide eyes didn't blink, and her mouth hung open.

I had to give her more. "Then you made me into a cross between a romance novel cover model and Jack Sparrow." I Pushed. Long hair, scruffy. I looked like I had when I pulled my helmet off at the school earlier in the day.

A short, throaty sound escaped from her covered mouth. Slowly pulling her hands away from her lips, she said, "A young, dark-haired Thor." Her voice was barely audible.

I stepped closer to her, her eyes still focused on my face. I Pushed again—the hair I showed up with tonight, with a slight scruff over my jawline. This was how I'd stay for as long as she knew me.

Josie's fingers grasped my forearm while her other hand shoved up my sleeve, revealing her brother's tattoo. Her eyes dragged over my arm to my face with extreme caution.

I cleared my throat so I wouldn't startle her any more than I already had, especially since she was so close. "You okay?"

The moonlight cast a blue, ethereal glow on her face. "My brother? You didn't get the tattoo with him?" she croaked.

"I'm sorry." I didn't. In time I could tell her what I knew of Nick, but not now…and that killed me.

Her eyes traveled up and down my body, over to my bike, and back to my face. She was trying to grasp what she'd seen, to understand. She seemed to be thinking, rationally processing what she couldn't wrap her mind around. Her index finger, lying at her side, pointed to me then to my bike. Yeah, she was trying to work this out logically in her brain. A crease formed between her brows, and her eyes narrowed. "You made all that other stuff appear. Can you make him…"

No. Don't ask. Don't go there. You will just be disappointed.

She shook her head. Of course she wouldn't ask. She didn't believe in this kind of stuff. It went against her very nature.

She needed to hear it, though. "We can't Push anything having a soul. Or once having a soul," I said slowly. "That's not how Pushing works." I wished we could. There were many people I'd Push alive if I could. Nick. My mom. Countless friends and mentors.

Her glassy eyes were almost more than I could handle. "I, I…" she whispered. "I don't understand what's going on."

I was too familiar with the longing in her voice. I'd been there. It was a fast downward spiral to a dangerous place. My muscles stiffened thinking about where I'd been two years ago, how I'd shut everyone out, how it had been easier to turn off my emotions than deal with reality. There was a time when I thought there would be more peace in death than wallowing in my grief and misery. I wouldn't let her even start down that path.

I leaned down, making sure she'd hear me. "Is this a bad time to hit on you, then?"

Her lips broke into a half smile.

Thank God. My shoulders relaxed away from my ears.

"You have some explaining to do. We're going to need more than"—she pulled her phone from her jeans—"ten minutes."

"Explaining?" I laughed. "You have no idea."

Josie stepped toward the bike, and a shadow darted out of the tree line. The figure held something shiny pointed at Josie. A gun.

I didn't think, I just reacted. I'd been Pushing a shield around Josie and myself, the energy leaving my body in a tangible pulse, since we got on my bike. Not taking any chances, I Pushed a bulletproof vest and a ten-by-ten brick wall blocking her from the assailant's view.

I sprinted toward Josie, simultaneously Retracting the gun from his hand and Pushing a straightjacket around the stranger, likely a Consortium goon. It didn't evaporate in the next second, so he wasn't an Anomaly, just a Pusher. That meant I had the upper hand.

My gaze flashed back to Josie. She now pointed a classic Glock at the brick wall. I hadn't Pushed it, which meant *she* had. The fight-or-flight chemical reaction in her body had kicked in, and standing firm in self-defense was her first instinct.

Seriously? Right on.

The ski-masked stranger wriggled, and the white jacket fell to the ground, revealing that he had Bowie knives in each hand. I didn't have time for this.

I pulled my hand back by my ear. He didn't see me Push my favorite blade into my hand. I had the advantage of accuracy and surprise. I flung the blade into his heart. He collapsed.

"Josie," I whispered. "Don't move."

Without pausing, I Pushed my gun into my hand. I flash Retracted all the trees in my line of sight. The trees disappeared and reappeared in a matter of seconds. *Clear.* Josie let out a strangled gasp, cutting through the silence. I pivoted and did the same to the opposite side of the park. Retract and Push. *Clear.* The action cost me. Pain cleaved my skull and dropped me to my knees. I could taste the blood in my mouth, feel it dripping out of my nose. I wiped it away before Josie could see.

I stashed the gun in my waistband. The pain had subsided, although I knew that action came with a hefty price tag. I jogged over to Josie, who was now peeking out from behind the brick wall.

Catching my breath, I crouched down in front of her. I slowly moved my hand into her line of sight so she could see my movements and empty hands. She had to trust me. Her chest heaved, and her face was drawn in disbelief. Cautiously, I reached for her arm, but she jerked away.

I didn't blame her for questioning my intentions or me after what she'd just witnessed. "I'm here to protect you, but we need to get you out of here."

Her bottom lip shook as she scrambled to her feet.

"Josie, there are very bad people nearby who want to hurt you, just because of what you are."

"N-no."

"You've felt it, Josie." I kept using her name, keeping my voice low and steady. She covered her ears and shook her head. "You felt it with the headaches, that sick feeling you get right before one of your thoughts becomes reality."

"The gun…"

"Yes, the gun. You Pushed it." And my hair and tattoo.

"None of this is possible," she said in a soft voice.

I held out my hand. "We have to go."

She stepped around me, avoiding my outstretched hand. I Retracted the brick wall. She crept over to the lifeless body, bent down, and touched two fingers to the person's neck.

"He's dead!"

Uh, yep. A nine-inch dagger to the heart tended to have that effect.

It started with a gasp. Then she slapped her hands over her mouth. She didn't say anything for several seconds, and then she just lost it. Tears overflowed from her eyes, streaming down her face. In a way, I wished she'd scream and wail. But she said nothing. And those soul-wrenching, silent sobs that she fought so hard to contain, they tore at me—what was left of me. Ripping the scabs off wounds that had never fully healed.

I wanted to reach out, to try to reassure her. I wasn't as cold an operative as I pretended to be. But I had to get her out of there—our safety came first. I Retracted all evidence that anything had happened: the jacket, the knives, everything apart from the body. I couldn't simply Retract a body. Objects, yes, but never the living. Or once living, as it were.

Josie's hand fell from her mouth, but tears still streamed down her cheeks. "We need to call the police." Her voice was raspy.

"Can't." It pained me to say it. We were talking about a dead human being, but it wasn't that easy. "The Consortium is everywhere, including branches of the government and law enforcement. We'd be giving you away. That's why he had to die—so he couldn't confirm finding you."

Her gaze flickered between the dead man and me. I Retracted the black ski mask. Caucasian, five feet ten, maybe closer to six feet tall. Average build, greenish-hazel eyes, dull features, short brown hair. Nondescript. The kind of twenty-something guy you'd pass in the mall or on the street and not give a second glance. There was nothing about him that would indicate he was a dangerous Oculi. A perfect Consortium goon.

I patted down his front pockets, coming up empty, but rolling his body to the side, I found a wallet in his back pocket that held a Science Industries ID card. Science Industries, called SI by most Oculi, was the public facade used by Schrödinger's Consortium.

Technically, I should've called this in, alerting the Hub to a threat in the immediate area. I needed to let them know our mission was compromised—but just as the thought formed, I shut it down.

The Hub would order me to retreat and return to base. They'd send in a different team to monitor the area. They'd post surveillance on Josie, use her as bait to draw out more

Consortium members. They'd wait to see if she was innocent or in league with the same people who had just tried to attack her.

Hell no.

"We need to leave, Josie. Now."

She didn't move. "Who is he? What did he want? Was he after you or me?"

I had to give her enough information so she'd understand the urgency of the situation, but not so much that it would freak her out more than she already was. "He was a member of Schrödinger's Consortium. They're comprised of people who have abilities like ours. They were trying to keep tabs on people like you and me, to police us. They think you may be a little different, though."

"Different how?"

How could I say they wanted her dead without saying it outright? "They think you're more dangerous."

She inched toward me. "They want to kill me." It wasn't a question. She stated it as a fact—and she was right. I nodded, and she bit her bottom lip, tears welling in her eyes again.

"I'm sorry." I needed to get her out of here. Either the mission was compromised, or there was a leak. Neither scenario was good. "Josie, we need to move."

Stepping between the dead body and the tree line, I Pushed a hole, six feet deep, directly behind the first tree. A grave was protocol for dispensing of dead Consortium, leaving no evidence of engagement, which in turn meant no questions from Plancks, humans without our abilities.

Josie stepped beside me, peering into the hole. A cherry-lacquered coffin appeared. *What the?* I swallowed my initial comment. Of course she could observe a coffin into existence; she knew what a coffin looked like from when Nick died.

My stomach rolled, and I stared at her in awe for a moment. No words were exchanged between us, but I understood what she wanted. Did I have time for niceties for an asshole who had attempted to kill us? Nuh-uh. That would be *no*. But if settling this scumbag in a box rather than the ground would help Josie sleep better at night, well, fine. I could spare a minute.

I jumped into the grave and wrenched the coffin lid open. Jeez, she'd gone all-out with cushioned pillows and plush linings. I reached up and dragged the man down. There was something about death that added extra weight to a body. Although the chest wound didn't bleed much, the scent of blood—sharp and oddly metallic—made me hold my breath. I situated the body into the cream-colored satin that lined the coffin, lowered the lid, and stood.

I stepped on the lower part of the coffin to vault out of the hole. Ignoring the pressure building in my skull, I Pushed dirt to fill the grave, followed by grass and plants so the ground appeared like the rest of the lightly wooded area.

Josie nodded soundlessly, like she was giving some kind of prayer or acknowledgment, and began walking back to the bike.

I stepped in front of her and whispered, "Stop. I go first." I grabbed my gun in one hand and, holding up the other to Josie, indicated she needed to wait. My infrared glasses appeared on my face and I did a quick 360. *Clear.*

"We're good. Stay close."

Josie didn't move or give any indication that she'd heard

me, though.

"I understand you're scared and you don't know what's going on, but you can trust me. I won't let anything happen to you." We stood there, staring at each other, and after a few seconds, something changed in her eyes and she closed the gap between us.

With my gun at the ready, I crossed the path with her, then grabbed the helmet for her to put on. Taking a step back, I scanned the bike. Someone could've tampered with it. Just in case, I Retracted the motorcycle and Pushed another identical to my baby. I straddled the tank and balanced the bike. After starting the engine and revving the throttle, I held out my hand and helped her get on. She was quiet and fast—afraid. I studied her over my shoulder. "You okay?"

"I need an explanation. I don't like not understanding." Her voice was monotone.

She intrigued me. Yeah, she was smart and beautiful, but there was something else—something others could easily overlook. Determination? Stubbornness? Compassion? I wasn't sure.

I faced forward but reached back for her hand, pulling it around my waist. She wound the other arm around me on her own. Her fingers sunk into my stomach. This time her hands didn't rest on my body, they held on like her sanity depended on it—and it probably did.

No pressure.

4.

JOSiE

We rolled to a stop in front of Marisa's house with about ten seconds to spare. I surveyed the stairs. Hannah wasn't anywhere in sight among the small crowd in the front yard.

I pried my fingers from Reid's body as he turned off the engine. I didn't want to let go. He was real, that I knew for sure, but I wasn't sure about anything else. Some of the kids yelled and I jumped, my heart rocking in my chest.

Reid looked at me over his shoulder. "You're safe." His words were strong, confident. They were the first we'd exchanged since leaving the park, and they held a certainty that I desperately needed. I hopped down, tugging the helmet off my head. With one fluid motion, Reid dismounted and took the helmet from me.

My pocket vibrated, sending my nervous system into hyperdrive. I was going to end up with one wicked headache from all the adrenaline ups and downs. I pulled my phone from my back pocket. Mom had texted: *Josie?*

Crap. I'd forgotten to check in. I responded: *I'm ok* 😊

It wasn't true, though. I wouldn't ever be okay again.

I felt Reid close behind me, so I hit send and turned to face him, my sinuses burning with threatening sobs.

His face was somber, his playfulness buried with the dead man. "Let's talk out here. We're safe surrounded by others, but we don't want anyone to overhear. Why don't you text Hannah and I'll text Santos."

I nodded like a lifeless bobblehead doll. I texted Hannah: *Out front w Reid. I'm fine. Take your time.* Reid's head bowed to his phone as he typed, his message taking much longer than mine, so I scanned the area for a quiet place to talk. My classmates were running amok. Some were just being silly, and some were probably drunk. I envied them a little. The veil of ignorance had been pulled from my eyes, but they still enjoyed it. *Ignorance is bliss.* Oh yeah. I'd never understood the full measure of that saying until now.

Tears trickled down my face, but I quickly swiped them away before anyone could notice. Reid's hand landed softly on the small of my back, and he ushered me away from the front porch and into the large front yard. "You're okay." His breath tickled my ear.

I was wrong. He'd noticed the tears.

When we reached several decorative boulders tucked into the landscaping, he gestured for me to sit. He faced the surrounding woods, his back to the house and the assortment of kids hanging out on the front porch. Those odd goggles appeared on his eyes, and he did a quick scan of the area. In a flash, they disappeared.

I blinked. All of these bizarre events felt like a hallucination, like some twisted dream in which reality warped and the impossible became real.

But these things didn't happen. A person didn't just think something, want something, and it appeared out of the ether. Infinitesimal possibilities existed for even the most statistically improbably scenarios, but, but…*still.*

I was crazy. Now *that* was a far more logical conclusion. I had been suffering headaches, and I hadn't felt quite right today— Holy shit, the "magic" popcorn and ice cream… maybe he'd drugged me! "What the hell did you do to me?" My knees started shaking, and it was all I could do to stand upright.

"Sit," he said, then, taking the choice out of my hands, he lifted me onto the stone ledge.

As soon as my butt hit the rock, the tears tumbled out of control.

"Take a deep breath," he ordered.

"That guy…" I tried not to let my voice shake, but I was doing a lousy job. "He's dead." I might be crazy or hallucinating, but I recalled the events in the park in vivid detail. That guy. The attack. "Y-you saved me." My voice squeaked. "What…what's going on? How did you—how did *I*—make that stuff appear?"

Reid held up a hand, indicating to stop or slow down, but my brain was on overload. I couldn't stop. "What's real and what isn't? Who else can do this?" The questions were piling up in my head. I couldn't spew them out quickly enough. And there seemed to be a direct correlation between the speed of my words and the pace at which my tears fell. "Am I losing my mind?"

"No, Josie. You aren't."

He raked a hand through his hair like he didn't know where to begin. He opened his mouth to speak, but I cut him off. "I made things appear. I made a gun appear in my freaking hand by wanting one in my hand. How? And how do I know I can trust you? How do I know you won't try to kill me, too?" I closed my eyes briefly, but all I could see was the dead body lying in the grave, a coffin I'd created with my mind, by simply thinking it into existence. And I lost it.

Giant sobs wracked my body, and I let my face fall into my hands. Reid pulled me against his chest. He whispered into my hair as he held me and let me cry. "I'll protect you. I won't let anyone hurt you, I promise. I'm going to teach you how to do this. You're not alone. Okay? I won't let you do this alone."

I didn't know if I should be scared of him or not. My gut said no, but I didn't go off gut feelings. I let observations, calculations, and analysis determine my actions. I needed proof that he was safe.

His arms wrapped firmly around me, my face resting on his shoulder even though my sobs had trailed off into uneven breaths and sniffles. I found comfort in this stranger's embrace, which went against everything I'd usually do. My warring feelings confused me just as much as everything else going on.

I slowly extracted myself from Reid's body. As my hand slid from his shoulder, he caught it, stuffing a tissue into my palm. I peeked up at him through my bangs, and his startling light eyes were already trained on me. He brushed my cheek with the pad of his thumb. The touch was gentle and soft.

A car came around the corner, the headlights temporarily blinding me, and it occurred to me that anyone, like the person in that car, could be after me or could do what Reid and I could do.

"Josie." Reid drew out the *O* in my name. Like the word sat in his mouth longer than it needed to.

My gaze drifted back to Reid's face.

"We're okay. Santos and I are both keeping watch." He knew I was watching, probably paranoid forever now. And Santos was like him. Like *us*. There were two of them and only one of me. My mouth went dry at this small, but potentially important realization.

"Let me try to explain this in the simplest way possible," he continued. "We're called Oculi. We can create reality through observation."

My stomach roiled and my lungs forgot how to work. *Holy shitballs.*

Reid

She hugged her stomach.

"Okay." Anxiety had a firm hold on my pulse. Maybe I shouldn't have been nervous, but I was responsible for quite possibly the most powerful person in the world, who just happened to be the girl I'd had a thing for since I was a kid. I'd made sure she wouldn't recognize me, but I was still terrified she'd figure out who I was before I was ready to tell her. I shoved my personal feelings aside, letting my training take over. "Have you heard of Bohr or Heisenberg, or maybe Schrödinger?"

"Of course, the fathers of modern quantum physics."

"Of course?" If I hadn't grown up in the Hub, I doubted I would've known those names, or anything about quantum physics. What normal person, especially at the age of seventeen, just *knew* about quantum physics? But, then again, she wasn't a normal seventeen-year-old.

"Okay. Well, have you heard of something called the Copenhagen Interpretation or Schrödinger's Cat experiment or—"

"You mean the theory that caused half of the physicists of the world to throw their arms up in dismay? The highly disputed and controversial theory stating that a system stops being a superposition of states and becomes either one or the other when an observation takes place?" Her mouth dropped open as she realized the words she'd said. She'd just made the connection.

I knew she was smart, but this was impressive. I was about to make sure she did, in fact, understand, but she continued. "When the act of observation is performed, *that* is what makes the wave function collapse into one of the two possible states. Is that what we're talking about?"

Shock at her understanding ran my blood cold. "So," I said, not sure how to continue, "you understand that in the theory, the transition from the possible to the actual takes place during the—"

Josie's words overlapped mine and we spoke in unison: "Act of observation."

She'd rendered me speechless, and I didn't think that'd ever happened. She whispered, "Heisenberg, 1958."

"How do you know all of that?" I asked, even though I knew the answer to the question. Her parents were scientists. But still.

"My dad is a physicist. When I was little, we had a dog named Erwin. Schrödinger's first name."

I stood and motioned for Josie to follow. I didn't like sitting still out in the open for too long. Josie's stare zigzagged around the yard. She was keeping watch, too. Quick study.

She followed my lead through the yard. "That's what we're doing," I said. "We're observing the possible into the actual. We're observing our own reality. We're ultimate observers, Pushing and Retracting reality. We're Oculi."

Her eyes scanned the opposite side of the street. "You're saying the theory isn't just a theory. Pushing reality, just by thinking it in our heads, then observing it with our eyes?"

"Exactly."

"Who are ultimate observers? Oculi?"

"Oculi. Latin for 'eyes.' We manipulate reality and are everywhere. We cover the Earth, in every possible country. Most of us are aware of what we do; few are clueless. Our race has been kept a secret from Plancks."

Josie paused under a street light on the sidewalk. Her emerald irises peered at me from under a flop of hair. "Plancks?"

"A Planck is a normal person, not an Oculi. You know, like Max Planck, another 'father' of quantum physics. He came up with Planck's constant in his equations. It's a constant. Unchanging. Boring. That's what ordinary people are."

She huffed out a half laugh, but her face was still punctuated with worry. "And where do I fit into all this? Why were you looking for me? How did you know where I was?" She tucked her hair back behind her ears.

For a moment, I was stuck. I got to really look at her. Even a couple years ago, I hadn't had that chance. I'd stolen glances of her when I could, but it was never anything this close.

A black ring outlined her green irises. A smooth slope, peppered with a few light freckles, defined her nose. Her lips, full. Pale skin. Curves I could get lost in. But I couldn't think of her that way. I needed to be her trainer, which also meant I was her rule enforcer.

"How did that guy find me?" Josie's hands tightened around her arms. "Who sent you? Why me?" Every word came out faster than the one before it, and her cheeks grew rosy.

I didn't blame her for wanting answers. Reaching over, I gave her a playful nudge in the shoulder with the tips of my fingers. "We have plenty of time for everything. Calm down."

"How can I calm down when you're talking about observing stuff into reality and you're"—her head oscillated on her shoulders like a fan—"keeping an eye out for people who want to kill me?"

She reminded me of Tinker Bell—sassy and cute until you pissed her off.

A high-pitched screech came from the porch behind us, drawing both our attention. "There you are!" Josie's friend yelled. She skipped down the steps toward us, Santos behind her. They strolled across the large yard.

I stepped back in front of Josie, giving us a few extra

seconds of privacy. "I just gave you a lot of information to digest. Why don't you practice Pushing tonight in the safety of your home, and I'll stand guard outside, keeping you safe."

Josie's brows scrunched. "Wait. What?" She grabbed the bottom of my shirt. "I need to know more. Now."

I stepped forward, Josie's mouth a breath from mine. The moment seemed to slow, or maybe I just wanted it to. I could almost taste her floral scent. I reached around her and carefully snatched her phone from her pocket and stepped away. For the sake of security, I'd Retracted my phone before we'd left the park, ditching it right along with the straightjacket and knives and evidence of the attack. I knew Santos's number by heart. Texted him to ditch his cell and Push another one, then we coordinated the numbers…That part was a bit more complicated.

"Key code?" I asked, needing to get "in" to her phone.

She rattled off a number. If I wasn't mistaken, it was pi.

I swiped down the screen and snorted at her *Guardians of the Galaxy* wallpaper, 'cause if the whole 3141 password didn't tip me off to her geek status, the screen saver would've. I peered down at her, her eyes squinting in anger. "I'm programming my number in your phone and memorizing yours. You need to rest. You've experienced enough for your first day. I'll make sure you get home." I returned her phone and turned to talk to Santos.

She whisper-yelled behind me, "Who are you to tell me to go rest?"

I twisted and lowered my mouth to her ear. "There are dangerous people out there looking for you. I'm your trainer, your teacher. Please trust me, listen to me."

Before I could reassure Josie any more, Hannah arrived. She looped her arm through Josie's. "Jo, why didn't you put your visor down? Your eyes are all watery and red."

Josie replied with a somewhat hysterical laugh.

I hoped she could keep it together. Hannah was a Planck. There were *serious* repercussions for exposing our powers to Plancks.

Hannah turned on a hundred-watt smile. "So he wasn't a mass murderer, I see," she said.

Josie turned, and her gaze locked on me. "Nope. Reid wasn't out to get me. If he were a mass murderer, he would've left me for dead."

A reluctant grin tugged at my lips. This girl…damn, she was sharp. Smart.

"Dude," Hannah hissed.

"Actually," Josie continued, "Reid and I have a mutual friend in Texas."

I walked toward the street, leading our small group. I followed Josie's brilliant story. "Yep. I was told Josie would help me settle in around here. Oh, Santos and I will follow you guys home to make sure you're safe."

"That's so nice!" Hannah gushed.

Josie's voice wasn't nearly as cheerful. "Yeah. So nice."

I watched the girls climb in the car as we walked to our bikes. "Bro, we've intercepted fourteen Oculi and we've never had problems," I said. "We've transferred the one Anomaly and trained the others in their locations with no problems. We've had no tails. We've changed our appearances; we've covered our tracks. It just so happens when we reach Josie, the most important charge in our history, we're tracked? I don't buy it. What if there's a leak?" My pulse quickened as I voiced my worries.

Santos saddled up. "Agreed. This had to be done from the inside. I think we need to go off the grid. At least until she's learned the basics. I don't want the responsibility of transferring a newbie to the Hub, especially if she is an Anomaly like they suspect."

Santos's thoughts mirrored my own, but I'd needed reassurance that I wasn't being paranoid, thinking up conspiracy theories and shit. I straddled my bike. "You think the Hub has been compromised? Because that...I wouldn't know what to do with that."

Santos held his helmet in front of him. "Not sure, man. But she's too important to put her in danger. Why run the risk?"

We *couldn't* run that risk. Josie was probably going to be one of the most powerful people in the world. If the Consortium got ahold of her, the rest of us Oculi were as good as dead.

5.

JOSIE

Hannah jabbered on and on about Santos on the way home, about how they danced and had fun together, all while I'd been discovering that our world wasn't what it seemed. I was so preoccupied with everything else and watching the guys on their bikes following us, I really didn't hear what she'd said.

Hannah parked in front of my house and gave me a hug. "Happy birthday." I gave her a hard squeeze. I didn't know what was real after the night with Reid, but I knew she was. I also didn't know if I was going to live to see her again. For all I knew, another random guy in a ski mask would kill me in my sleep...or maybe Reid would. I wanted to trust him. The rational part of my brain knew if he'd wanted me dead, he could've killed me in the park. That thought kept me from freaking out, from forcing Hannah to drive me to the nearest police station—where my recital of events would either land me in jail or a psych ward.

I stepped out of the car to the thundering rumble of Reid's and Santos's bikes. Reid was watching me in their headlights. He'd parked opposite my house, his gaze analyzing my two-story brick suburban home, and the houses on either side.

I crossed in front of the car. Hannah waved before taking off down the street, Santos following her, but Reid cut his engine. Was he going to finish our conversation and tell me what he was supposed to teach me, to train me for, or was he going to try and kill me himself? I wasn't quite as confident now that we were alone. And I was having serious doubts about coming home, because if he was as evil as the man in the woods, then I'd just allowed him to follow me to my doorstep. I should've known better. I *really* should've known better.

His leg swung over his bike and he placed his helmet on the seat. I didn't run. If he did want to hurt me, I knew I couldn't escape. I knew what he could do with a knife, or even a thought. He closed the distance between us in a few steps.

My porch light reflected in his eyes as he stared at me, and after a few long seconds, he cleared his throat. "The Consortium wants to control all Oculi, and they want those who are the most powerful dead. You need to train in order to protect yourself, to master your abilities, and to fight the Consortium for our lives." Urgency laced his voice.

He stood like he was ready for a brawl, his hands open and loose at his sides and his stance wide. There was no hint of a smile, no joking.

Terror paralyzed me—my thoughts, my body, my breath. I couldn't form a coherent thought, let alone words. The world tilted a bit, and Reid's hand grasped my elbow.

"I know." His voice was gruff and close to my ear. "It's a lot."

Was he for real? Was *this* real? By the *USS Enterprise*, things would be easier if I *were* crazy or drugged. And really, who wishes for *that*? But I'd checked my pupils in the rearview mirror on the ride home. I'd counted my pulse and felt no nausea or dizziness. Granted, those symptoms only appeared when I was, you know, *making* things appear, but for now, I think I could rule out mental illness or intoxication. Then again, my perception of being sane could just be a symptom of—

"Hey, snap out of it."

"Huh?"

"You're mumbling incoherently," Reid said. "And no, you aren't tripping or suffering a *paranoid delusional psychotic break.*"

My mom was a neuroscientist, and while I didn't know much about her research, I had studied up on some of her old textbooks and that whopper of a tome, the *DSM-5*. Reading that thing was worse than checking out WebMD.

"Mental illness is nothing to be ashamed of. One in five Americans suffers from some form of mental illness. There are treatments, doctors, prescriptions that can—"

"Josie, focus. *Please.* I understand that you want to grasp a more…plausible scenario. But denial is not going to change who you are and what you're capable of doing."

I swallowed hard.

"It won't change your circumstances," he said.

And cue the flashback of the attack in the park…

His hand fell from my arm, and I hadn't noticed how

warm his touch was until it was gone. He bent to make sure I looked him in the eyes. "You are in danger. But Santos and I are here to protect you."

Dead. A group of people wanted me dead. I'd have to join others to fight for my life. I couldn't process the concept.

"Why don't you go inside?" he said.

I mindlessly made my way to the garage with Reid a step behind me. "For now," he whispered, "stay alert and be careful. But I'll be on watch, so do try to get some shut-eye."

I punched in the garage code and ducked under the slowly opening door. I slammed the garage door button and watched as it shut out the world. It was amazing the type of numbness that could be achieved through informational overload. And, I won't lie: I rather enjoyed this blank, blissful state of shock.

A warm glow cast soft shadows around the kitchen. Mom had left the light above the kitchen sink on for me. She'd also left a note out on the kitchen island, detailing my chores for tomorrow. A second, hastily penned message said there were leftovers in the refrigerator. I wasn't hungry, but I opened the fridge and considered the takeout container of pad Thai. I stood there for light-years, cataloging the condiments and counting the containers of yogurt and the apples in the fruit bin, letting the cold air wash over me.

But all too soon, the events of the day slipped into my mind, repeating like a scratched DVD, and I gently closed the door to the fridge and paused in the center of the room.

A man was killed tonight. A man who'd tried to kill *me*. I'd given him a coffin with my thoughts. And other people, an entire group of people with superhuman powers, were after me. For a sci-fi fan, this had all the makings of some Marvel comic or something à la George Lucas.

My eyes landed on Eli's Iron Man figurine on the counter. *My brother.* I was jolted from my temporary paralysis, from the shock of everything, from this whole disconnected sense of reality.

I had to protect my family.

My mind looped back to the scenario in the park. I'd Pushed a gun into my hand. I didn't know what kind of gun it was, but I'd blinked and given a Push from within myself. I thought about the gun in my hand.

Heat.

Pain.

Nausea.

And cold metal in my hand.

My fingers wrapped around the handle. The gun was real. Heavy and cold against my palm. I didn't know much about shooting, or even how to reload this thing with bullets. But I'd learn.

I set the gun on the counter and flew to the back hallway door, the door to my mom's lab. It was locked as usual, so I yanked the tiny message window open. Dark. That meant Mom was upstairs in her room.

I ran to the back door, twisted the dead bolt, and entered the code in the security system, then sprinted to the front door. It was already locked. I knew locks probably didn't matter if someone really wanted to get to my family or me, but I had to do everything I could to slow someone down. I flittered around the first floor like a manic hummingbird, pausing at every window to make sure it was secure.

With the first floor as safe as I could make it, I crept up the stairs, with the gun tucked into the back of my pants, to check on my family. A sliver of light stretched across the hallway from my parents' bedroom. With measured steps, I peeked in the doorway. The desk light above Mom's computer shone down on her silky strawberry-blond hair, her head resting on her folded arms in front of her computer screen, iPhone next to her. She'd fallen asleep working and waiting up for me. The size of my parents' bed behind Mom seemed larger. It wasn't, though—just empty.

I worried about her. She worked so much and she seemed more distant, lost in her own thoughts, each day. I wanted to tell her everything that had happened tonight, like I would have before Nick died, but I couldn't. She'd think I'd lost my mind. Maybe I had, despite Reid's protests to the opposite. And she didn't deserve that.

Still, it hurt. The truth bubbled from my stomach and wanted to break free. Mom was like me; she understood facts, theorem, science. She would understand, or at least be willing to listen...But I swallowed back the words, the disbelief clawing up my throat.

"Mom," I whispered.

She practically fell out of her chair and glanced to me with one eye closed. "Everything go okay?" Her words were rushed, alarmed.

I wavered for a moment. Man, I wanted to tell her everything, but her eyes were glassy and unfocused. With everything she was dealing with—Nick dead, Dad gone, her health failing, my brother and I being far from normal...I cleared my throat. "Yeah, Mom, it was fun. I'm home—you can go to sleep now."

She nodded, stood with the help of her cane, and gave a strained smile.

"Night," I whispered.

I continued down the hallway and edged into Eli's room. He was curled in a ball under his blankets facing the wall. I checked his window and placed a kiss on Eli's forehead before I slipped into my room.

I flicked on my light, shut the door, and my Benedict Khan and Benedict Sherlock posters welcomed me home.

I went straight for my window, pushing the blinds back to check the lock, and there was Reid, walking the perimeter of my yard in the dark. Was he keeping people out or keeping me in? His face snapped up, and his eyes locked on mine for a moment before he continued his patrol. The lock was secure, but that wasn't going to be enough to make me feel safe.

When a guy could create and destroy things with his mind, was anyone really safe?

My hands automatically went to the gun at my back. The weight of the weapon surprised me all over again. I thought of the metals—iron, steel, copper. Heavier elements. But would this be enough to protect me? Could anything in my limited knowledge suffice?

Flopping on my bed, I set the gun next to me, opened my laptop, and started searching handguns. I wanted to know what type of gun I'd made appear and how to use it. As soon as I found the picture of my gun, a standard-issue Glock for many police officers, a light blinked in the lower right corner of my screen. Security. It was time to update the firewall for my computer.

My cursor paused over the button as panic stilled my body. I'd thought about the security of my house, but what about the security of my computer? I closed out of the window. If the creeps after me monitored my computer, my internet searches could give the impression that I was an Oculus to those looking for such signs. I couldn't put my family in more danger than they already were.

And there it was. The moment in which I accepted what I had seen and what I could do.

I wouldn't delude myself or deny what I'd seen. What I had done. I recalled my zombielike state when I'd learned that Nick had died. But I couldn't dwell in that painless, oblivious place. And I couldn't deny the truth now. Not with my brother's and mother's safety on the line.

I might not understand all that I'd seen and done today, but that didn't make it any less true. Great Tesseract, there were so many things in the scope of this universe—heck, in the multiverses—that I couldn't wholly comprehend or explain, but that didn't make them any less real.

Real was the gun weighing down my hand.

I'd done all I could to keep us safe: secured our house and Pushed a weapon. What else could I do to prepare my family or myself? Practice. I could practice Pushing. Like Reid had said. Best to start simple, though.

I leaned over the edge of my bed to the bottom of my nightstand. I yanked the basket up into my lap and carefully pulled out my stuffed puppy I'd had since birth, followed by one of his severed legs. It'd been slowly tugged away from the body from years of play, but I never had the heart to toss him out. The picture of the mended stuffed animal was a fleeting half thought. Then heat, pain, nausea.

The leg was secure, mended. My stuffed dog sewn into one piece, without the use of needle and thread.

A tiny thrill danced up my chest. If I could create a gun and a mended toy, what else could I do?

I set my sights on the floor in front of my dresser and pictured a boulder like the one I'd sat on in Marisa's front yard, then gave a small nudge from within myself. The painful trio of heat, pain, and nausea came and went in the same time as it had with the gun, but the severity was more intense than when I'd Pushed the leg onto the stuffed dog. I opened my eyes from a long blink, and the rock I'd imagined sat on my bedroom floor. Mossy limestone. It was bigger than I'd realized when it was outside. Crap. I could hide small things, but how was I going to hide a boulder from my mom?

I concentrated on the rock vanishing, making it disappear as I'd witnessed Reid do several times. It didn't move or blink out of existence. I concentrated and gave that nudge from within me again, that want, that desire. A dull headache throbbed in the back of my head and behind my eyes, matching my heartbeat, almost like it was laughing at me.

I was done trying to make it go away for now. Instead, I slipped off my bed to touch the weathered limestone. It was rough under my hand, but the moss was like velvet.

It was real.

My room went out of focus and my breathing became labored.

I should've been relieved after successfully Pushing my personal weapon, mended puppy, and landscaping rock. Instead, fear crept into my room and wrapped its tentacles around me like a giant squid. Fast and graceful, the terror enveloped me. I took a break from Pushing, letting the headache subside, changed into comfy clothes, and spent the next several hours combing every scientific book I owned, trying to make sense of what could be possible within this new ability. I made lists and gathered everything I could from around the house to make emergency backpacks for my family and myself. If a group was out to get me, we needed to leave and be able to defend ourselves. Passports, hats, dark clothing. I Pushed two bulletproof vests and a smaller one for Eli. That took some effort. It had been difficult to visualize and even more difficult to Push. I quietly retrieved our stash of maps from the kitchen to add to the backpacks and opened a map of the city.

What would be our escape route? We'd need to flee town, seen by the fewest amount of people possible. Every route north would be watched. If we took Highway 41 east, instead of 75, there would be less traffic. By then, Mom could help me figure out where to go from there. Or, if Reid were truly here to help me, maybe he'd have an idea of how to escape. But what if he didn't let us leave? What if he wasn't safe, either?

My phone vibrated on my nightstand and startled me so much, I jumped and dropped my light saber pen on the map. There was no picture on my phone screen, just the word *Reid* and his text: *u r safe*

I typed back, *hard to believe when the Empire is after a young Jedi*

My phone vibrated with his response. *Lol. U r fine. promise*

Me: *You don't understand.*

I tiptoed to the window and peeked through the blinds into my yard below. Wedged between two bushes directly across from my window, Reid leaned against the fence, his phone lighting up his face. His head slowly drew upward, and his gaze latched onto mine. My phone vibrated through my palm.

I hit the button and read his message: *I do understand. Would it make you feel better if I stood watch in your room? say the word and I'll come up.*

Would I feel safer with him in my room? I wasn't sure if I could trust him, but I knew I didn't trust the people trying to kill me, and he seemed to be against those people. He definitely seemed to be on my side. If that warranted my full trust, I wasn't sure, but I *would* feel better with him closer. He'd already protected my life once. And for as much as I vacillated like a pendulum, he *had* saved me. If I had been a target, he could've killed me at any time. Yeah, so I kept needing to reassure myself. A guy who could erase a forest and conjure items out of the air—he could do a lot more than stand guard outside my home.

And, hello, if nothing else, he could deal with the boulder in my bedroom.

My fingers trembled as they hovered over my phone keyboard. I typed, *Come up.*

I pulled the string for the blinds and they slid up. Reid ran toward the house. Stairs appeared, one at a time with each step he took, raising him higher and higher toward my room. Reid was three stairs away when my window was suddenly open. Taking a step sideways, I gave him space to climb inside my room. He straightened and, with my next blink, the window was closed and the blinds drawn.

"Hey, Luke," he whispered. His eyes fell to my shirt.

I wore my Vader tee with the words WHO'S YOUR DADDY? printed across my chest. My cheeks burned and my stomach flipped. Of course, of all nights, that was the shirt I'd chosen…

His head swiveled around, taking in my mess of a room. The maps, books, and backpacks earned me a grunt of approval. Then he saw the boulder and muffled a laugh.

"I was practicing," I mumbled.

"Sorry. I didn't expect to see Mount Rushmore in here." One corner of his mouth pulled up in a grin.

Having a boy in my bedroom wasn't allowed. And I'd just welcomed a hottie with superhuman abilities inside. I'd broken all kinds of rules. That had to be why my heart thrashed against my ribs like a caged animal. That and the whole Oculi "out to get me" thing. Trying to ease my panic, or whatever it was, I inhaled deeply and massaged my temples. The stress of everything and the proximity of said hot boy did not help the constant dull headache that was now setting up camp in my skull.

"How about I—" Reid paused mid-sentence and froze like he just got hit by Iceman. I followed his gaze…to my gun. "What are you doing with a Glock? You don't know how to use that thing. Could you even pull the trigger when it came down to it?"

My throat felt thick, making it difficult to form words. "If someone tries to come between me and my family, yes, I'd pull the trigger."

He let out a puff of air, and his eyes were sympathetic. "Look. I get it. Really, I do. But this is exactly why you have to train, to learn how to use your abilities in order to protect yourself and others. This"—he nodded to the gun—"is just an accident waiting to happen."

I closed my eyes and rubbed my temples again. "I don't know what is going on. I don't understand. And—"

I flinched when his hands landed on my shoulders. I sat on my bed with him beside me, his larger body settling him toward the middle while I leaned off the edge. My eyes fluttered open when he squeezed my muscles. "You need to relax. Freaking out isn't going to help the headaches." My stomach dipped as he moved his strong hands. It had taken me weeks to let Tate get this close to me.

His thumbs worked in neat rows up the back of my neck, while chills tingled down my spine. "I...I don't know what is real and what isn't. Anything could be an illusion." None of this was logical or rational, meaning I couldn't process it, understand it. I wrapped a hand around my stomach, trying to calm the uneasiness.

His hand swept over my head, smoothing my hair. I knew he probably only meant to move my hair so he could see my face, but the motion was slow, and the way his hand swept down my back felt like a caress.

"Hey."

I closed my eyes.

Reid grabbed my hand, threaded our fingers. "I'm real, Josie."

I opened my eyes, but I couldn't meet his gaze, so I focused on our hands instead. I felt the calluses along his palms, the thickness of his knuckles between my fingers, the soft pads of his fingers moving over the top of my hand. His steady heartbeat thrummed from his wrist to mine.

We stayed that way for moments—minutes?—until his hand retreated, until only our fingertips connected. We were barely touching and yet the contact was intense, magnified. I gasped a breath.

Reid shook his head. He released me and stuffed his hands in his pockets, flexing his triceps, and said, "I should teach you a few things. Ready for lesson one?"

"Uh, sure."

He stepped to my magnetic chalkboard. My whole life was there. Pictures of my family and me. Photos of my friends. Undergrad Physics Achievement Award certificates. Homework assignments. Brochures on summer programs from all of the top universities blowing up my mailbox with "Come join our state-of-the-art physics program" letters. Usually the wall made me smile—it was proof I had a life, unlike all those years we were homeschooled. Tonight it seemed like a reminder of how much of our world may not be real.

A second later, the wall and everything were gone, replaced with a whiteboard. Reid tapped the board with his marker. "The three rules of the Resistance." Reid scribbled, his back toward me. And I tried not to watch the muscles in his shoulder twitch under his shirt as he wrote. I was relieved when he finally finished and faced me. "One, cause no harm. Two, never reveal Oculi abilities. Three, don't play God."

6.

Reid

Doubt shadowed Josie's face. She wasn't a rule breaker by nature, and she knew she'd already broken rules. Good. It would help keep her safe.

I scribbled the word *Oculi* across the board. "There are three types of Oculi." Josie's eyebrows arched. Was she surprised or overwhelmed? I couldn't worry that much. I had to treat her like any other Resistance member. The marker squeaked as I wrote *Pushers*, then *Retractors*.

Josie sat cross-legged on the end of her bed, resting one elbow on her knee. "Retractors?"

I dragged in a long breath, readying myself for the explanation and her possible breakdown. "Pushers Push reality, make the possible real. Retractors Retract reality. Basically, they make shit disappear. They're pretty rare, but they exist. If the Pusher was a pen and created, then a Retractor would be the eraser. *But* Retractors can only Retract what's been

Pushed. They can't erase what a pen hasn't created. Get it?"

Josie straightened her posture. "Yeah."

I spelled out the word. *A-N-O-M-A-L-Y*. "And then there's—"

"Some people can do both." She shot off the bed.

It was a little spooky how she could figure out what I'd say next. "How'd you—"

"You continued. It was the most logical step in the sequence."

"Okay, *Spock*. Yes. We call those who can do both Anomalies. They can Retract anything whether it was Pushed or not, just nothing with a soul. They're rarer yet."

Josie crossed her arms. "That doesn't make sense. By definition, an anomaly is something different from the norm. Pushers and Retractors are so not normal."

"Actually," I said, popping the cap back onto the marker, "in *our* reality, it is the norm."

"Do the abilities come on at once? Like, I tried to make the rock disappear earlier but I…Well, it's still there." She gestured to the boulder.

"Oculi abilities start around age seventeen. An Anomaly can usually Push first, and the Retracting comes soon after, usually within days."

Hitching her hands on her hips and cocking her head, she said, "I'm assuming a lot of the unexplainable phenomenon in the world can be explained by Pushers, Retractors, and Anomalies?"

"Not all, but yeah. A lot." I scooted past Josie to her bedside table. I picked through her stack of books, some novels, some nonfiction physics and theory textbooks. *Jackpot.* I held up a book titled *The Physics of Star Trek*. "Are you a VIP card holder to Club Nerd?"

Josie stomped over and snagged the book out of my hand, her cheeks pink. "Nerds don't know they're nerds. I know I'm a…well, I prefer to be called a dork, thank you."

I turned away from her, trying not to laugh at her adorable nerdiness. "All the random or freak stuff, like a boat in the middle of the desert? Pushers who were new, or lazy, or careless. Something is there one minute but not the next? You think your eyes are playing tricks on you. A Retractor could've done that."

"Okay then…" Josie's voice was directly behind me. I spun, trapped between her and the bed. "What about people walking away from an accident unscathed when they should've died from the impact or whatever?" Josie asked, her face tilted up toward mine and her brows furrowed. I could almost hear her neurons firing.

Being so close to her in her room next to her bed made me think of things I shouldn't be thinking about. I stepped to the side. "That's usually chance, fate, a greater plan, or whatever you want to call it. We can't move vehicles with humans inside. That would make them aware of us, or of *something*. And that's rule number three—don't play God."

Josie followed two steps behind me around her room. "What about wishing for someone to do something, say something, making a decision on something or—"

"No."

"Why not?"

"We Push and Retract reality, but people still have free will. We can't control their minds."

"Got it. No bending will."

I stood by her dresser where a picture of her, Nick, and

Eli sat in a frame. My chest hurt. I hadn't seen a picture of Nick in a long time.

"What about that?" Josie asked, pointing behind me.

A pile of money. The top bills were hundreds, which meant Josie had Pushed at least a million bucks. She started toward the heap of cash, but I blocked her way. "You want to draw that attention to yourself? You want to tell them exactly where you are? Go ahead. But the quickest way to pop on the radar, Consortium or not, is to Push a million."

The green of her irises darkened and the whites of her eyes expanded.

"I told you, the Consortium has infiltrated all branches and levels of government and society. There aren't many of them, but they are strategically placed." Josie's mouth opened to say something, but I put my hand up to stop her. "Why do you think the IRS has rules for deposits over ten thousand dollars? Red flag." Her mouth closed. "Every action has a consequence, and some of these consequences can be seen—monitored." I didn't want to sound mean, but I needed her to understand.

"Oculi can live quite comfortably, but we have to be smart about it. You Push as you go. The more extravagant, the more attention you'll draw. And we don't want attention." Josie nibbled on her bottom lip. "But, by all means, if you want to live it up, Push a few mill, just know you'll be dead sooner rather than later."

Josie shifted to see around me. The money was gone; I'd already Retracted it. "You didn't have to be a dick about it." She flopped back on her bed and rubbed her temples.

I crossed my arms. "I'm saving your ass." She was hurting from all the Pushing she'd done. "Speaking of consequences, that headache is from using your abilities so much today. You can probably already tell that the bigger or more intricate a Push or Retraction, the more severe the pain. The pain and nausea will lessen. You'll be able to see a difference in the next day or two. But from here on out, you have to remember that Pushing and Retracting take energy and that energy comes at a price."

"What's the price?"

Taking a seat on the boulder, I leaned forward in an attempt to make this part more conversational. "We observe through the use of our eyes, and the information travels through the optic nerve to our brain. I'm sure you know that's oversimplified. Anyway, the amount of energy we use with our abilities fries our nerves, which leads to degradation of the parietal lobe, cerebrum, and cortex." And the occipital and frontal lobes, and, oh yeah, it causes blindness, neurological degeneration, and a boatload of pain. But I didn't say all that. Still, she had to know the risks. "The energy for our Pushing or Retracting is stored, almost like a savings account. Over time and usage, that supply of energy slowly dwindles. The more we use our abilities, the more energy we use, the faster we'll physically deteriorate, go mad, or…die."

The color drained from Josie's cheeks. "Die." She said it a fraction of a second after me. She understood.

Most Oculi simply lost their powers at some point. They reached the finite expanse of their abilities and then one day, they ceased to be able to call on them. They lived the rest of their lives as Plancks, no one any wiser. It was the peaceful end to a rare gift. Others…for others, the end was anything but peaceful.

Josie's gaze shifted to something behind me. Over my

shoulder, I caught a glimpse of a photo of her and her family. "How am I an Oculi, Reid? Where do we come from?"

I'd let her draw her own conclusions, and she had. "It's an inherited trait."

Her whole body seemed to tense, and she pulled her trembling hands into her lap. A deep crease formed between her eyes before she dropped her head. Yeah, learning your parents were in on the "lie," that was a bitter pill to swallow. Kinda right up there with the whole red pill/blue pill scenario from *The Matrix*. Swear to God, if given a choice, I would've gone the blue-pill route and not known about any of this. Plancks didn't know how good they had it.

I stepped forward, not sure how to comfort her. Josie lifted her head, and her lower lip gave a little shiver. It really shot a hole in my stoic, I-don't-give-a-shit trainer facade I was trying to maintain. And if her eyes welled up again…forget it, I was a goner.

She bit her lip, squeezed her eyes shut, and let out a long sigh. When she opened her eyes, her usual unshaken, calculating face was in place. Either she was as tough as nails or she was a damn good actress. "I'll talk to my mom. Should I do that now?"

It was after four in the morning. "Why don't you try to grab a couple hours of sleep? I have a feeling tomorrow will be a long day. I'll keep watch. You'll be safe. Santos is on call close by, too. Do you want me to stay inside?"

She nodded quickly. "Please."

Of course I'd stay. I needed to talk to Josie's mom after she did—I needed to convince them both that it was in our best interests to go off the grid…if they wanted to live.

7.

JOSIE

Sleep didn't come, and I wasn't sure if it'd ever come again. After an hour of tossing and turning and exchanging long, awkward looks with Reid from my bed—he sat across from me with his back to the wall, watching me, and, really, how was I supposed to catch any shut-eye like *that*?—I shoved up to a seated position. I'd been thinking about how my parents knew about all this and the lies I'd been told. My chest hurt, like the Hulk had my torso in a death squeeze. It was probably psychosomatic. I also thought about the "cost" of using our abilities. Seems I was just a tad premature in thinking myself delusional—my mental problems would inevitably come, just not right away.

Reid watched me, and I finally asked the question I'd pondered for at least five minutes. "How did you Retract all those trees in the park? If a Retractor can only Retract what has been Pushed?"

"I'm an Anomaly, Josie."

Right. And Anomalies seemed to be able to do just about anything. At a cost… "If all the Pushing and Retracting subtract from our so-called savings accounts, then why did you Retract all those trees in the park? That was pretty massive."

Reid, sitting on the boulder he hadn't Retracted yet, shrugged, then leaned onto his forearms. "I needed to make sure you were safe."

I didn't know how to respond to that. My tongue felt like a cotton ball in my mouth. The entire night, every time he'd Pushed or Retracted, it had been for me. He'd tapped into his own energy bank, inching his way closer to a physical or mental breakdown, draining his brain of power—for me. Overwhelming gratitude bubbled in my stomach and moved into my chest. I needed to convey how much that meant, but I'd just sound ridiculous or I'd muck up the words, so I settled for simplicity. "Thank you."

A lazy smile pulled at his lips. My thank-you wasn't enough for his personal sacrifice, but he acted like it was.

"I can't sleep and I need to talk to my mom." It was easy for me to connect the dots. Reid talked about neurological issues, something my mother specialized in, then said this whole phenomenon was inherited. Which meant my mom knew. "Does she know about you?"

"Yeah." One of his hands combed through his dark waves. "I'll give you some time alone with her, and then I'll need to talk to you both."

Part of me wanted to stay in bed, dreading what I'd learn from my mom, but part of me wanted to march into her room and demand answers. That seemed to be my MO for the last two years since Nick died—stuck in a constant limbo with my mother, never getting anywhere with her. The two parts of me usually warred with each other and I never initiated anything, didn't ask the questions I needed answered. Not this time, though.

I pinwheeled my feet to the floor and beelined for the door. Glancing over my shoulder to Reid, I saw there was something in his eyes, an understanding maybe, that reassured me.

Mom's bedroom door was open, revealing a dark, empty room, but my brother's door was closed. This was my mom's usual—going to bed late and getting up early. The smell of coffee hung in the air and I followed the scent downstairs. She had to have heard Reid and me talking in my room.

I rounded the corner. Mom rested a basket of clothes on her hip as she hobbled from the laundry room into the kitchen. Paused in the middle of the floor, she stared at me, the creases in her face seeming deeper and her eyes tired. "What do you know?" She set the clothesbasket on the counter and sat at the island.

I rehashed almost everything since meeting Reid at school yesterday, but I left out the way he made my insides do funny things. I didn't share that kind of stuff with my mom, or anyone, really.

She let me talk without interruption, and I ended my summary of recent events with Reid's whiteboard lesson. I thought maybe she'd say something about Reid being in my room, but that didn't seem to faze her. She cleared her throat and said, "I never wanted to have this conversation with you. I hope you understand, or will someday, that this was not our wish for you. We didn't want you to experience or know any of this. That's why we didn't tell you anything—in the hope that you wouldn't be affected."

I wasn't sure if that was the truth or not, but, besides the birthday cake she'd attempted to make, this was one of the most affectionate things she'd said to me in a long time.

Mom inhaled slowly as she stood and limped over to pour a cup of coffee. She made her way into the living room and waited for me expectantly before she settled on the couch. The size of the couch seemed out of proportion for just the two of us. I remembered when Nick, Eli, and I would all pile on this couch with Mom and Dad on Saturday mornings. I wanted that back. At least that feeling of security and predictability, anyway.

I sat, and Mom's green eyes found mine. "Twenty years ago, your dad and I both worked for Science Industries, he as a physicist, me as a neurologist, both of us Anomalies. We were individually recruited to work for SI. At the time, we didn't know the goal of the Consortium was to control Oculi, specifically Anomalies. No one really did. Your dad and I were under the impression, as was everyone who worked at SI, that we were doing research that would benefit Oculi and, in turn, aid humanity. We didn't know the Consortium wanted to keep Anomalies in check until I was asked to experiment with ways to strengthen and weaken Anomalies."

I shoved a pillow in my lap. I wanted to know more…yet I didn't.

Mom sipped her coffee casually and continued. "I worked on a vaccination for Anomalies, basically to strengthen their characteristics. It worked on a cellular level, affecting the DNA of the Anomaly recipient. After months of experiment-ing and testing, I determined the inoculation would enable an

Anomaly to do more, Push more, Retract more, make reality *exactly* what they wanted it to be. Move beyond the limitations Anomalies had, which really weren't many. That's when I realized we needed to dig deeper to figure out what was really going on at SI, because this vaccination would make an Anomaly Godlike. Nearly invincible.

"We discovered that the Consortium, though it was a small organization, was integrated into all aspects of life—law enforcement, government, banking—and their purpose was to keep Plancks safe through policing Oculi. As this was all happening, your dad and I fell in love. We didn't like the direction things were moving within SI, within the Consortium. No one should have the power I'd created, nor should they have their power weakened. Who were we to play God?"

Anxiety simmered in the pit of my stomach. I didn't like the direction this story was headed, either. I prepared for what was coming next.

"I wanted to quit my job, but a place like SI is not easy to leave. Your dad and I planned on exiting the company, but we couldn't do it simultaneously. We kept our relationship a secret and planned on my leaving first.

"On my last day, your dad was in my lab when security raided it. They wanted the enhancer. They approached, armed with loaded weapons, and I was holding the syringe with the enhancer. I gave your dad half the syringe, then stuck myself, knowing if the enhancer worked, your dad and I wouldn't abuse our abilities. We were moral people who'd never use it in the wrong way. We Pushed and Retracted our way to the window and jumped two stories, me taking a gunshot to the thigh." She patted her leg.

"A gunshot—after what Reid had told me, I assumed…"

"You thought it was the debilitating aftereffects of over-usage of my Oculi abilities."

I could only nod.

The tiniest of smiles tugged at my mother's lips, there for a second and gone the next. "No," she said. "I don't have that problem."

"Mom…"

"Let me finish," she said. "After our escape, we slowly assembled those like us, Oculi who didn't want to be controlled and manipulated, and planned to take down the Consortium, knowing it would take time to do so."

Mom paused. She shoved off the couch with the help of her cane. "Something to drink?" She couldn't sit for too long without having to move, due to the pain in her leg.

My head swimming in new information about a life I never knew my parents had, I hadn't noticed I was already following Mom without question.

I grabbed myself orange juice and Mom topped off her coffee. "Will you get that for me?" she said, pointing to a small wooden box on a high shelf. I retrieved it and placed it on the kitchen island.

We stood across from each other. Mom took a long gulp of coffee and sighed. "Shortly after we escaped from the lab, I found out I was pregnant with Nick. Before we were married."

This was a surprise. From what Mom had told Nick and me, Nick was a honeymoon baby. With everything else she was revealing to me, though, I shouldn't have been shocked.

Mom filled the silence. "I guess you could say Nick was a

pleasant surprise."

"You didn't plan on having children?"

"No," she said. "Your dad and I didn't think it was safe. But then Nick came along, and he was so healthy and happy. And so were we. We discovered a joy unlike any we'd known. Parenthood changed us." She took another sip of coffee and avoided looking at me.

I sipped my OJ and tried to swallow.

"When Nick was a normal baby with absolutely no side effects, we eventually made the decision to have other children. We wanted a family and thought, if we stayed away from the Consortium, we would be safe to do so."

I slid my shaking hands from my cup into my lap. "And?" Deep inside, I already knew the answer. Something happened with Nick.

"After we had Nick, we met with other Oculi like ourselves, trying to fly under the Consortium radar. As we moved around the country, homeschooling you guys, we slowly helped form what is now the Resistance, and—"

"Wait." I coughed, nearly choking on a swig of juice. "What do you mean by *we*?"

Mom swirled her coffee again. "Your dad and I, along with several others."

"What others?"

Mom slipped the lid off the box and pulled out a few pictures. Laying the photos between us, she said, "These people."

I spread out the old photographs. Deanna and her daughter, Stella. Stella and I used to play when we were little. The Ross family. Their son was my brother's age, his good friend, and I'd had a crush on him growing up. Mr. and Mrs. Davis. They were the grandparents we never had. The last time I saw any of these people was at Nick's funeral more than two years ago. Nick had a role in this, bigger than I'd ever imagined. A drip of sweat rolled down the back of my neck.

I peeked up at Mom. "They're all Oculi?"

Mom took another sip and nodded. "They all helped us start what is now the Resistance. None of us wanted to be controlled by the Consortium."

Even the family friends, who visited us all over the country, were a part of it. It was overwhelming—everything right in front of me, but I'd never seen it. I didn't know what to say or to think.

I thoughtlessly took another sip, and Mom continued. "The Resistance grew, as did the Consortium and their efforts to obtain power. About twelve years ago, we found out their plans to eliminate Anomalies altogether, and that pushed the Resistance to organize, to mobilize. Things at home were fine. Nick and you knew nothing about what your dad really did on his business trips, which was to help organize the Resistance efforts…until your brother turned seventeen and we found out he had Oculi abilities. Then he died."

She twisted her lips, seemed to ponder something. "Once we moved here, your dad spent a lot of time in the Denver Resistance Hub. The Council, which is exactly what it sounds like, decided they needed to get someone on the inside of the Consortium, and who better than someone who'd started there in the first place?"

The orange juice soured on my tongue. "Dad."

"Yes, your father has gone undercover into the Consortium to spy and report back to the Resistance. But, as you know, we haven't heard from him in a while. At all. We don't even know if he's still alive at this point." She kept her eyes on the coffee mug.

I refused to believe my dad was dead. For the first time, I was starting to understand my family's past and our future. Neither were fairy tales.

Mom cleared her throat, pulling my attention back to her. "When Nick was a toddler, we thought we were in the clear. Eventually we had you, then Eli. Your dad and I didn't want to raise our kids in a Hub, so we took turns training at the biggest Hub in Denver and moved our family regularly to avoid the Consortium. Since your dad and I took it upon ourselves to train Oculi, we exhausted our abilities. We can no longer Push or Retract." She pinched the bridge of her nose and squeezed her eyes tight.

I'd been right. She didn't have abilities. Neither of them did. But they had in the beginning.

It would take time—years, probably—for me to be able to process the multiple knowledge bombs Mom had just dropped in my lap. I mean, my entire life had been built upon lie after lie. I hated her for that. And on the heels of that burning hate was a pain that cleaved straight through the heart of me.

But I wouldn't dwell on my emotions. They wouldn't help me to process this information. These feelings wouldn't help me assess anything. Events had been set into motion before I was even born. Those were the elements I focused on.

I needed to know what I was supposed to be training for. "What is the Resistance's *cause*?" Whatever it was, was it worth risking my life?

8.

Reid

I turned the corner in just enough time to hear Josie's question to her mom. I could answer that one. "The cause? Our lives and every Planck life on Earth."

Josie whipped around on the stool to face me. She should've looked tired, but she didn't—every part of her was awake, seeing most of her world as it really was for the first time.

Mrs. Harper's cold eyes swept over me. "Reid." The resemblance between her and Josie was uncanny, but Josie's face was much warmer, brimming with just a tad less hatred.

"Mrs. Harper." I saluted her. "We need to move your family. Our cover has been blown—there's a leak. We were attacked in the park last night."

She snagged her cane, shoved off the stool, and wobbled. I started toward her, but she held up a hand. "I'm fine." She positioned the cane under her more securely and straightened.

Josie's mom shuffled to the back hall leading to the garage. "Eli is still asleep. Is your partner outside to take over safety surveillance?" I gave her a deep nod. "Follow me, then." She opened a closet and shoved aside several jackets. She moved her hand along the back wall and a panel slid open, revealing a second door with a keypad. Mrs. Harper placed her hand over it. I caught the flickering blue light of a retinal scan as she leaned her face toward the panel. High tech.

The partition opened.

"Close the door to the closet," Mrs. Harper said.

In the darkness, only the blue from the panel illuminated our faces and maybe a foot or two into the corridor.

Josie flipped on the flashlight app on her phone. "I can't see anything, Mom."

"That's the point. What can't be 'seen' can't be Pushed or Retracted."

Josie and I followed her mom through the weird door into a sterile hall that reminded me of a hospital with its antiseptic smell, only all of the walls were blacked out.

I thrust my arms forward to gauge the width of the hallway, which was four, maybe five feet wide. The light from Josie's phone made me think the ceiling was pretty high.

Running lights appeared on the floor in an icy blue color that lit up the ground in a line. "That leads to a dummy panic room," Mrs. Harper said. "You reach the end of the hallway, hit the panel with your hand, and it will open."

"A dummy panic room?" Josie looked at me questioningly. I just shrugged.

Her mom swept by the two of us in the opposite direction, farther into the darkness until we butted up against a black wall. She bent and touched the ground, her palm flush against the floor. It activated another sensory panel. The black wall in front of us slid open.

"Whoa."

Yeah. I kinda had to agree with Josie on that one. I'd seen a lot of high-tech security at the Hub, but this was surreal.

It took Mrs. Harper a couple of seconds to reposition her cane and rise back to her feet. I took a step toward her, and in the dim light of Josie's phone, I saw her mother's features harden. *Okay, I won't help you up.* Apparently Josie knew better than to offer. I probably should've learned my lesson when I'd tried to help her in the kitchen.

"Where are we going?" Josie asked. Although she was already following her mom.

Mrs. Harper stepped into the elevator—I was able to discern that much when I followed Josie into the tight space — and she didn't look at either of us as she pushed a button and the doors closed.

"Mom, where are we going?"

"Down."

Uh, this was Florida. Between being at sea level and the low water table, a subterranean basement? Um, not so likely a scenario. As if reading my mind, Mrs. Harper glanced over her shoulder. "Amazing what a couple of good Pushes can do, isn't it?"

I grunted more than responded. If Josie could take this all in stride, so could I.

Josie made a sputtering sound, like her thoughts were moving too quickly for her to speak them. So maybe she wasn't quite as cool about all of this as she seemed.

I couldn't imagine how she was feeling at the moment. She had to be second-guessing everything—including her mom, who was just as impersonal as she had been two years ago, if not more so.

Once we hit the bottom, the elevator doors dinged open and Mrs. Harper slipped a series of switches on the wall, lighting a pristine white room. High-tech communication devices, several computers, machines, and a dozen surveillance televisions lined one wall. The rest of the sterile room was a science lab. Bottles, jugs, containers, microscopes, an assortment of various science-looking machines. Josie's face said everything I was feeling—complete disbelief. *This* was under their house? A heavy metal door anchored the opposite end of the room, with shelves to the side of it.

"This is your lab," Josie accused.

"It is…among other things." Mrs. Harper shook her head. "The space off the family room, the other 'lab' that you're used to seeing me use, that's just for show. It's a decoy."

Right. Decoy lab. Dummy panic room. There was a friggin' labyrinth of tunnels and spaces running under this house. And, really, had I expected anything else? A person didn't maintain her anonymity, manage to break away from SI, form the Resistance, *and* keep off the radar without some serious precautionary measures.

I took stock of the room, imagining what I would have to Push or Retract to maintain the integrity of it. If one didn't know it was here and couldn't observe it, then it was virtually indiscoverable. I wanted to believe that, but…

Josie headed to the shelves and held up a box. "Mom? Hair dye." Well, since she could no longer Push or Retract,

Mrs. Harper would have to change her looks the old-fashioned way. I crossed the room and watched Josie's hands move quickly through the shelves. Stacks of money, clothes, and a lock box labeled DOCUMENTS. One shelf was entirely filled with medical supplies like IV bags, syringes, boxes of bandages, and multicolored bottles of medication. I opened the small closet door next to the shelves, revealing various guns and ammunition.

I turned to Josie, and her gaze settled past me to the weapons. "This is for a fast getaway, isn't it, Mom?"

"Yes. The door at the far corner of the room opens to an escape tunnel. Two passages. One opens into the shed at the back of the house. The other will take you into the drainage system and let you move beneath the streets."

Drainage system? This was Southwest Florida. Something told me any underground water or sewer lines would be cramped, or have components of the reptile variety. Anomaly or not, I wasn't about to drag Josie into alligator-infested waters.

"Mrs. Harper, this safe house, how secure is it?"

A smile so much like her daughter's tilted her mouth for a moment. "My husband designed the space. It's state-of-the-art technology. It'll open for Josie or Eli, or me. Nothing else will get through those doors. It's thirty-six inches of solid steel reinforced with two feet of concrete. The air and water circulation systems are self-contained and close-circuited." She pointed to something in the far corner of the lab that looked like a pool filter. "This is your safe zone in the event of an attack on this house." She gestured to a panel beside the door from which we'd entered. It had a big red button beside it, with a glass shield covering it. "Hit that, and this place goes on lockdown. It can sustain four people for four months."

I had no intention of holing up in here. Maybe in a pinch, but when it came to the Consortium, no amount of steel or concrete would keep them out—not indefinitely. I got that the space wasn't "visible" and therefore couldn't be Pushed or Retracted, but that wasn't good enough for me.

"We should leave here," I told Mrs. Harper. I still wasn't certain if that Consortium thug in the park had been following Josie or me. "We'll go off the grid, head west. Once Josie has mastered her abilities—"

"No," Mrs. Harper said.

Huh? Maybe I wasn't explaining the situation correctly. "Ma'am, the Hub may be compromised. This house may be compromised."

She shook her head. "I need to stay, and I need Josie to stay with me. This isn't up for discussion."

A whole bunch of swear words rattled in my head. It was a good thing thinking words didn't Push them out of my mouth.

"You have a problem with that, Reid?" she asked, taunting, pulling rank.

Hell yeah, I had about a hundred problems with that.

Josie's gaze darted between us. I could tell she didn't really grasp everything that was going on, but she was definitely cueing in to our body language. Me, I was pissed. My hands had clenched into fists and, without meaning to, I'd shifted my weight to the balls of my feet. Mrs. Harper? She looked like she was about to sit down for High Tea. All calm and sweet. Except for her eyes—they were glacial.

"Mrs. Harper," I said in the calmest voice I could manage. "I respectfully request that you rescind that decision."

"Um, Mom, what about the Consortium?"

"We are now in a position where we're just as strong as the Consortium."

Josie moved so she was standing in front of me, a buffer between her mother and me. "But I thought the Consortium held important offices, and—"

"And now we do, too," she said to Josie. "In six days, the vice president will present you your physics award before his presidency campaign speech. The VP is a part of the Resistance. I need you to make a delivery to him."

What the hell? If the Consortium had even a hunch about the VP being in the Resistance, that would put Josie in direct danger. Josie's face twisted with confusion and hurt.

My hands balled into fists at my sides. No way would I let Josie be more of a target than she already was.

"Let me do it instead. Whatever her role is…let me take her place."

Both their heads snapped to me. Mrs. Harper seemed surprised.

"No. It needs to be Josie." Mrs. Harper moved to a stainless steel panel. She punched in a couple of buttons, and it opened with a hiss. "This is the serum." She extended a short vial filled with an opaque yellow liquid. "When you accept your award next week, you need to slide this into Vice President Taylor's hand."

"What does it do?" Josie asked.

"It's the key to preserving Oculi abilities and neural function so degeneration doesn't occur."

I couldn't stop my gasp of surprise. There, in the palm of her hand, was the cure. The key to continuing to use my powers. My mouth watered, I wanted it so badly. I muttered a curse, disgusted with myself. Josie's mom watched me carefully. Yeah, she was weighing my reaction, but whether I passed whatever test she'd just pulled or not, I didn't know. The thing was, I believed in our existence as it was intended to be — finite, limited. If we started manipulating ourselves to prolong our abilities, we were no better than the Consortium. We'd be abusing the very laws we were tasked to uphold, and I wouldn't do that. There was a balance in the system, and this would disrupt that status quo. And if it fell into the wrong hands…

"You should destroy that," I said.

Mrs. Harper nodded. "Probably. But that decision is neither yours nor mine to make."

I still didn't know how I felt about anyone having this "cure." But she was right. There were a great many things above my station as an Operative. I had pretty high rank in the Hub, but that didn't mean I knew the true logistics of what we were up against. And if it came down to an all-out war between the Consortium and us, well, the Resistance would need every advantage.

"Why can't the VP just Push some of this stuff for himself?" Josie asked.

An excellent question. And exactly what I wanted to know.

Mrs. Harper slid the serum to me. "Try and Push this, Reid."

I concentrated on the vial, on the viscous liquid it contained.

I envisioned the healing properties of the serum. I focused and...nothing.

"It's a form of gene therapy, isn't it, Mom?"

Mrs. Harper's icy visage warmed by a couple of degrees. "Yes."

"Mind filling me in?" I said. I considered myself intelligent enough, but in the presence of these brainiacs, I might as well have been a preschooler.

"The serum works by targeting cells and inserting specific genes," Mrs. Harper began.

"It's viral, Reid," Josie cut in. "You said that nothing living can be Pushed or Retracted. Viruses aren't technically alive, as they can only replicate inside a living cell."

"Alive enough, it seems," I said.

Mrs. Harper reached across the lab table and claimed the vial. "I can only produce it in very limited quantities. Hence, the serum needs to be administered to the person who can benefit the Resistance best." She leaned against the table and absently rubbed her bad leg. "The VP is our best shot at surviving as a species, and we have to give this to him. If the Consortium continues their hunt and execution..."

Yeah, it had been a witch hunt for several years, and, if the stories were to be believed, the Consortium had been locating and killing Anomalies and Resistance members for a couple of decades before that. I understood the urgency, the need to take a stronger offense.

Then I glanced at Josie. She was an innocent. A friggin' pawn in this deadly game. God, it made me sick to think what they'd do to her, knowing who she was—what she'd be carrying. She didn't deserve to be manipulated like this, thrust into the limelight and used as some glorified drug mule.

"No," I said. "Josie doesn't need to do this. I can change my appearance—"

"It isn't that easy," her mom snapped. "Do you have any idea how tight the security is going to be around *the vice president*? It'll take more than an external adjustment of your appearance, Reid."

Josie spoke up for the first time. "She's right. I already had to be fingerprinted and photographed at school. We're receiving special admission badges and have to go through a certain screening prior to the award ceremony. I thought it was just heightened security for terrorist purposes…"

The Consortium was another breed of fanatic. I raked a hand through my hair. "What do we have in terms of reinforcements?" I suspected a breech in the Hub, and if I was right, then Josie would be a sitting duck at that event, with enemies coming at her from all sides. Damn it all to hell, if the breach went far enough, then the VP had a giant target on his back, too.

"We're only calling in a few of the best, you being one of them."

Okay, at least that would somewhat lessen the chances of us inviting the enemy into our backyard. But it still didn't mean that we were safe or that this safe house was any more secure. "If there's a leak in the Hub—"

Mrs. Harper cut me off. "These Resistance members aren't associated with the Hub. I'm more than capable of rallying support without it coming through the central processing net. Think about it, Reid. The Hub may have instructed you to locate my daughter, but it was my encrypted call that brought you here."

True. The Hub had narrowed Josie's whereabouts to a five-hundred-mile radius, but it was the anonymous call that brought me to Oceanside. My mind raced with the possibilities surrounding this proposed serum handoff.

"You'll need to train Josie here and continue with her usual daily routine like nothing is out of the ordinary until we complete this delivery."

My mind calculated the logistics. Hiding in plain sight. The probability of drawing more attention with an immediate evac. Training Josie before we completed the drop.

"Let's move, then," I said. Mrs. Harper tipped her head to me in affirmation, and I started to turn, but a cement barricade that hadn't been there a moment before blocked my way. Another tall concrete wall cut off Josie's mom.

Mrs. Harper froze, staring at Josie, who rubbed her temples.

"Sorry," Josie said. "I wanted both of you to stop. Don't make decisions for me when I'm standing right here. Please."

Shit. That hadn't been my intention. I knew the Harpers ran a tight ship and things were tough in their house. I didn't want to add to it. "I'm sorry."

Mrs. Harper's lips puckered like she was trying not to smile. She nodded. "Josie," she said. And when she looked at her daughter, there was pride and tears and something I couldn't describe shining in her eyes. "Reid can train you well and protect you. You won't get hurt. I wouldn't put you in this position if I thought it would get you killed." She paused. "Or you can leave if you want. Reid can take you far away from here."

She was giving her daughter a choice.

With the way she'd been on a roll, I hadn't expected that. I waited, barely breathing, searching Josie's face for some indication of what she might decide. Long seconds passed as Josie stared at her mom, then her gaze slowly shifted to the vial of serum. Finally, she turned to me.

I wanted to grab her and run. To hell with the war, the Resistance. I wanted to take Josie away and keep her safe.

She lifted her chin and held herself a bit taller. "I'll make the drop."

She strutted past me, paused, and the concrete barricade disappeared. She'd just Retracted for the first time. And that poker face while she did it? Hot.

Shit. I wasn't supposed to let her affect me that way…or any way.

I couldn't wait. I'd have to show her who I really was earlier than I'd planned. I just hoped she didn't hate me for it.

9.

JOSiε

The drive in my old Honda Civic to Reid's place was short, which I appreciated because all I could think about was how my parents had lied to me for years and how my dad was probably dead.

No, my dad wasn't dead. I refused to believe that. I would know it, would sense it somehow. Yes, that completely defied all reason and rational thought, but I clung to this belief with every bit of my will.

Reid had insisted that my father was alive. Before we left my house, he'd made a point of telling my mom and me that the Council had received no news to suggest that my father's position in SI had been compromised. All correspondence and communication had been purposely terminated by the Hub, several months ago, to prevent against such a breach.

My mom had collapsed onto the sofa upon hearing that, smiling like I hadn't seen her smile in years. It wasn't definitive.

We didn't know for sure that Dad was okay, but it was something.

And I latched onto that one morsel of good news like Thor's hammer, Mjolnir.

The rest of our discussion, well, I was still processing that. My own mother had hid a safe house and escape route under our home and was willing to sacrifice me to smuggle a vial to the vice president. I mean, I understood how important the serum was, but she was asking me, a new Anomaly with no experience—*her seventeen-year-old daughter*—to complete a task fit for a Special Forces veteran.

Was I that disposable? Had she hardened that much since Nick died?

A wealth of memories surfaced—my mom spending hours teaching me math and science, the way she'd been so proud when I placed in my first swim meet. The way she'd fought back tears on my first day of high school at Oceanside. How she'd held me every night until I'd fall asleep in those first weeks after Nick died.

I *knew* she cared about me. And Eli. We might have our differences and differences of opinion, but I didn't doubt that she loved me.

And if making this "handoff" would help the cause, if it would help my dad or somehow keep my mom or brother safe—how could I possibly say no?

I couldn't. Not really.

So I'd hopped in my car, my personal version of an X-wing, like when Anakin first embarked on his new life to train as a Jedi, and followed Reid.

Reid pulled up to an old warehouse. An oversize garage

door took up most of the front wall, a large, windowless door to the left. Windows circled the top of the building, near the roof. No one could see in or out. A chill shimmied down my spine, leaving goose bumps in its wake.

The asphalt was unmarked. No lines for parking stalls, no indication that anyone lived or worked here, besides Reid. He shoved up the industrial-size garage door.

Reid motioned for me to follow him in as he climbed back on his idling bike, and I followed, driving inside and parking to the right of the door.

It took a moment for my eyes to adjust as I moved from the afternoon sun into the old warehouse. Light filtered in through windows around the top of the newly renovated space. I would've never guessed from the outside that it was so clean and updated inside. Completely unassuming.

"Hey, you okay?" he asked.

I glanced at Reid. The question was so absurd, I couldn't stop the laugh that bubbled from my throat and broke free.

"Stupid question." He smirked. "So, back in your mom's 'hidden lair…'" The way he said that—accompanied by actual finger quotes, using a Dr. Evil voice—it loosened the vise that had clamped around my heart. We both laughed for a second, and then his expression turned serious again. "Look, what you did…what you're choosing to do…it's…cool."

Now it was my turn to smirk. Yeah, I got it. He was proud of me. Funny how his reaction, how that one small bit of praise, could make me feel more confident.

"Thanks."

"So are we good? You wanna talk about anything?" he asked, his blue eyes assessing me. He'd shifted back into "trainer mode."

I ran through the checklist of discoveries that my mom had so unceremoniously delivered, as if she'd been reading her post-grad dissertation.

1. You and your brothers were "experiments." Oh, and your dad? He's likely dead. Well, we think he's safe, but there's no way to know for sure.
2. Tucked beneath our home is a Batcave.
3. Don't mind all those guns and grenades—save 'em for a rainy day.
4. Under attack? No worries. Hunker down here for a third of a year, or take your chances in the drainage system.
5. And while you're hiding from the evil Oculi Consortium, make sure to make a handoff of a super-serum to one of the most powerful people in the world.

I was tempted to recite my crazy list to Reid, but, really, there was no need. He'd been lucky enough to have a backstage pass, admit one, to the Harper family saga. I wouldn't whine about it.

"I'm good," I said.

He nodded in that way that told me my answer pleased him.

"Let me show you around." He crossed the vast length of the warehouse toward what I assumed was the living quarters. My eyes gravitated to a kitchen, something straight out of *Top Chef*, that ran along the back wall, accompanied by a table and chairs. A hallway was tucked to the right of the kitchen. I guessed bedrooms. Coolest. Living room. Ever. Industrial and simple. Yeesh, the flat-screen TV was almost as big as me. Basic glass tables. Huge black leather sectional. Total bach pad.

The closest corner hosted a workout area. Machines, weights, a punching bag, sparring cage, everything a gym had and more. The Rock would've been jealous.

But the majority of the space was empty. Wide open, tall ceilings, clean. Why did they need a building so large?

Before Reid could say anything else, Santos rumbled through the open garage door, parked his bike next to Reid's, and jogged toward us. "Like the kitchen?"

"Love it," I said. Santos gave Reid a wide grin. That's when I realized they'd probably done everything themselves— they'd Pushed and Retracted the interior. Realizing this prompted me to look more closely at everything. The details of their living arrangements were astounding.

"If you haven't guessed," Reid said as he moved toward the kitchen, "Santos is the cook and designed the kitchen." I caught up with him, meeting them both at the table.

"Well, it's amazing," I told Santos.

"Thanks! I think so, too."

Reid rolled his eyes at Santos and pointed to the living area. "Over there is where we relax, obviously. Help yourself to the kitchen or the bathroom."

Reid crossed his feet, shoved his hands in his pockets, and nodded to the other doors. "Our bedrooms." My cheeks warmed at his words, which was silly. He looked past me. "That's the workout and training area."

I rotated, taking in the massive space. "Did it take you

long to do this? To make it the way you wanted?"

Santos held out a box of crackers, and I shook my head. "Not long at all. It gets easier the more you practice. Besides, when you're an Anomaly like you and Reid are, it's even easier. You'll find that out soon enough when your Retraction comes."

"She already Retracted, bro." Reid shoved off of the doorframe so he loomed over me. Anyone could tell he was in good shape, but it wasn't until he stood directly before me that his size registered. His shoulders looked like they could hold one of those giant concrete walls I was becoming so fond of Pushing.

"You want to take it easy today?" he asked.

Why? I knew I wasn't exactly graceful under pressure, but all things considered, I thought I was holding up okay. No, I didn't want him to go easy on me. It wasn't like we had a lot of time. The National Physics Honors Awards ceremony was six days away. "Do *you* need a break?" I said instead.

He didn't grin, but I could tell he wanted to.

"All right, then," he said. "Let's get started."

I followed his gaze to a giant whiteboard easel.

"You really like dry erase boards, don't you? And you think I'm a nerd." He didn't laugh at my joke, but Santos did.

Reid pulled his hand out from behind his back, and there was a marker in it. "I'm trying to make this as painless as possible. I thought a drawing game would be more fun than verbal commands, but, by all means, if you'd rather—"

"No. Pictionary is good."

Reid pointed over my shoulder to Santos. "Santos will keep time. Speed matters."

"Speed?"

Santos wielded a stopwatch. "Yeah. You need to be able to think and observe quickly, faster at times, depending on the situation. The faster the better."

"So you draw, and I Push what I see?" Seemed easy enough.

"Correct."

I held up my index finger. "Before we start…if our abilities are limited, won't this physically deteriorate me or move me closer to the edge of Crazyville?"

"In the grand scheme of things, what you're Pushing this week isn't much. It's not going to dip into your supply of energy much. Besides, you need to train, to know how this all works and how to handle it safely for yourself and others." Reid turned to the easel, his marker raised. "Ready?"

"Go!" Santos yelled.

He scribbled. I Pushed a piece of broccoli on the table. Santos yelled, "Time."

Reid turned to view my first Push. "What the hell is that?"

"What's it look like? It's a broccoli floret."

"I drew a cupcake."

"Then why is it all bumpy on top?"

"Okay, you two," Santos warned like a parent. "Try another one. Go!"

The muscles in Reid's arm twitched as he drew hastily. Cup. Bowl. Fork.

We went through some items that were much easier for me to identify from his sketches.

Tennis racket.

Chair.

"Me thinks you're taking it easy on her," Santos said.

Reid grunted. "Something to stretch the mind, then…" He drew a car.

So I Pushed a car.

"Time!" Santos shouted.

Reid spun around. "I don't see it."

Santos chuckled behind me. "Yo. Over here." He pointed to the coffee table.

I'd Pushed a Hot Wheels.

Reid shook his head. Santos laughed.

I glanced between them. The makings of a headache pulsed behind my eyes. I knew nausea was a side effect. As a precaution, I inched closer to the bathroom. Better safe than sorry.

"Okay, Josie." I really liked the way Reid said my name. The little smile that wanted to come out? I flattened it.

"Yes." I kept my voice even.

"That little model car—not quite what I had in mind." His body blocked the easel as he hastily sketched something. "Let's see how you handle this." He stepped aside from the whiteboard. A giant swing set, complete with slide, monkey bars, and fort? Seriously? A freaking playground?

Santos started counting off the seconds.

"Don't think of the size or complexity," Reid said. "Size doesn't matter."

Santos laughed so loudly it echoed through the warehouse. I tried to concentrate, I really did. But the chuckle rolled out of me into a full-bellied laugh. Man, did it feel good.

Reid's lips twitched, but he didn't have some insecure freak-out. He rolled right over the immature joke. "The size of the object doesn't affect your perception of it. Don't limit your mind. Accept that the observation is just the observation."

Right. Okay. Santos's laughter died down.

"Picture it and Push, Josie."

I concentrated on the whiteboard, envisioning the swing set and slide in my mind. Then I allowed my vision to go hazy as I focused past Reid and his easel, toward an empty spot in the center of the warehouse. A shooting pain arced from my eyes to the back of my skull.

Chills.

Nausea.

A full-size playground.

"Time!" Santos whooped. "Hell yeah! You rocked that!"

I couldn't really believe it. I walked over and touched the plastic slide. I jumped onto the monkey bars and swung from one rung to the next. They held my weight. The swing set was solid. Real. I'd even Pushed a pile of sand to cushion the ground beneath it.

"Good execution," Reid said. He stood with his arms crossed, eyeing the construction. "Take a break for a moment." A bottle of water appeared in his hand. He twisted the cap to break the seal and handed it to me.

I wasn't really thirsty, but the water helped to ease that queasy feeling in my stomach.

Santos climbed the structure and took a spin down the slide. "I don't know," he said as he landed, kicking up sand. "Seems like you aren't challenging her enough, boss."

"Maybe," Reid agreed. "What do you say, Josie?"

Uh, my brains felt like they were going to slide out of

my nose—ancient-Egyptian-mummification style. I didn't say that, though. Reid and Santos were staring at me like I was some moron. They waited for me to respond.

"Go big or go home," Santos taunted.

Deep breath. "This isn't so hard," I said, all nonchalant. I threw in a shoulder shrug for good measure.

Reid's lips twitched again.

Santos approached Reid with an extended hand. "Lemme give it a try."

Reid handed over the marker and accepted the stopwatch.

"Go," Reid yelled. Santos scribbled a tree. Really? Easy.

I Pushed the tree. The branches fanned out toward the ceiling of the warehouse. Notches in the wide trunk. Some roots spearing out like vines across the warehouse floor. Not too shabby, if I did say so myself.

"Hold up there, sista." Santos stopped my celebration before it began. "We ain't through yet." He turned back to the easel, and the marker squeaked against the whiteboard. He jumped aside with a flourish, waving his arms all Vanna White style, and, like on *Wheel of Fortune*, he revealed a single word in block letters: FOREST.

Huh. It seemed to me that he was cheating, but the word conjured the thought, and I repeated Reid's words, *an observation is just an observation*, like it was a mantra. No limits. Just Pushing what my mind could see.

Forest.

I Pushed. Heat licked at my brain, then came pain, nausea. My stomach rolled into my throat.

With my next blink, the entire warehouse was full of red oak trees. My favorite tree in autumn when we'd lived in the Midwest. And, since I'd conjured thoughts of fall, the leaves changed from green to red—another shooting pain zinged through my head—and a breeze rustled through the warehouse, dislodging the leaves from the trees in one big gust, sending them whirling like a crimson blizzard. Oops.

Pain erupted in my head again, and more red oaks started popping up. They rose from the warehouse floor and sprouted toward the ceiling, crowding out the room, crushing the workout equipment and the sparring arena. A branch whipped out and shattered the flat screen.

"Stop!" Reid shouted the command, and I tried to shut off my thoughts.

He Retracted the worst of the offenders but didn't clear the whole room.

Santos let out a long whistle. I heard him, but I couldn't see him through the trees. A moment later, the *grr-grr-grrrrr* of a chainsaw echoed through the warehouse. "I'm yelling timber!" Santos sang in his best Kesha voice. "You better dance."

I knew better than to laugh. Santos didn't.

He toppled one of the most obnoxious trees and brandished the power tool, singing and dancing like a loon with wood chips flying. *Ax Men* meets hip hop—now this was a sight I would remember.

"Put it down before you saw off your own arm," Reid growled.

"You're no fun." Santos turned off the chainsaw and left it on a stump. One of the tree limbs had snapped off a corner of the whiteboard. Cool as could be, he capped the marker and placed it on the easel. "I, uh, think I'm going to chillax in my room for a bit."

A couple of red oaks blocked the hallway to the bedrooms. Reid Retracted them, and Santos beat a hasty retreat.

A ring of trees surrounded us, and Reid's feet crunched over the fallen leaves as he approached me. He crossed his arms. "While Santos's methods were a bit crude, he used his abilities to formulate a solution. He's a Pusher. So he Pushed the chainsaw to cut his way through the trees. Okay, now what was going through your mind when you Pushed?"

"I...I don't know."

He nodded. "And that's the problem. You have to be concise, intentional. Pushing requires your undivided attention. Full concentration."

"I get it."

"Even as you're Pushing something, you need to be calculating the next Push or Retraction to counter that action. Do you understand?"

I could clearly deduce that I would need an equal and opposite reaction. I thought of magnets and opposing forces, the concepts inherent to the Law of the Conservation of Energy. But Reid was in operative mode, and he wouldn't appreciate my lengthy mental dialogue, so instead I said, "Yep. Got it."

"Okay, then let's try Retracting those trees. Focus. *Observe* the act in your mind."

It was like pulling energy from the world around me and sucking it into the middle of my being. A really bizarre feeling rolled through my body, I blinked, and half the trees were gone. The other half toppled and collapsed onto one another, carpeting the warehouse floor like it was some desolate logging camp.

My stomach and head fluttered. The lightheaded rush reminded me of one of those whirling carnival rides where the floor drops out and the centrifugal force keeps you glued to the walls. I held my stomach like that would keep the contents of it locked in there.

Reid's eyes trained ahead to the decimated mini forest. I stepped in front of him so he'd look at me. "I don't understand. What did I do wrong?"

His arms fell from his chest. "It wasn't really wrong—it just wasn't enough. You have to Retract with the same preciseness as the Push if you're trying to undo a goof like this."

I resented that he was being critical. It wasn't like I knew what I was doing. "I'm just learning, Reid. I'm going to make mistakes. I'm not *trying* to goof up."

Reid muttered a curse.

"It's not fair for you to get mad at me!" I hated that he seemed annoyed, because if he was, I—or my lack of expertise—was the cause. I wanted to hide my face, now heated with embarrassment. I hated when people made me feel like I wasn't adequate enough in something. Perfectionist problems.

"Hey!" Santos popped his head out of his room. "I feel like I'm in timeout," he whined. "And it's boring."

He offered me an understanding smile as he shuffled out of his room. His interruption eased the tension between Reid and me. I wanted to thank him for that.

"Nobody nails a forest," Santos said. "Most Oculi can't even Push a tree on their first day."

His words made me feel marginally better, but it was

the disappointment and censure in Reid's expression that I struggled with.

"He's right," Reid agreed. Like the flip of a coin, his mood seemed to change. He even flashed that lopsided smile. Whoa, whiplash. I didn't call him out on his whole Dr. Jekyll routine—Hannah would've been so proud!—instead I kept my expression blank and waited.

His gaze shot past me, pulling my attention in the same direction. Santos had snatched up his chainsaw again, and it motored to life. "Hold up!" Reid yelled.

Santos shrugged. "Come on, you know you want to try…"

A momentary look of amusement slid across Reid's as he shook his head. He Retracted the remainder of the trees and Santos's chainsaw.

"Let's try something kind of…experimental."

His tone was different, more playful, and—dare I say?—suggestive.

"Uhh." I slowly spun toward him. The first thing I saw was his broad chest and strong jawline, so naturally when I thought of experimental, I thought of his body. *Dear Star Lord. What is wrong with me?* Heat flashed in my cheeks.

One corner of his lips curled in amusement. "Get your head out of the gutter."

"I…psh…ha." I shook my head, denying that he'd just caught me making a total and complete fool of myself. Damn it, Hannah hadn't coached me through this kind of awkwardness.

"Instead of Pushing something static," he said, "why don't we try something in motion?"

"Liiiiiike…?"

He leaned toward me. "We've got a moving target right there." I followed his eyes to Santos, who was now climbing up the stepladder to the playground fort. "Show me what you can do."

Well, not like that wasn't putting me on the spot. Who'd he think I was, Data? I didn't have infinite answers for everything. I'd just proven that. And could his instructions be any vaguer?

Okay. Um. I focused on Santos. His clothes. I could change his clothes.

I Pushed. The pulse of energy was less painful, but a dull headache was settling in the back of my skull and taking up permanent residence.

"Hey!" Santos tumbled down the slide. He wore a clown suit, big shoes, a rainbow wig, and a big red nose.

I glanced over, and I thought something was wrong with Reid. He was buckled over, holding his stomach. Laughing.

"Yeah, yeah," Santos yelled as his shoes flopped our way. "Laugh it up. It's all fun and games until the funny guy is turned into a..." He looked down at himself.

"A funny guy," I said.

Reid stuck out his fist. I hit mine to his, and for some reason that seemed like some award in its own right.

"Do it to Reid. If I'm a clown, how would you dress Reid?"

"I—"

Reid lowered his chin and watched me through his dark lashes—daring me. "Go ahead."

"I didn't even think about what I was making his clothes," I blurted. "It just happened." Shit. I'd probably screwed up again. I frowned, thinking of his reaction to the maple forest.

"Josie." He touched me under the chin. "That can be a good thing—you not having to think so hard."

"But I don't understand. You told me to concentrate. To be specific in my thoughts."

"Yes. But you won't always have to do it that way. For the big-ticket items and for your first observations, yeah, it has to be precise." Reid crossed his arms again. "But as you master your skills, it'll come more naturally."

"So I won't have to try so hard?"

"Exactly." He tipped his head to me again. "Go ahead."

Right. Just swap out his clothes the way I had with Santos.

"Hey." He stopped me. "Lay off the dark-haired Thor stuff." The reprimand was delivered in a gruff tone, but his eyes sparkled.

For a moment, I debated pranking him, but before my mind could conjure ball gowns or a Wookie costume, I Pushed and the headache revved like an engine in my head. In the next moment, Reid stood before us in a full army uniform— fatigues, boots, helmet. Okay, so we were going with my true impression of him.

Santos erupted in laughter, while Reid's head bobbed in tiny nods. His gaze was on the floor, as if thinking. "I get that."

"What would you dress me as, Reid?" And why those words came out of my mouth, I didn't know.

A grin spread across his face, slow and mischievous. "Wouldn't you like to know."

My stomach kissed my heart. It just shot straight up. Yeah, I would've liked to have known. Then again, maybe not. His impression was probably an old-school nerd with broken glasses, pants up to my bra, and a pocket protector.

In the next instant, the boys' clothes were back to normal and I was still staring at Reid.

He cleared his throat and said, "Let's take a break, then hit the mats."

10.

I took a few minutes in the restroom to freshen up and wrap my brain around everything that had happened over the last twenty hours. My conceptions of the world were shattered. With my mom's mad scientist lab, Dad, and everything I'd just Pushed into reality, I was barely keeping it together.

Reid was right. Physically working off some of the stress and frustration would be a good thing. I wasn't a gym rat, but I could appreciate yoga or hitting a treadmill. Hannah and I went to an intermediate yoga class twice a week. I practiced my forms.

I stepped out from the back of the warehouse, and music reverberated in my chest. My eyes scanned the floor as I rounded the corner. All good. Reid and Santos had restored the warehouse to its former glory. Flat screen intact. Not a leaf or swing in sight. What I *did* see, well, *whoa*. Two shirtless guys beating the crap out of each other.

The moves almost appeared choreographed. They struck and retreated so seamlessly, their strong bodies a blur of kicks and punches and retreats, but when my gawking in the doorway nabbed Santos's attention, Reid kicked Santos in the stomach, sending him to the floor, cursing.

Nope. Not choreographed.

Reid held out a hand, helping Santos up. Both of them sauntered toward me in tempo with the song. It didn't seem like they did it on purpose, but it added to their badassery and reminded me of the way they'd walked up to me on their first day of school—by the *USS Enterprise*, had that only been yesterday? How the whole world could just up and shift on its axis in the span of a day…

Santos was built. Lean and muscular and only wearing blue Adidas shorts and sneakers.

I took in Reid's defined chest and the dips and ripples in his abs. Jeans rode low on his hips, exposing the black waistband of his underwear. A thin, dark trail started at his belly button and disappeared into his pants. Insta–face burn. I tried not to stare but, Thor Almighty, how could I not?

"I don't have workout clothes. You want me to Push—"

"Josie, you need to learn to fight in street clothes. This isn't a workout session." His eyes flicked to the front of my shirt, and he walked toward the training area. Okay, so no free weights, then.

"Shoes on or off?" I bent down, prepared to take off my Sperrys.

"I said street clothes. That goes for footwear, too."

I was starting to think I'd prefer Santos over Reid. Reid was so stringent.

I approached the mat. I'd never done any extensive sparring, but I wasn't a total nube when it came to self-defense. The tae kwon do I'd practiced for years with Eli had to count for something. I hoped.

A heavy footfall pulled my attention back to Reid.

An arm came at me from the side. Without thinking, I ducked, punched under the incoming arm, and swung my shin at the ankles in my sights. Reid's legs swept out from under him, and his hands shot out to catch himself. He landed on all fours.

I gasped for a breath of air, my chest heaving. Evidently I held my breath whenever I was attacked. Reid's eyes locked on mine. Finally some eye contact. And then he gave me a shitty smile.

"What the hell?" I snapped. Reid stood and didn't stop moving until he was in my face. I didn't let myself flinch. "Just because you're pissed at me, did you really need to try and take me out? I know you think insta-immersion works best, but maybe it doesn't for me. Maybe, just maybe—"

"Will you shut up?"

I hitched my hands on my hips. "So rude."

"Five days, Josie."

That shut me up in a heartbeat. What the hell was *wrong* with me? I hadn't lost sight of the goal. The awards ceremony was—I glanced at the wall clock in the living room—125 hours and fourteen minutes away. Reid shouldn't take it easy on me. He couldn't afford to.

"I'm sorry," I began.

"Stop." Reid didn't budge, but he crossed his arms, too. "I was going to give you a compliment, but you won't stop thinking or talking long enough for me to get a word in edgewise."

Oh, oops. "Proceed."

He shook his head, closing his clear eyes for a moment. "You are a piece of work."

"That doesn't sound like a compliment."

Reid barked a short laugh. "Because it wasn't. I was going to tell you that you did a good job earlier, you know, with the whole Pushing Pictionary thing. And this?" He pointed behind him, where I'd taken him down. "How did you know what to do?"

"My parents made us take tae kwon do. Like, for years and years. I guess it just kind of comes naturally." A hint of pride fluttered through my muscles. And with that pride, just a smidgen of hope. Like maybe I could do this. Maybe I could actually pull this off.

"Mmm."

Reid stood so close that I had to angle my head up to him. My shirt was already sticking to my sweaty stomach. And he still didn't have a shirt on. I had to make a conscious effort not to look at his body. I could barely focus on what he'd said.

In no way, shape, or form had I lost sight—no pun intended—of the big picture. I remained focused on the end goal. Reid was just, well, a wee bit distracting, that's all. And perhaps that was a good thing. Yes. If I could focus around Reid, then that would only better serve me in a real-world environment, when I faced other distractions.

Yep, that was my story. And I was sticking to it.

"Let's work more on hand-to-hand combat. See what comes not-so-naturally, natural."

Giving him a nod, I pivoted toward the mats. Feeling his presence behind me and hearing the swish of his jeans as he moved, I stopped short. I twisted, throwing a punch toward his lower jaw. He shifted out of the way, grabbed my wrist in midair, and twisted it around my back. Thank the moon of Endor I was pretty flexible.

He yanked my arm farther up my back. His opposite arm wrapped around my waist and tugged me into him, his bare chest pressing into my back.

Pain and exhilaration shot into my nervous system. I was stuck. My heart beat wildly, but I wasn't scared. It had to be the rush of adrenaline into my bloodstream and the fact that a half-naked guy held me in a death grip.

Reid's exhale tickled the back of my neck as he steadied his breath. "Nice try." His voice came out in a rough whisper. His arm tightened around my waist again, his fingertips singeing my skin through my tank as they dug through the material, drawing me in to his body.

"What's the matter, Josie? Can't move?"

A chill danced down my spine when he pulled in a deep breath and his chest expanded against my back. I should've been shrugging out of his hold, but I didn't. My body had locked up in response to his presence. And it pissed me off, because even though he could be an underwear model, I would've rather made out with a Romulan. Similar personalities.

Okay, I can do this.

I rolled my body to the right and down, and Reid loosened his embrace around my waist and dropped the hand holding my wrist. I turned to face him, his fingers sliding across my stomach as I twirled.

He could flip from flirty to field marshal? Yeah, well, so could I.

I took another step backward and bounced on my heels. "Okay," I said. "Again. Come and get me."

Reid cocked an eyebrow and nodded. A smirk curved his lips upward. "Challenge accepted."

Reid

Okay, so the girl had skills.

Pretty mad skills, if I was being fair.

Like most trainees, she sought approval, positive reinforcement for her accomplishments. But if I'd learned anything from the dynamics in the Hub and in the Harper household, it was to keep the niceties to a minimum. The Hub treated trainees like army recruits. Mrs. Harper treated her daughter with equal measures of discipline and objectivity. Not really the style of parenting a kid should have to put up with, but, considering the responsibilities Josie would have to shoulder, it would be better for her in the long haul if she could handle setbacks and disappointment now. I'd also sensed that Josie dealt better with information and explanations rather than emotion. Part of that came from her analytical mind, but I also think that harkened back to her upbringing.

Contrary to popular belief, life as an Oculi wasn't all Pushing posies.

"Again," I commanded when she retreated to the opposite side of the mat. "But this time, you're attacking *me*."

I watched Santos flip his thumbs up before heading toward his room. He Pushed a pizza and a liter of soda.

A foot came at my face, but I caught it before it hit. I could've twisted, throwing Josie off balance or even breaking her ankle if I wanted, but, again, I didn't want to hurt her. Quick little thing, though. That was certainly a strength.

I smiled as I held her foot in the air, and she flashed a fake grin back to me. I released her foot and waved her on, silently saying, *Come on*. She circled me slowly, one foot creeping in front of the other, constantly moving, so that front foot was always able to plant if need be, or to shift her weight backward if she needed to retreat. Smart.

I matched her turn, her eyes focused on mine and not my body. She approached slowly, and when she was close enough, she threw a left punch. Blocked. Right punch. Blocked. Her foot slammed into my gut, shoving me back several feet. She advanced again, but I Pushed a long dining room table between us.

"Hey!" she yelled. "Cheater!"

"Just checkin' out your skills." And that wasn't all I was checking out.

Instead of Retracting the piece of furniture, she hopped onto the table and ran at me. She was thinking outside the box. We had to use what was there or not there. I had to press her harder, though. At the last second, I Retracted the table, but another showed up in front of her mid-stride. Just as she launched at me, feet first, I jumped out of the way, and she landed with a grunt. I paused, watching her closely for any indication of pain or strain.

"Remember," I said. "This is training. We can't afford any

injuries."

With that in mind, I didn't Push any other obstacles. Better to be safe than sorry on this first day.

She lunged forward. Punches, blocks, kicks, and more blocks. She could take care of herself. She had both my hands. I pulled back my head to throw a head butt—nothing hard—but a catcher's mask appeared over her face before my forehead could make contact.

Not gonna lie. That hurt a little.

But her quick thinking and innovation were worth it. A little fazed by my head hitting her metal mask, she took the opportunity to plant a foot, and then pulled her knee up to my groin. She halted the impact—and I jumped back. Yeah, I was going easy on her, allowing her to land some moves. The confidence would suit her in a real-world fight.

She balanced on one leg and kicked with the other. I caught her knee. Oh, this girl.

"Quit holding back," she said.

"You first," I taunted.

She grumbled like I'd insulted her. Again, that angry-Tinker-Bell analogy popped into my head. Shifting my weight forward, I pushed off the ball of my foot, charging Josie head-on. She widened her stance and bent her knees. As soon as I was within reach, she jumped laterally, so instead of safely tackling her to the mat around her middle, I caught the bottom of her tank top. I yanked and pulled her into me, my body already moving in a forward motion. We fell to the mat, me twisting to take the impact and then rolling, until I stopped on top of her, pinned. I straddled one of her legs; my torso lay on half of her chest and one of her arms.

I turned my head to evaluate her reaction and condition, my mouth by her ear. It was a fine line. I had to test her, challenge her, but I didn't want to inflict pain. "You okay?"

With our chests joined, I felt both our hearts going crazy. I could've stayed like that for longer, but I probably would have received a knee to the crotch sooner rather than later. Shoving off, I helped her to her feet.

Josie's physical contact skills soared. Sure, she was naturally athletic, but I wasn't convinced her black belt had taught her instincts she didn't realize she even had. No doubt it was the inoculations. She moved like her body already knew how to defend itself. She moved like Nick. Josie was actually better than Nick.

And the thought terrified me.

11.

Reid

Once we situated Josie at home with her mom on guard, Santos and I took off, heading north toward the Panhandle. I had to contact the Hub, but we needed to ride far enough away that we wouldn't reveal Josie's location and put her in danger. We stopped in a small town about four hours from Oceanside.

Nothing was open beside the usual late-night digs: gas station, bars, fast food. We weren't about to make this call inside, where anyone could hear, but it was usually best to be in a populated area. The fast-food parking lot seemed the least shady option.

We stayed on our bikes. Santos parked closer to the street, where he pretended to play on his phone, but really he kept lookout on the road and gave me privacy for my login. I punched the number, then the security code. I was prompted for my voice verification through my password. Passwords weren't something we shared, not even with other Resistance members, as a safety measure. My contact, one of the Council members, picked up right away.

He answered, "Secure."

"Leak possible."

"Bring her in."

"Not possible. Orders from Mrs. H. to educate her here and make delivery."

"We—"

Shouts pulled me out of my conversation. My heart jump-started, and a second later, a *thwamp* sound echoed off the houses down the block.

"Hold." I Pushed my gun and held my phone with my shoulder.

Waiting for the sound again, I watched Santos. He was on it. His hand went to the back of his waistband where he kept his weapon. Nice thing about this state: concealed-weapon permits were easy to come by. Not that we'd bother with paperwork when we could Push the weapon into hiding or Retract it altogether. But at least being seen with guns on our persons wasn't going to raise any immediate alarms.

A group of kids came around the corner, jabbering in hushes. I Retracted my gun before they saw me, to be safe. One of the kids bounced a basketball, and the sound reverberated down the street.

Am I losing it? I could've hurt one of them.

"Sir. I'm here," I said into the phone.

The kids disappeared into a house. A rustling sound came from behind a truck parked in front of the kids' home. Something reflected light, moving into the shadows. It wasn't a kid this time. Someone had been watching us.

Santos's bike started—he'd seen it, too. Text from Santos. *Trailed. Out.*

I Pushed my shield, and the bike rumbled to life under me. I took off in the direction of the movement, my heart speeding in unison with the engine. Staying on the street, I followed the shadows darting among houses and through bushes. The grumble of another street bike told me whoever trailed us was no longer on foot. Tires squealed, and I cut my bike in the direction of the sound. One person, it seemed. But there could be more.

Santos completed his lap of the neighboring block and rode beside me. He motioned that he was going around to the other side of the street. Divide and conquer. Good plan.

I trailed the guy for several blocks into what appeared to be a business district. From the dark, overgrown lots and lack of signs, I didn't think any companies flourished in this area. If there was business taking place amid these abandoned buildings and rundown homes, it was of the illegal variety.

Turning left, I found myself at a fenced dead end, a small space between two buildings. This Consortium person must've Pushed the fence. There was no gate, but I saw him drop his bike on the other side and take off on foot. I Retracted my bike out from beneath me, then Retracted the fence.

I ran. About halfway down the alley, I stepped on a slippery trash bag, and my body pitched backward. Although I Pushed padding behind me, I didn't judge the trashcan jutting out, and it clipped the back of my head as I fell.

The cut stung, and I could feel blood dripping down the back of my neck. I shoved off the ground.

Several dogs barked in the distance, maybe a block away.

It had to be the Consortium dude. I ran to the street, pausing to hear the barks, then followed the sound to a group of houses with a shared green space. Much like the stores and shops had looked vacant, these houses appeared abandoned. Weeds rose knee-high, and half the windows had been boarded up. Slowing my pace as I approached, I heard the barks cease. I wandered around the open area, but there was nothing but a bench and landscaping—no dogs. Either their owner had silenced the animals, or they were smart enough to know that something slightly more than human was coming their way. Chirping crickets filled the night air between distant rumbles of traffic.

My phone appeared in my hand. I didn't bother pressing the buttons; my text to Santos blinked into existence on the screen.

Need backup—GPS on

I shoved the phone into my back pocket, and then I heard it. Running feet—more than one set—coming straight for me from the bushes and trees between the houses. Taking a wide stance, I faced their incoming direction and Pushed my gun in one hand, a knife in the other. My heartbeat pulsed in my head wound, throbbing.

A flash of color dashed out of the bushes, and I let the knife fly. A big man came at me, my knife sticking out of his shoulder. My shield Pushed and ready, he wouldn't be able to really hurt me. We collided in the center of the green, and I used the force of my momentum to knock him to the ground. The knife in his arm must've cut an artery, because he didn't put up much of a fight. I locked him in an arm bar around his neck and held until his struggles ceased.

I caught movement in my peripheral vision as a second goon appeared. I Retracted the weapon in his hands before he could fire off a shot. Another gun—a rifle by the look of it—appeared in its place. I Retracted that, too. Then Pushed a steel net on top of him. Let's see if he could do anything about that.

The net pinned him to the ground. Ahh, not an Anomaly, then. Good. I'd keep him alive. We could use one of these scumbags for questioning.

I approached the assassin with my gun drawn. "No sudden moves," I warned.

"You should take your own advice." I spun toward the sound of the new attacker. He stood not ten feet behind me. I didn't have time for a standoff. And if he was Pushing a shield like me, this would be no easy brawl. Already, I could hear the other goon scrambling to break free. Another figure pounded out of the darkness and tackled the man in front of me. The two figures rolled. *Santos.*

I pulled up my gun, but with them grappling, I didn't have a clear shot. The guy Retracted Santos's weapon—he could have an advantage over my friend. I started toward them to help Santos, but he rolled on top of the man, Pushed another gun, and pressed the barrel to the man's head. I sucked in a breath as the all-too-familiar *pop pop* sound from a suppressor cut through the quiet night.

Santos spun in my direction and fired again.

I pivoted to see the first attacker crumble.

Santos dropped his gun and slowly turned to me, still on top of the attacker. "You okay, man?"

I clasped his hand and hauled him off the dead body.

"Yeah. Thanks."

Three dead men. What a mess.

Adrenaline rushed through my veins with no outlet. I braced my hands on my knees, hunched over, letting the feeling pass. I was pretty sure that hit to the head wasn't helping matters. Once I knew for sure I wasn't going to puke, I limped over to a bench with a mega post-adrenaline-high headache. I dropped my head into my hands.

"I got this," Santos said. "You take a minute."

"We need to dispose of them."

Santos Pushed gloves on his hands and searched the pockets of the deceased. Then he Pushed a black tarp to cover the bodies, while I Retracted all weapons.

He claimed my phone and his and stomped on them. Then he Pushed two new phones and handed them to me. "Can't be too cautious."

No shit. My first instinct was to program Josie's number and shoot her a text, but seeing as how our phones might be compromised, her number would've been in my call log, so her phone could be compromised, too—ugh, just thinking about it made my head throb harder. Despite his arguments to "stop and sit," I helped Santos.

We moved the bodies together. Santos Pushed a hole and rolled the bodies in. Hub protocol. This part of the job...I didn't think I'd ever get used to it. The smells of wet earth and death, the *thump* a body made when it dropped into a six-foot hole. I'd pretend like I was immune, but killing would never come easily for me. Santos Pushed dirt and patches of dead grass so the grave blended in seamlessly.

"Thanks, bro."

Before we left the area, Santos Pushed ball caps and different jackets. In true Santos fashion, he whined about me bleeding all over the fan gear of his favorite team. Served him right for liking the Patriots.

We walked back to Santos's bike. I checked the perimeter and quickly examined the windows within this rundown area. No surveillance cameras. No one seemed to be watching. I Pushed my bike, but I paid for it in the form of a whopper of a headache.

"Aw, what's the matter, Reid? You didn't want to ride with me? '

The jerk. A brief smile tilted my lips, but it didn't last long. This was just confirmation of how much Josie needed protection. Once you were on the Consortium's radar, you would always be a target. I tried to imagine how I'd feel if Josie had been here with me, and that sick feeling in my stomach crawled into my throat. I didn't want to think of her in harm's way. I didn't want to think of what the enemy would do if they caught her.

I straddled my bike and turned to Santos. "Thanks again."

His head shook. "I got your back. I think we may have bigger things on our plate, though. Check this out."

Leaning over, he extended a rumpled newspaper clipping to me. "I pulled it from that last jackball's pocket."

DEL MAR HOTEL OCEANSIDE

I only caught a glimpse of the words. Instantly the details clicked into place. I glanced to Santos.

"These guys and the rest of the Consortium are willing to kill for whatever is going down at that ceremony," he said.

Yeah, and that meant Josie was right in the middle of it.

12.

I slept through the afternoon and night and woke midmorning to a text from Reid saying Santos would follow me to the warehouse to practice. After a shower, I found my mom and brother at the kitchen table.

Eli brushed hair out of his eyes. "Got you some grub," he said around a mouthful of quiche I recognized from the nearby coffee shop.

"Thanks, buddy." I slid into the seat next to him, where a closed container sat.

Mom placed a to-go cup in front of me. "Salted caramel mocha, right?" It was my favorite.

I hadn't talked to her since I left her lab upset—you know, when she'd told me my life was basically a lie. I really didn't know what to say to her at this point. Not only had I been thrust into this crazy world and told my dad could be dead behind enemy lines, but now she was intentionally putting me in harm's way by making me deliver the inoculation. I didn't know how to process this, but I knew my favorite coffee drink wasn't going to make it better.

And, yes, she'd been *so kind* to offer me a choice in the matter of the serum, but really, my family's safety was on the line. Not to mention the whole scope of the Resistance…it wasn't like I could say no. And, yes, *yes*, I knew that made me sound awful, like the worst kind of person, but the feelings were there. I was trying to work through them. Truly. But the pain and hurt and all the regrets, those emotions were difficult to suppress.

Eli played his video game while Mom and I ate in heavy silence. There was so much I needed to ask, to say—but I couldn't right now.

I snarfed down my food, guzzled half my drink, cleaned up my area, and grabbed my shoes. "Mom," I said, passing through the kitchen to the front door and hoisting my purse strap over my head. "I haven't grocery shopped. You need to figure out something for dinner."

She turned in her seat. "You don't need to worry about those things this week. I'll take care of it. Be careful."

Thank Asgard the drive wasn't long, because all I could think about was Mom telling me to be careful, and I was ready to blow a gasket. She'd thrust me into this position, to face danger head-on, and she had the gall to tell me to be careful? I promised myself I'd stop this pity party, but my bruised feelings didn't want to be suppressed. If she'd just exhibited a little bit of remorse, it would've gone a long, long way in helping me deal with this situation.

"You wanna ride with me, Josie?" Santos asked from his

position parked in my driveway. "Or should I follow you?"

I jingled my keys to show him I intended to drive.

He glanced at me quizzically, no doubt reading my oh-so-foul mood. But he didn't comment any further, donning his helmet and revving his bike while I slid into my Civic.

A couple of cleansing breaths—compliments of the Mediterranean Spa air freshener that Hannah had stuffed in my car a few weeks ago—and I almost had my temper in check. I wasn't normally so volatile.

I reversed out of the driveway and waited for Santos to pull up behind me.

The ride across town didn't take long. Crossing over Main Street, I moved with the flow of traffic. At a light, I drew even with a minivan. Two kids strapped in car seats stared at televisions in the back of the headrests. One older boy, five years old or so, dark hair, dark eyes. And a little sister with bouncing brown curls. The familiar strains of the *Princess Sofia* soundtrack echoed out of the open minivan windows. Normal people. Innocent kids. *Plancks.*

I'd always known I was a bit different—weird, geeky, whatever you wanted to call it. But recognizing such profound differences between myself and the kids in the minivan, a weight of obligation settled on my shoulders with the force of a landing Y-wing. Those kids, *Plancks*, my brother…so many people depended on the Resistance.

The light changed, and I drove forward.

Santos followed me to the warehouse. He pulled beside my window. "Leave your car here. You can go in around the back."

Huh, this was new. "Oh. Okay."

"I can park it in the warehouse for you."

"Sure."

"Oh, hey, before I forget, here's a new phone."

Uh, what was wrong with my old one?

"I'll swap your numbers over for you," Santos offered amiably. Which totally triggered my Spidey-sense. Something was suspicious, but I handed it over before I thought better of it. If my number needed to change, there was likely a very good reason for it.

"Nice cover," he said. "You want the same one?"

"Umm, okay."

He scrolled through my phone—what, reading/memorizing my contact list?—then he focused on the new phone he held in his other hand. A few seconds passed, then he handed me the new phone. "All set. I Pushed texts to all your contacts, letting them know your mom changed cellular plans, and this is your new number."

Uh…

"Good luck, Josie." His smile brightened his whole face. I could see why Hannah liked him. And speaking of my BFF, I really needed to call her. I'd woken to a text from her this morning, asking if we were going to yoga class later. That probably wasn't happening.

I got out of the car and tossed Santos the keys. He grinned and slid behind the wheel.

Santos wishing me good luck tipped me off to the likelihood that my alternate entry into the warehouse was likely a test of some sorts. Immediately, my senses sharpened.

Using the brick wall as my guide, I followed it toward the back of the building. A metal fence, barbed wire twisting along the top, stood like an impenetrable wall. When the fence went no farther, I found a door, almost camouflaged, and pulled. Nothing. It wouldn't budge.

I tried again. Bending, I examined the lock. If I knew how it worked, I could Push a key or something. As I contemplated how to break in, I thought about how such an act was actually *breaking a law* and it felt wrong, even if it was only to enter Reid's place. Although I'd been instructed to "go in," so maybe opening this door *was* the test. I studied the lock for a second. Wait. I could Retract the deadbolt…

Heat, pain, nausea.

The lock clicked, and the door crept open with a quiet *squeak*.

A rush washed over me. I'd broken into a place by *thinking* it. In the next second, though, guilt crashed my little party. What was happening to me? I'd just silently celebrated breaking into a warehouse. I wasn't Catwoman. This was so not right.

I scanned the alley. I didn't know who I didn't want seeing me, but I knew I needed to be careful.

I squeezed through the gate door and closed it behind me.

"Hello?" The warehouse was silent. No sign of Reid or Santos. Not in the living room, training area, or what I could see of the kitchen. The place was eerily silent. Spidey-sense, indeed. I stepped away from the door and moved slowly across the vacant space.

A bell rang behind me. I spun, but there was nothing there. The door remained sealed. There was nothing at the far end of the warehouse by the bay doors where Reid and Santos had parked their bikes. Where my car was nestled in beside their rides.

I spun back around and started toward their living quarters. My pulse hammered in my veins. Something wasn't right.

Another bell rang. I spun wildly, searching for the source, and my foot slipped out from under me. My left foot joined my right, sliding down a rocky surface.

A scream tore past my lips.

My brain fought to figure out what was happening as my hands gripped for something—anything—because I was falling. My head swiveled.

I couldn't comprehend the giant, gaping crack I'd fallen into. A fissure in the ground at least eight feet wide. My fingers sunk into the cracked concrete, barely holding on. Sliding.

Then I looked down.

No end in sight. An abyss.

Everything around me blurred, and all I could see was black. And in that blackness was the one thing I was terrified of: death. My stomach pitched and my chest heaved, but no air moved in or out of my lungs. I was suffocating.

Ripping my eyes away from the darkness, I focused on my hands, still grasping at the gravely terrain crumbling beneath them. My right foot slipped, and my fingers dug deeper into the ground. It was a mixture of rock, and mud, and I didn't know what. It felt like glass shards were being shoved under my fingernails.

I dug in with my toes, using the muscles in my legs to slow my descent. I slid to a halt, but the rocks and substrate continued to crumble beneath me. I searched blindly for a sturdy foothold. My foot found a rocky lip, but as soon as

I thought it was safe, it gave way. My right silver flip-flop plummeted into the darkness so eager to swallow me.

Attempting to force my gaze upward, I focused on the contrast of the dark surrounding me and the bright light above, the line where they met. Technically, I'd die in broad daylight.

"Think, Josie." The voice was strong, demanding. It took a second for it to register. "Josie, look at me."

Reid. Reid was here. That's where I was. I was at Reid's place. I'd come here to train. *I'm an Oculi.* It all became clear as I broke free from the terror.

I wrenched my head toward his voice, my gaze meeting his. He crouched above me at the surface, his eyes my lifeline because he didn't offer a hand. He wasn't about to coddle me. That wasn't his style. He said, "Breathe. Think."

Dragging in an uneven breath, looking into his clear eyes, something clicked in the far reaches of my mind.

Stairs.

I Pushed with no effort. No headache, no nausea. I blinked, and stairs carved themselves into the side of the chasm, jutted out as if they'd always been there. With great hesitancy, I climbed the stairs on all fours, close to the wall. I could see the surface, right within my reach.

Whoosh.

The stairs were gone.

I felt myself tumbling, falling. Flailing along the wall of the abyss with nothing to stop my descent.

"React, Josie!"

Think.

I focused on the surface, on the light growing dimmer the

farther I skidded. *Earth*. Ground beneath my feet. I Pushed. And Pushed.

Pain. Nausea. Dizziness.

Thunder sounded below, like the darkness of the chasm was rising up to swallow me whole. Something hit my feet so hard that it tossed me in the air.

Up. Up. Into the light.

My thoughts didn't coalesce clearly, but I felt myself rising. The pain behind my eyes made my vision waver. I shot to the warehouse floor. Reid reached for me as I collapsed.

My lungs rebelled, and tears burned trails down my cheeks. Dirt covered my hands and caked beneath my fingertips. One fingernail had broken to the quick. It bled sullenly. I wasn't about to look weak in front of him, though, so I held out my arm to ward off his offer of help. I stood tall on trembling legs.

Reid closed the gap between us, his arms extended like he would embrace me. "Josie —"

The light streaming through the warehouse windows dimmed and flickered. Darkness edged my periphery. I balled my trembling fist and slammed my knuckles into his cheek. White heat shot through my hand before everything went black.

My eyes cracked open to dust floating in beams of diffused afternoon light. The fuzziness fell away as I blinked. Santos was in the distance, punching and kicking a bag, and music played in the background, alt rock with a heavy guitar riff.

My whole body was sore; my heartbeat pulsed beneath my broken fingernail. My right hand ached, and my knees were tucked in toward my chest. My hands were clean, and a bandage covered my forefinger. A heavy hand lay along my ribs. My pillow moved a little. I drew in a breath and, with it, a crisp, clean scent.

Not a pillow. Jeans. Reid's lap.

His fingers ran over my ribs, down the curve of my waist, and up my back, as if he was tracing my hair. If I didn't hurt so badly, I'm sure his touch would have brought on more tingles than it did. Still felt good, though. I didn't know he had it in him to be so gentle. I slowly rolled to the back of my head and looked up.

Reid's chest expanded and his eyebrows pushed together. A red splotch sat along his cheekbone. Guilt bubbled in my stomach…until I remembered why I'd punched him.

His hand brushed hair out of my face, his fingers stilling behind my ear. The sound of Santos hitting the punching bag stopped.

"Are you okay?" Reid's voice was gruff.

I cleared my throat, making sure he could hear me loud and clear. "You are an asshole."

Santos walked past and whispered, "Awwwwkward."

Reid

I pulled my hand off her waist, wondering if my touch had freaked her out, and repositioned my arm on the back of the couch. "It'll probably come as no surprise, but I've been called worse. You didn't have to punch me. That's gonna leave a mark."

I could Push to cover it and alter my appearance, but I didn't say that. I'd done that with the gash I received from the Consortium dude up in the Panhandle. The three-inch cut on the back of my head didn't show—but that didn't make it hurt any less. Josie threw a decent punch. Of the two, my cheek hurt worse.

She struggled to sit up from my lap, and my hand instinctively slid under her arm to help her. She tugged away from my touch and swung her legs around, dropping her bare feet to the floor, and quickly jerked them back up. "Floor's cold," she muttered. Josie sat so close that I could feel her body heat. "You owe me a pair of flip-flops."

I tried not to laugh, but I couldn't help it. "You're concerned with your sandals?"

"No. Not really." Her elbows rested on her knees as she leaned forward.

I Pushed pink Hello Kitty slippers onto her feet. To my surprise, she didn't chuck one at my head. "You have to at least admit that was awesome training?" I said. "It showed you to be aware of your environment, required you to think outside of the box, to react instinctively…"

Josie shot off the couch, standing in front of me. "I. Could. Have. Died."

I shook my head. She didn't get it.

She turned toward the door, but before she could take a step, I stood, snatched her wrist, and tugged. She crashed into me and immediately tried stepping back.

"Hey. I know you're mad, and maybe you should be, but this walking-away thing has to stop." She'd pulled this storm-off routine when I snapped at her over the oak trees. Oculi, we took orders while we were training. We weren't in the Hub, so there was no need for strict formality, but that didn't mean I'd tolerate her walking out on me every time she got frustrated or upset.

With a hand around each of her arms, I kept her there, planted in front of me. Anger raged in her eyes and flushed her cheeks. "Let me go."

I held her long enough to illustrate that she wasn't escaping until I allowed her to. Oh, yeah, I knew it pissed her off. But I was angry, too. For a second, I thought she might force her point or try to instigate a fight.

I had to make her understand. I lowered my forehead to hers. "I will *never* let anything happen to you. Ever. As long as I'm alive, I'll look out for you. Do you understand?"

She glared at me.

"Say you understand, Josie."

After a few seconds, she nodded. "I understand." Her jewel-colored eyes softened by degrees.

I loosened my grip on her arms, but my fingers didn't want to leave her warm skin. There was more I could say, but I didn't. And if I stayed this close to her, I'd do something I couldn't undo. I eased away from her. "You did well today. Better than I did with this same exercise."

Her eyes widened. "You've…done this? The same thing?"

I gave her an affirming grunt before plodding back to the couch.

To my surprise, she followed. "Oh, this I've got to hear!"

Did I really want to tell anyone about my own training? No. But it was Josie. In the short amount of time I'd spent with her, she'd had this effect on me—like I couldn't tell her no, like I couldn't deny her anything. It was the most bizarre feeling. One I'd never known before. And I fought that feeling with everything I had. Every. Freaking. Time.

Moving back onto the couch, she slid onto one of the cushions at least a foot from me, tucking a slippered foot beneath her. I needed to assure her that everything would be all right.

Telling her about myself, about my own experiences, would help her understand what I was trying to do. It may also make her trust me more. I wasn't sure if I could look at her, though. Instead I focused on her slippers.

"When my mom died, I was sixteen." She knew that. She and her family had been at the funeral. "Consortium related." She didn't know that. I hadn't really told this story before. Santos knew bits and pieces, but I knew I could share the whole of it with Josie. "I wasn't about to let her die in vain, so I told my dad to initiate me by fire. I wanted to be the strongest I could possibly be so I could show them we weren't going to be controlled. Dad didn't go easy on me. I think he wanted me to be as strong as him. Or maybe strong enough for both of us."

I chanced a glance at her. Anxiety masked her face as she nibbled on her bottom lip.

"My dad did the exact things I've done to you. Scared the crap out of me with that chasm. Unlike you, I didn't Push my way to the top. I hit rock bottom. He left me there in the dark."

She sucked in a breath. "That's terrible!"

"That's training." I didn't want her sympathy. "And that

wasn't my point. When I faced the chasm, Josie, it took me a lot longer to calm my mind enough to Push my way out. I Pushed a ladder. Most Oculi, hell, most every trainee I've ever encountered, Pushes something basic—ladder, rope, stairs. That's what Pushers do. Retractors remove the earth to create handholds and footfalls. Simple solutions. Pushing God only knows how many tons of cubic dirt like you did—yeah, that's a first."

Placing my fingers under her chin, I pulled her face up to meet mine. "I didn't stage that trial to hurt you. I'm doing this to make you stronger, like my dad did for me. I'm doing this for your own good. It's to prepare you, to keep you safe. There are people out there who are coming for you, who'd prefer you dead. If for one second I didn't think you could handle the practice, I wouldn't do it. I'm the last person you need to worry about hurting you."

I hadn't noticed that I'd leaned in to her. Six inches, at most, separated her parted lips from mine. And she hadn't moved.

Forcing my attention somewhere, anywhere, else, I relaxed away from her and focused on the punching bag hanging from the ceiling in our training area.

"I'm sorry about your mom," Josie whispered. "And I'm sorry your father left you in the dark."

Man, she was killing me.

"I'm Pushing pizza. Want some?" Santos asked from around the corner, sending Josie and me apart. It wasn't like we'd been doing anything, but we both acted like we'd been caught doing *something*.

"Not now, Santos!"

"No thanks," Josie said.

She readjusted, sitting on both feet, pretending she hadn't just recoiled like a spring to the far corner of the couch. "Um, w-what…" She stuttered for a moment. "What, uh, what happened to your dad?" An edge had crept into her voice. Her thumb bounced in her hand, like she couldn't sit still.

Everyone at the Hub knew I didn't talk about my personal life, but they also knew why—dead mom, dead friend, kidnapped dad. But Josie didn't know any of that. She didn't know not to ask.

"My dad? Well, unlike you, I grew up knowing about the Consortium and the Resistance. I've lived my whole life pretending around Plancks. Like your dad, my dad wasn't on the council but was head of training at the Hub in Denver." She was hanging on every word. "He disappeared about four months ago."

Her brows furrowed. "Does the Consortium have him? Where was he? Was—"

"I don't know." It came out harsher than I intended.

She eased farther away from me, not that there was much farther she could go without landing on the floor. "Man," she huffed, her cheeks flushed. "You throw up steel defenses faster than Iron Man."

A laugh burst free. "You're one to talk, Miss I-have-to-guess-everything-you're-thinking." She chuckled, which made me happy. There was so much dark, we had to find the light in small things. "I didn't mean to snap. I don't know what happened to him, and I don't like not having answers. But I intend to find out."

Yeah, the fact that my father was being held by the

Consortium or dead, like Josie's dad, wasn't lost on me. And by the look in her eyes, that coincidence hadn't escaped her overly analytical brain, either.

There had to be a connection to both our parents, parents of Anomalies, being in the same situation—Consortium hostages. After this serum drop, finding that connection was next on my agenda. That was, if we didn't end up hostages ourselves...or dead.

13.

JOSIE

Reid followed me home so I could have some downtime before I was supposed to meet another local Oculi that evening. Mom and I were driving together, and Reid would meet us there. Hannah was babysitting my little brother, thinking I was doing something physics related for the award ceremony, and Santos was keeping watch on the house. Of course, Hannah and my brother didn't know Santos was pulling security duty, so he had to stay on the down low. Pity for Hannah; I was thinking she would've loved a little time with him.

Mom hadn't told me whom we were meeting and Reid didn't give any indication that he knew, either. I wasn't going to ask my mother because I'd find out soon enough, and I really didn't feel like conversing with the person who was making me the sacrificial lamb, so to speak.

Bad, Josie. Bad. I got it, I did. I rationally accepted all the reasons why she was doing this, but, damn it, it...hurt.

In between the hurt, I was hit with flashes of terror, because more than dying, I feared failing at the task.

We drove south of the city limits and parked in front of a tiny coffee shop, close to the hotel where the award ceremony and vice president's campaign speech would be hosted. We went inside to order drinks, and I was surprised when I didn't see Reid.

Mom paid, and we went out the way we'd come. Instead of climbing back into the car, though, I followed my mother, who hobbled down the sidewalk.

"Mom?"

"Yes?"

"What are—"

"Well, hey!" Mr. McIntosh, my physics teacher, said as he rounded the corner. "Funny bumping into you. You DVRing the new *Big Bang Theory* tonight, Josie?"

Crap. This was not the time to run into people I knew. My head swung to Mom. What was I supposed to do?

Mom extended her hand to Mr. Mac. "Nice to see you. Thanks for meeting us."

Wait. What?

He shook her hand, smiling. "Meg. Of course."

Mom turned to me. "Mr. McIntosh started at Oceanside the year we moved here...to help protect you at school."

My stomach churned. My sweet drink didn't seem to fit this epic realization. My parents had agreed to send me to that specific public high school because of their stellar physics program—but now I knew it was due to Mr. Mac's astounding résumé. I wasn't discounting my teacher's amazing gift for education, but he'd been placed there. For me.

All the pieces snapped into place:

1. *Tae kwon do*
2. *Homeschooling*
3. *The constant moving*

It was all in preparation for an Oculi life. My parents had taken steps to prepare us…just in case. I hadn't thought my life could get any more jacked, but I was wrong.

Reid moseyed up on the sidewalk behind Mr. Mac. He gave a short salute to my mom and extended a hand to our physics teacher. "Sir. Would you like to lead us?"

Mr. McIntosh ambled down the sidewalk beside my mother, and Reid fell in next to me as we followed a few steps behind them. "You don't look so good," Reid said to me.

"Gee, thanks. This is what 'my life is screwed' looks like."

"You're doing fine."

I glanced down at my bandaged hand from my time in the chasm. A sarcastic laugh punched out of me. "Yeah, I'm doing fine."

He didn't respond, so I peeked at his face. His light blue gaze was steady, waiting. "Really. It may seem like an impossible situation, but in order to succeed, you have to believe you can do it."

He was now offering the kind of advice printed on fortune cookies? "You gonna tell me what my lucky numbers are next?"

"I'm serious. It's mind over matter." His brows arched playfully. "On many levels."

A giggle burst out of me, and I was surprised when Reid laughed along.

Mr. Mac and my mom slowed in front of us. "Now," Mr. McIntosh said, clasping his hands just like he did before the start of an intense lecture. "On Sunday, you two will want to drive separately and park down one of these side streets. Josie, your mother and I will be seated in the audience. But you will have to go to the back staging area." He pointed across the street to the side entrance of the hotel. "You'll be ushered to the security check in the back. Reid, I've worked out your position as the school journalist. I already submitted your fingerprints and all the necessary documentation. Obviously, do not appear as if you two are together."

Mr. Mac continued walking. It was always weird seeing teachers outside of school, but he wasn't just a teacher—he was an Oculus. This made me wonder who else in my life, or random people I passed on the sidewalk, were Oculi.

This was how paranoia started, I was sure.

We turned the corner away from the busy street, as if we were on some after-dinner stroll around the neighborhood. Though my physics teacher didn't turn around, he continued talking loudly enough for Reid and me to hear. "Josie, you'll want to treat your week at school like any other. However, from here forward, you are not to travel without an Oculi accompaniment."

"Okay. But what about Hannah?"

Mom halted in front of me, causing me to bump into her back. "She checks out—I've done a full history check on her, her father, and her lack of extended family. But you can't tell her."

My mother had done background checks on my best friend's family? Hannah literally didn't have any family. It was just her and her dad. Oh. Was that why she was a safe Planck to hang out with? My parents had allowed me to spend time with her because she was, in fact, benign and posed no threat. Even my best friend was preapproved. *Everything* had been orchestrated for me, and I never saw it. I thought I might hurl my coffee drink.

I hadn't thought it was possible to be more upset with my mother, but I was wrong. I couldn't even look at her. I handed my coffee to Reid. "You can have this."

Reid seemed a bit perplexed, but he accepted the insulated cup and dutifully took a sip.

Staring at a big crack in the sidewalk, I nodded. "Give me more credit than that, Mom. Please. Of course I wouldn't tell her. I meant that I had some things scheduled with her this week." I wasn't stupid.

"I…" A long sigh hissed from my mom. "That's not what I—"

Reid cleared his throat. "Josie will stick to her regularly scheduled week, and I will be with her." He was trying to diffuse the tension. "If she has individual plans with Hannah, Santos or I will provide security." He eyed me. "You won't even know we're around."

Right. Like he was easy to ignore. Instead, I mumbled, "Thanks."

"Now that Josie knows who she can trust at school and where we need to go on Sunday, are we free to go?" Reid asked.

"Oh, yeah, sure," Mr. Mac said in a quite chipper tone, seemingly oblivious to the weirdness between my mom and me.

My mom leaned on her cane while the other hand held her drink, her critical eyes softening for a brief moment. She gave us a curt nod.

As soon as her head bowed, Reid's hand touched my elbow and softly guided me back the way we came. When we rounded the corner, I finally dared to glance at him.

"What?" he asked without looking at me.

"Thanks." This time I meant it sincerely.

He didn't respond. When we passed a trashcan, he chucked my drink, led me to his bike, and took me home.

It wouldn't have meant much to some—him kind of saving me from a frustrating situation with my mom—but it meant everything to me.

14.

JOSIE

Reid, Santos, and I were scheduled to practice using my shield—whatever that meant—before school, since I had plans with Hannah later. That morning, Santos followed from my house to the warehouse, where I found Reid pacing impatiently.

"Time to practice," he said.

"Defenses up." That was one of the first things we'd learned in tae kwon do—the importance of defending oneself. I wouldn't let him, or anyone else, see how scared I was.

"You were right," Santos said. "She is tough." Maybe it shouldn't have, but it gave me some kind of satisfaction to know that Reid had called me tough. And I think he knew that, because Reid walked away, saying nothing. I turned toward Santos, who shrugged. "He gets grumpy if he doesn't get enough sleep."

I smiled.

Santos waved me on to follow him. He was easy to be

around, always making jokes and smiling. I liked that about him. So did Hannah, who'd already texted me about Santos this morning. I told her we'd talk later. It pained me to think it, but with everything going on, my bestie's love life—that wasn't even a blip on my radar.

Santos glanced over his shoulder as he continued to the middle of the warehouse floor. "Now, you're an Anomaly, which is rare. But during this exercise, try not to Retract. You're going to be like me, a Pusher, for this lesson."

Huh. The ability to Push but not Retract…interesting. And, I imagined, a skill that was more difficult to control. If I made a mistake, I could "erase" it. If Santos screwed up, he'd have to continue to Push to correct it. That would be much harder.

I was mid-step, and deep in thought, when cinderblock walls magically appeared stacked on both sides of me, about twenty feet long and at least fifteen feet tall. Walls I hadn't Pushed. I whirled around and found another wall, boxing me in. My stomach dropped and I turned to run, but Reid and Santos took the place of the final wall, making a dead end.

"What are you doing?" My voice was steady despite the fear turning my blood to sludge.

"Training," Reid said, his face expressionless.

A basket of tennis balls snapped into existence next to Santos. He pocketed several balls and held three in his hands.

Reid stepped over to the basket and copied Santos, shoving balls into his pockets, palming as many more as possible. "Pushers and Anomalies have their own defensive mechanisms," he said. "'Defenses up' means many things. We need to always be aware of our environment." Santos glanced at Reid, raising an eyebrow, but Reid didn't bite. "Gather as much information as possible, especially when first engaging Oculi you don't know. That may require thinking outside the box. You need them to show you if they're a Pusher, a Retractor, or an Anomaly. And the most important part of being on the defensive is actually Pushing your shield."

A shield. I focused my thoughts.

Heat, pain, nausea. The sickening feeling was passing faster, though.

I Pushed a round metal shield into my right hand, one I'd seen in my history textbook when studying the Vikings. The shield appeared and instantly weighed my arm down to the cement floor. I hadn't thought that through. I dropped the heavy shield and Pushed Captain America's shield, which was much more manageable, not to mention the coolest piece of memorabilia I'd ever touched.

Santos bent over, dropped his tennis balls, and grabbed his belly, laughing. Reid turned away from me, his shoulders silently heaving.

"What?" I shrugged. "The first one was too heavy. And how badass is this?" I struck a Captain America pose. Total selfie material.

Both shields vanished and I felt naked. How was I supposed to protect myself?

Reid eased back around, still grinning, and said. "Not that kind of shield. Ours is, uh, not usually seen by the human eye. Only if the light catches it just right."

"So you mean it's basically invisible?" That contradicted the notion of *observing something into reality*.

His stance was wide, his arms crossed, and his face stoic.

Intense. "Yeah. Not seen by the human eye. Do you know anything about magnetic fields? They are electric currents that can be measured, *observed*, if you will."

"Yes, I know about magnetic fields, but that just sounds crazy."

Reid's eyes opened wider. "Like the rest of this isn't crazy?" Then he beaned me with tennis balls. Like full-on dodgeball style.

I jumped, ducked, swerved, arched my back. I did everything I could to avoid the balls, but I was getting walloped. "Ow."

"And no Retracting allowed, Miss Oculi Genius." This from Santos. The jerk.

I glanced at Reid, but white blurred my vision. Four or five balls flew toward me. Reflexively, I Pushed. My go-to concrete wall popped up, barricading me from the haze of tennis balls. In a flash, it was gone. *Damn it, Reid!* I cowered from the balls that were inches from pelting me, but they never made contact.

"What's with you and the barricades?" Reid asked.

A good question.

"You know," Santos said, "I'd heard you like to put up walls with people, but I didn't expect you to do it quite so literally."

His infectious chuckle made me smile.

Reid was all business. "Try again," he instructed. "No walls. No Marvel comic merchandise."

He and Santos Pushed more balls into their hands. A basketful of them appeared between them.

"Ready?"

Uh, no.

They let loose, and I focused, or tried to. My thoughts flip-flopped from Pushing to Retracting the little neon suckers. But I couldn't concentrate. A hazy, flickering light of sorts was there for a moment, and then faded into the space around me. I braced for the impact of a ball to my face.

The pain never came. The ball was gone.

Reid let the balls in his hands bounce to the floor, and he stepped to the side. He'd stopped the ball before it collided with my nose. *Maybe he does care about the status of my face.*

Then Santos stepped up. And a tennis ball machine appeared beside him.

I didn't know why Reid wasn't participating in my beat-down anymore. Something didn't seem right, and my stomach agreed. I didn't know how to create an invisible shield, and until a few seconds ago, I wouldn't have guessed it was even a possibility.

I was powerless.

Reid

"Josie," I said, trying to grab her attention away from Santos and his machine. "You have to Push energy out from your body. It doesn't have to be far. Just enough that whatever is thrown at you won't actually harm you."

Her eyes widened as she caught the word *harm*. She was one smart cookie, but I didn't dare tell her that. Pretty sure she'd kick my ass for calling her a cookie.

Santos cleared his throat, and I nodded. He unleashed a fury of balls at her. I Retracted most of them, and from the way she jumped and twisted, she avoided the others.

This wasn't working.

I Retracted all the balls to give her a chance to gather her thoughts as I walked the length of the training area behind Santos. "Instead of envisioning what you want to Push, think about extending your skin beyond your body. That's what helped me at first. It's going to feel weird."

I'd trained dozens of Oculi, and it'd never bothered me. But this? This wasn't just torture for Josie—it was for me, too. I wouldn't let anything devastating happen, but I also couldn't purposefully throw danger at her. That's why Santos had to do it this time.

Josie stopped trying to avoid the balls and stood up. Santos paused momentarily. She stilled, and her eyes met mine for an instant. She was Pushing a shield. I couldn't see it, but I could tell from her face. Her eyes concentrated on one spot and her jaw clamped down.

The ball chucking resumed, but the balls hit an invisible wall about two inches in front of Josie's body and fell to the floor, bouncing away.

Santos flicked the ball machine lever up to decapitation-by-tennis-balls mode. Balls hummed through the air at a dangerous speed. Josie's face twisted in surprise, and I knew her concentration had broken. Two balls pelted her in the leg, then a ten-by-ten brick wall appeared. Again.

I Retracted the wall. Josie hesitantly peeked at us from around her forearms.

"You can't use something as obvious as this wall for

your defense. You'll reveal yourself to Plancks, thus getting yourself killed."

She ran her hands over her face and let out a quiet growl. She was frustrated and probably scared shitless.

I wanted to assure her everything would be all right, but I didn't know that and I couldn't promise it. I stepped into her personal space, wanting to touch her, but I knew I shouldn't. "You have people after you. You need to be able to protect yourself—against anything. Anyone. And they will use whatever means necessary to harm you…including your family."

I could almost see her resolve harden.

"Be ready," I said. "Push your shield."

After I walked back to Santos, he zipped a few more balls at Josie, and they fell to the floor before reaching her body. In the next blink, the balls were gone and replaced with a bucket of hatchets. Santos gripped a sharpened tool in his right hand, another on deck in his left.

Josie faced us head-on, pointing, frozen. "Are you *serious*?"

"I didn't say it was going to be easy…" Santos hurled the first hatchet at Josie.

My stomach knotted. The hatchet turned, end over end, slicing through the air as it approached her torso. I was ready to Retract it. The hatchet hit her invisible barrier and clanked to the floor. Ten inches away from her body. *Yes.*

Santos flung another hatchet at her, and it also fell. He now held four hatchets in his left hand and one in his right.

Rapid-fire round. Initiation by fire.

My heart drummed in my ears, and I focused on the space in front of Josie. I had to be just as prepared as she was, in case her shield failed and I needed to Retract it at the last second.

One. She didn't flinch. Two. She didn't blink. Three and four were almost simultaneous. I wasn't sure she was breathing. They all fell in a heap to the floor.

Beyond impressive. No one did that on the first day. "Nice work." I clapped.

Her gaze darted to me at the same moment the last hatchet left Santos's hand. *Shit.* If she didn't see it coming, she wouldn't have time to Push a shield if it wasn't already up and holding.

I saw, thought, and Retracted the last hatchet three inches from her beautiful face and simultaneously Pushed my own shield around her. I almost pissed my pants.

It didn't take any effort on my part to Retract the hatchet, but it could've scarred her for life, in a couple different ways.

Santos and I both stared at Josie. She let her posture relax and looked confused. "I'm okay," she said. "I was still Pushing a shield. I'd just pulled it closer to my body."

Of course. Of course she was able to shift her shield with seemingly little effort on the first day of trying, making her a prodigy. I shouldn't have expected anything less.

"Let's see if you can Push a shield against something a little more threatening," I said. Santos lifted his chin toward me, signaling he got the order.

"More threatening than a sharpened metal blade targeting my head?" she squeaked.

"Uh-huh," I confirmed, nodding. "I don't want to be a dick, but we're under some time constraints." She perched her hand on her hip, tilted her head, and gave me her best "you've got to be kidding" look.

Santos tossed a hand grenade up in the air, giving Josie enough time to figure out exactly what it was. She could handle this; she'd just proven it. I Pushed my own shield around her, making sure she was safe. I needed her to practice within a highly dangerous situation so she could have experience when, or if, something like this happened in the future. My shield covered my own body so I could watch her without the threat of having shrapnel as a permanent accessory. Pieces of the grenade and bits of cinderblock flew away from the point of impact, sliding across an invisible umbrella protecting Josie.

Santos's arm swung out, launching another grenade directly at Josie. She'd be fine between her shield, mine, and both of our abilities to Retract, but anxiety clamped onto my stomach and constricted my airway.

The weapon slid down Josie's shield and dropped to the floor in front of her. Her gasp echoed through the warehouse. She was good. I held my breath, ready to help like I would be with every other Oculi I'd trained, but this was different. She had to train faster and harder than anyone before her.

The grenade detonated. Pieces of cement, metal, and plastic stopped short of hitting her body. The air was full of debris, yet she remained dirt free, her protection still in place.

I knew this wasn't easy for her, being a new Oculi. It never was. But this was months, hell, even years of training condensed into a week. Part of me wondered how much those inoculations her parents took affected her Anomaly abilities. Knowing the Harpers had been involved with SI, knowing the testing that had taken place there prior to them breaking free—exactly how unique was this girl? Quick on the heels of that thought, my mind turned to the serum. What powers did it contain? How much stronger, faster, more powerful would it make an Oculi? There was a draw to that kind of power. Like a drug.

Josie slowly unclenched her fists. She considered the mutilated wall and debris around her, and then locked eyes with me.

"That's enough for today," I said. "Santos, meet ya at school?"

"Yeah, gonna catch a few winks. I'll be there later." Santos Pushed a kid's scooter and footed himself toward his room. He yelled to Josie, "Don't take me throwing weapons at you personally. You rocked it." His head swung to me. "Later, boss."

"Time for class. Your regular schedule awaits."

JOSIE

I was struggling. And shield training…sucked.

I tried to embrace my inner Hannah, to find that silver lining, that spark of positivity in every situation, but, man, it was tough. Don't get me wrong, I'd just deflected bombs— and how badass was that? Plus, the whole ability to focus on most anything and make it appear? It was like magic, only it was science, and no matter how I rationalized it, it was pretty. Flippin'. Awesome.

Years of being a comic book and sci-fi junkie, only to

discover I had some superhuman powers of my own—amazeballs! But those hatchets had been *real*. The threat to myself, my family, to innocent people...*real*. And imminent. Suddenly, the perks of being an Oculi weren't so awesome anymore. I rubbed at a spot on my left thigh where two tennis balls had pelted me—yeah, it was gonna bruise—and I tried to smooth away the pain.

"This..." I ran a hand over my face. "This is..." I couldn't verbalize the intensity.

"I know. It's insane."

"It's...I don't know if I can do this." My last word came out as a whisper.

"You can." No hesitation.

"The shield I Pushed—" I began slowly.

"The Viking or Marvel comic one?"

"The...field. Following the theorem of Oculi existence, if I can Push that shield, then a Retractor should be able to—"

He shook his head. "It has to do with the wavelengths of energy, the range of the spectrum. A Retractor wouldn't be able to lock into that. It's too variable for someone to Retract."

That alleviated at least one fear. I considered the logistics of measuring EMF fluctuations and the types of machinery required. In the time it would take an enemy to lock in on my shield, I could disarm him or escape. Well, theoretically, at least.

Which brought me to my next question: "How long do Oculi abilities last?" In other words, how long would I be capable of defending myself before I was forced to go off the grid and live in a subterranean panic room? Just how many pints of chocolate peanut butter fudge could I Push on a whim?

"Again," Reid said, "it's variable. Depends on usage, on the inherent amount of one's natural stores of energy. Most Oculi begin to experience the degenerative effects in their early thirties. Operatives are lucky to keep their skills past twenty-five."

"Why do you train people if it reduces your abilities?"

He shrugged. "Somebody has to."

He crossed his arms, and his lips thinned. Okay, so that wasn't a happy conversation. I hadn't truly accepted that I had these Oculi abilities, so losing them wasn't my concern right now. I was concerned for Reid. But his expression told me he didn't want my sympathy. "What will happen after the award ceremony?"

"After the handoff, we'll need to take you somewhere safe. If there is a leak, I don't see how we can take you back to the Hub. I'm working on the rest."

He didn't have a definitive answer because we still didn't know who could be trusted. I got that. But I didn't like non-answers. I thought we needed to find my dad, but I'd keep that to myself for the time being.

He pressed his lips together in a sort of sad smile, like he felt bad. Something in his expression was comforting, vaguely familiar.

"This will sound ludicrous," I said. "But I feel like I've known you forever." I couldn't believe the words came out, but now that I'd started my bizarre thought, I'd better explain it. "I know people say that all the time and I never thought I'd think or feel something so cliché. I...I don't usually have gut feelings. I'm even a little disappointed in myself for thinking it. But…"

Reid flashed me that sexy, lopsided grin I hated loving. "That's because you have." I leaned closer, examining his face for signs of delirium. He said, "You've known me for a long time."

"I don't call a day a long time."

"I don't, either," he said. "I've know you much longer than a day."

Lovely. My trainer-slash-bodyguard had lost his mind. "You do know basic math, right?" That got me a chuckle.

"Yes. And according to my calculations, I met you for the first time when you were less than a year old."

I felt my face twist in disbelief. "Have you been eating paint chips?"

"Are you ready?" Reid asked with a strange excitement in his voice.

"Ready for wh—?"

His complexion darkened. His hair changed to a lighter shade of brown, and his light eyes turned more of a green-blue than a sky blue, but the shape didn't change. His nose narrowed, but his mouth stayed exactly the same.

My stomach spasmed. "Impossible," I whispered. Nick's best friend, Callum Ross. Cal, who I'd known since birth and had a crush on since I was eleven, sat across from me. His family and mine had been friends forever. I hadn't seen him since before Nick died. I thought back to the photos Mom had shown me of the people who had started the Resistance with them. I opened my mouth again, but nothing came out. My head wasn't just spinning, it was turned upside down and running backward.

"It's me." His fingers squeezed around my fist. "Once everything went down with Nick, I had to go into protection—meaning I had to change my name and looks. I'm on the Consortium's Wanted List. Wentworth is a distant family name."

I had so many questions that I didn't know where to start. As I stared at Cal, like a puzzle, pieces clicked together, forming pictures from my past. The Ross family lived in Denver. They often visited us as we moved around the country and were the closest thing we had to family. They'd visit six or seven times a year. We never visited them. Now it was obvious why. They lived in the Hub.

Then, when Nick turned seventeen, he went to a private school in Denver, which, I could now see, was really the Hub. My parents had told me they were comfortable with Nick going to the school because the Ross family lived close by, and Cal would be attending the same place. Again, the Hub.

Cal's mom had died a year or so before Nick. I went to her funeral. I went to Reid's mom's funeral. My mind was blown. My parents had said he was away at some university in Europe.

I'm not sure how long I sat there thinking, staring. It felt like I revisited every second I had known Cal as Reid. Or Reid as Cal.

With my next blink, he appeared as the Reid I knew.

He leaned forward, and my heart leapt into my throat. His soft lips pressed against my forehead, spreading heat over my face, bringing his neck incredibly close, along with his clean smell. He slowly pulled his mouth away from my forehead.

"I'm sorry I left after Nick died. I wanted to stay, to support you and your family. But I had to leave, to lure away the Consortium. They found Nick, so they could find you. Someone had to allow for you and your family to escape."

"What? You were bait?" He'd been protecting me—from both near and far—for a long time. He'd already saved my life, but that was nothing compared to him giving up *his* life to save my family and me. I couldn't believe someone could be that selfless. I stared into his eyes, now recognizing that familiarity I'd seen there before. I had no words.

So many emotions swirled inside me, I didn't know what to do with them all. He was someone I knew, someone I'd trusted, someone I'd wanted to be mine. He was here, in front of me, and real. I didn't know how to express to him the overpowering feelings I'd experienced in the last twenty-four hours, but I could try. "This was the best thing anyone could've told me after last night. I…I'm so happy."

My body acted without my consent. My arms flung around his neck, and he pulled me against his chest. I'd lost him once already, and I was terrified to lose him again…

Reid

I inhaled Josie's gardenia perfume, flowery and fresh. Telling her who I really was let me breathe easier. I was about to tell her more, to explain my other duties as her trainer, but it would have to wait. That news would deflate the moment. I wanted to revel in the feeling of her in my arms, the sensation of a dream realized.

She'd practically jumped at me, and I thought I was going

to dissolve under her excitement. This, her touch, I'd craved it for years. But I wasn't sure it meant the same to me as it did to her. The lines were blurred.

Warmth simmered in my chest as I loosened my grip, my palms sliding across her back. I didn't want to pull away from her, but there was so much I needed to say.

Her gaze bounced around my face, inquisitive. She shook her head in disbelief, then her face broke into a wide grin. Her tiny giggle infused the stale warehouse with luminous energy. "That's how you knew about my favorite ice cream."

I laughed with her, relieved she wasn't furious. "Yeah, I remembered from a couple years ago that you were an ice-cream junkie." I'd been around the Harper family enough to know that Josie had an ice-cream addiction, deplorable taste in movies, and an incredible amount of love for her family. I'd been devastated for her when Nick died. Unlike me, the Harpers weren't submerged in the Resistance life. Being homeschooled and moving so often, Nick and Josie hadn't just been siblings; they were best friends.

Yeah, I'd had a full-fledged soft spot for Nick's little sister. As we got older, though, it became more than that. Of course, no one knew.

I sucked in air in an attempt to calm an unexpected nervousness. "I wanted to tell you sooner, but I couldn't. It would've complicated things. I don't want you to think I meant to deceive or trick you. I changed my appearance for everyone's safety—most importantly yours."

"After the funeral, we moved to this house, and Eli and I started public school. It wasn't easy for either of us. They told me you were traveling, but I checked Facebook, and I did some searching online."

I shook my head. "Any information like that would've been restricted. You were probably logging onto dummy sites. There's no electronic trace of me left."

She opened her mouth to say something more, but nothing came out. Her cheeks flushed and her eyes dropped to her hands, a soft smile playing on her lips. "I…" She lifted her head, and a ray of morning sun through the windows lit up her face, her lip gloss sparkling. It took everything in me not to taste those sparkles. "I missed you," she whispered.

15.

Reid studied my face and finally said, "I missed you, too." Then he abruptly leapt from the couch, like he'd gotten caught with his hand in the cookie jar, and jogged across the warehouse. Okaaay. I replayed the discovery, trying to process the news that Reid was really Cal. The garage door to the warehouse opened.

Reid straddled his bike, looking like some cologne ad. He tipped his head forward and watched me through dark lashes, flashing a flirty half smile, and my stomach somersaulted. "What?"

"Your shirt."

I looked down. I was wearing one of my favorite tees. Set Phasers To Stun was screen-printed across my chest.

Reid laughed. "Well, you certainly stun. You're the only person I know who can make nerdy look so sexy." My cheeks burned and my stomach decided to step up the somersaults to double handsprings. His face seemed to deepen a shade, too.

"We're taking training outside today." He examined the blue sky. "Follow me in your car."

"What about school?"

"You never cut class?"

I shook my head. "I had to fight and argue with my parents just to go to high school. I never miss a day."

Reid grinned. "Well, technically, your mom called you out. We chatted a few minutes ago." He flashed a postcard-size piece of green paper. "Doctor's note."

He started his bike. I climbed into my Civic and pulled out behind him.

I followed, but not too closely, with the radio blaring and the windows rolled down. The wind blew my hair around like a red storm. I stuck my hand out the window, playing with the air velocity flow, trying not to let my mind wander to all the things that were screwed up about this situation and my world. The wind pushed at my palm, and I angled my hand so the air passed over it smoothly, then twisted my wrist so I could feel the resistance. My life wasn't much different than the extension of my hand. I could "go with the flow," as it was, or resist. The choice was mine to make.

Not that I really had a choice.

W e headed west and slowed as the paved roads trailed off to sandy dirt. I'd been under such a microscope since moving to this house that I hadn't really explored the countryside in

South Florida since getting my license.

Eventually we ended up in a cypress grove with the bright sunshine blocked out by the dense tree coverage. Beautifully skeletal trees, draped with Spanish moss, rose out of the shallow marsh as if tiptoeing on their gnarled roots. These were *way* different than the red oaks from my last home, but no less lovely.

I turned down the volume on the radio, and the eerie silence, apart from an orchestra of insects, sent tingles over my scalp. Reid rode his bike off to the side and idled until I pulled even with him. I took in the beautiful layers of greens and grays surrounding us, waiting for him to speak.

He leaned on the edge of my open window. "You need to drive forward for your test."

Drive forward where? The dirt road cleaved a path through the cypresses for as far as I could see.

"I'd roll up the windows," he said, "so you don't get carried away by a mosquito." His eyes held my gaze as he stepped back from my car, and I closed the windows. I didn't like not knowing what my training was, especially after being pelted with various objects to practice using my shield. And that whole abyss scenario—scared me senseless.

I pressed the gas pedal with great caution, scared of what was to come and wanting to be prepared for anything. My white knuckles punctuated the dark steering wheel like my own silent exclamation points.

Looking in my rearview mirror, I no longer saw Reid. Perfect. My gut twisted.

I jolted forward as the car fell, my stomach dipping like I was landing in an airplane, and the moment almost seemed to slow. My head snapped back, my view out the windshield momentarily obstructed. In a flash, the road in front of me was gone. Water rose along the windows and poured in through the air conditioning vents. Cold water covered my feet. Glancing down, I saw dark liquid rising through the floorboards, gushing in from every crack.

Pulling my gaze forward, I realized the windshield was already fully submerged. The bright green algae appeared almost neon in the murky water. The gnarled roots of the trees looked as if they were the tentacles of a large beast.

I could Retract the water. I could Push a raft, a yacht, a freaking mountain of concrete out of the swamp—but I couldn't move. I couldn't breathe. Fear had a grip on my heart, tethering me to my seat, disabling me.

Nick's car had gone off the road into a river and he'd drowned. I could still picture his distorted face in my mind, images from the autopsy I was never meant to see. It was the image that I'd seen every time I closed my eyes in those first weeks after he died. Those memories, etched into my brain, weighed me down.

Cold, gritty water rushed in, steady as the rush of my heart. I fumbled with the seat belt, the water rising. My clothes clung to me. The liquid smelled of mud and grass and decay. It brushed up to my neck. If I didn't get out, I'd drown like Nick. The seat belt unlatched, and I thrashed through the water, reaching for the door handle, but it didn't budge. I pulled and pulled. Nothing. I let myself float to the surface of the rising water in my Civic, sucking in oxygen from the four inches of air still left, and then I kicked. I kicked the window repeatedly, depleting my energy.

Pressing my face to the surface, I found one last sip of oxygen, only half a breath, from the air pocket. My lungs burned. I was going to drown like my brother. Panic shot through my veins, congealing my blood.

I had causes to fight for, people to protect. This wasn't the way it was supposed to happen. I wasn't ready for death. I tried to blink away the darkness closing in around me, fast and steady. And then I welcomed it.

Reid

I simultaneously Retracted the car and the water and Pushed an air mattress directly under Josie's floating body. "Damn it, Josie!" I yelled. The mud squished through my shoes as I sloshed forward the first couple steps, then I snapped out of my shock and Pushed a sidewalk to Josie and sprinted. My heart flailed around in my chest, out of control.

Slipping my hands under her, I collapsed to the mattress and pulled Josie's limp body into my lap.

Yeah, I knew with the car crash, the drowning might be a trigger. But that was exactly why I had to exploit it and force her to move past her fears. Son of a bitch, I'd made a mistake. A grave mistake.

I rocked, hugging her to me. She didn't deserve this. Josie was smart and witty and wonderful in so many ways—and she didn't ask for any of this. She'd already lost so much. Her dad, Nick...

I maneuvered behind her and locked my hands together

around her midsection. I heaved once, twice, and then water shot out of her mouth like a fountain.

"Gross," she mumbled.

Oh. Thank God.

"Reid, uh…" She coughed. "If you don't loosen your arms, I'm going to pass out again."

I let my hold go slack, but I didn't let go. She leaned against my chest. I think my breathing was as strained as hers. Sure as shit, I'd been just as terrified.

"I'm sorry, Josie."

She glanced over her shoulder at me. "For what? My car?" Her lips curved into a semblance of a smile. "Guess now I can Push a new one."

"No." I inclined my chin to the cypress swamp surrounding us. "For this. You weren't ready. I put you in danger."

A soft sigh. "It's the water. I used to love it, you know."

I did know. When I'd spent time with the Harpers in Phoenix, they'd had a pool in the yard. Even when the weather began to change in September, Josie would take to the water like a fish.

"It's because of the accident…because of Nick."

I knew that, too. Mrs. Harper wasn't just analytical about her lab. She'd kept files on her kids, detailed accounts of their strengths and weaknesses, their flaws and fears. When I'd spoken with her this morning, she'd issued orders for me to incorporate water into one of Josie's training exercises, said her daughter needed to be ready for anything. I had already known about the water phobia—I could recite Josie's friggin' profile, I'd read her files so many times. Spiders and snakes weren't high on her list, either. But most Oculi weren't out to play games or to terrify her. They would plan to kill her. And like an asshole, I'd thought this literal "sink or swim" approach to the water would do her good.

She shivered in my arms. And I hated myself.

"You weren't ready," I said. "I never should've done this."

Her hands rested atop mine, like she was trying to calm me instead. "I have to get past this; you're right about that. I can't let what happened to Nick control my life. Too much is at stake."

I brushed her hair back from her forehead. She'd nearly drowned, had been tossed into her greatest nightmare, and here she was putting on a brave face and being so friggin' pragmatic about the situation, it was all I could do not to scream.

She leaned to the side toward the trees. "There're maybe six inches of water down there—just how much did you Push?"

Her concern for me made me hate myself more.

She shifted a little in my arms, almost facing me directly. "It's okay, Reid."

No. None of this was okay.

"Shh." She touched my face.

Shit. I'd said that out loud?

"I know you'd never intentionally hurt me. I know you'll always keep me safe—"

I cut off her words the only way I knew how. With my lips.

16.

JOSIE

My first day back to school and I was terrified. I tried not to demand, or think in general. I didn't want to accidentally Push something into existence. Today, I ventured to actually talk and interact.

Plopping down on the bench across from Charles and Lauren, I opened up my lunch box. Marisa and Hannah showed up, gabbing about the VP coming to his hometown during his campaign. Since they were both involved in student government, no surprise for them to be discussing the Veep's bid for the presidency and the blah-blah-blah details of his campaign. I engrossed myself in one half of my wrap, pretending to be too hungry to care.

"Josie." Hannah sighed. "I'm talking to you. Are you in there?"

I pivoted and fought the urge to throw my hands around Hannah, hugging her until she had to pry my arms away.

I stared at her, the first person who'd really liked me despite my dorkiness, and wanted to spill everything that was happening. And I'd have to keep wanting that, because I simply couldn't.

Something nudged my butt, and I almost choked.

A deep voice behind me grunted out a fake cough. Reid.

I took a moment to swallow and wipe my mouth. "Yeeeees?" I said without turning around.

"Will you introduce us to your friends?" he said in a sweet voice. Man, he could turn the charm on and off like a switch.

And he had yesterday, with a kiss.

His breath had whispered across my lips as he'd said my name. His mouth had been firm, soft—yes, somehow both—and he'd held me frozen in place with just his lips. One second his mouth was pressed against mine, his strong arms anchoring me to his chest. In the next, he was ten feet away, cursing up a storm and ranting about how that would never happen again.

'Cause my life didn't suck enough without getting rejected to my face.

It wasn't even a "real" kiss. It was just a fleeting second of our lips connecting. No tongue, not even a taste.

"Josie."

I peeked over my shoulder. The guys were holding trays. Reid or Santos had already followed me everywhere I went that day, besides the girls' restroom, so I knew I needed to invite them to sit with us.

Lauren sat up straighter. "Santos, Reid? Friends." I waved my wrap in the air to gesture. "Friends? Santos and Reid." Lauren, Charles, and Hannah chorused a drawn out,

"Helloooo."

Reid placed his tray down between Hannah's protein shake and my vintage *Star Trek* lunch box. He stifled a laugh as he climbed over the cement bench, then continued bumping his hip into my side as he wriggled his butt down next to me. My stomach tumbled over itself with each bump.

His messy dark waves, light eyes, and the way he carried himself were almost too much to handle. Why did he have to be so attractive even in jeans and a tee? I wasn't the only one who'd noticed. Girls all over the courtyard shot me death stares. And the really crazy part was, now that I'd seen him as Cal *and* Reid, I could see how similar they were. The exact mouth and same eyes, just a different color. They were one in the same now, indistinguishable to me.

Everyone else at the table made room for Santos, who, not surprisingly, wedged in beside Hannah. Her curls bounced as she scooted over, and a huge smile stuck to her face.

Reid's forearm brushed back and forth across my bare arm as he leaned forward, half standing to extend a hand to everyone around the table, performing his usual Reid McCharming intros.

I wanted to resent him. But he was doing his job, and I was the one attaching emotional sentiment to the logistics of something bigger than either one of us. And emotional attachments weren't my usual, which seemed to tick me off even more.

I took another bite of my wrap and chewed slowly. My brain had to breathe before thinking about anything else.

I watched both guys stab at our school's version of meatloaf. Reid gave up, popped a few tater tots into his mouth, and rested his hand over a mystery Styrofoam container. Santos moved on to slurping down the rest of Hannah's shake. These guys really believed in the Resistance's cause, otherwise who would be so masochistic that they'd go back to high school lunches?

But then again, Reid actually looked like he was enjoying himself.

Without turning my head, I watched him eat his last tot and then crack open the Styrofoam dish to reveal the best-looking protein-packed salad I'd ever seen come out of our cafeteria. No doubt he had Pushed it after he tasted the meatloaf. In my most nonchalant voice, I said, "How's your first day *back* in high school? You like being the new kid, don'tcha?"

His eyes darted around the courtyard, to the street, and back to his salad. Without looking at me, he said, "This is my first time in a public school. I can be a people person."

Of course he could be a people person. Me, I'd been a virtual recluse in my first days at Oceanside. Reid was here less than a week and he'd probably nab a prom court nomination. I rolled my eyes and forced myself to gab with my friends and pretend life was normal. I explained an advanced physics problem to Lauren and listened to prom talk.

When Reid stood to return his tray, I followed to continue our conversation without the worry of being overheard by my tablemates.

We walked in sync with each other, side by side. "This is hard, the whole pretending-to-be-normal-at-school thing," I admitted. He side-eyed me, returned his tray, and gestured with his head to follow.

I turned the corner and leaned against the wall, relieved to be away from people for a few minutes. Pretending to be a

Planck was exhausting.

Reid placed a hand on the cinderblocks next to me.

"Santos will follow you to the warehouse after school today." I swung my head to him, and his closeness surprised me.

"Hannah asked to drive me home. I, uh, had to tell her something when she asked why I didn't drive. I said the battery was dead." Letting my bestie in on the fact that an Oculi trainer had sunk my car in a synthetic swamp—yeah, not going to win me any points in the trust department. Plus, there was that whole "keep Plancks in the dark" policy.

He grunted. His jaw moved as he appeared to process what he wanted to say next. "Okay. Catch a ride home with your friend. I'll arrange the surveillance."

Alone at no times. Got it.

The bell rang, and Reid's lips twisted into his flirty half smile. He stared at me for a moment before he held out a hand, gesturing for me to move ahead of him. He walked me to my next class, where Santos was waiting to babysit me.

The school day progressed like normal, or as normal as it can when you're scared senseless that one wrong thought would Push or Retract something. Oh, yeah, and if I did screw up and do that in front of my classmates, well, then the Resistance, who I'm working to help, could come after me, too. Good times.

Santos chaperoned all of my afternoon classes except advanced physics. Reid was in that class. Of course he'd placed himself in my favorite class, because apparently he lived to make my life hell. Or, at least, more complicated.

Mr. Mac bustled into the classroom, his mannerisms

brusque but patient, his voice carrying that odd cadence like he had to purposely slow his words, or else he'd talk too quickly for people to understand. Before heading to the whiteboard for our lecture, he paused in front of me. "Oh." He addressed the class. "And check out the new poster."

He directed our attention over the board. THIS POSTER IS IN LATIN WHEN YOU'RE NOT LOOKING. Only a few students chuckled, Reid and me being two of them.

Reid didn't look at me, let alone talk to me the whole period. That was fine. For some reason, though, even being pissed at Reid for kissing me then acting like I was a freaking leper, I was more relaxed in that class than I had been all day.

So, maybe Reid deserved my crappy attitude today for blowing so hot and cold, but in the scheme of the Resistance versus the Consortium, there was nothing that could stand in my way—or his. He was just doing his job. And I'd have to do mine. I needed to scale back my annoyance and promise myself to keep my feelings under control.

Easier said than done.

Hannah dropped me off at my house after school. I tried not to show the happy surprise I felt when we pulled up and my car—the car that had drowned in the swamp the day before— sat in my driveway.

I pulled Hannah in for a tight hug. She wrapped her arms around me. "Aw. I think I've made you a softie, J!"

"Ha. Ha." I leaned back to the open passenger side door. "Text ya later."

I waited for her to reverse out of my driveway and watched her drive down my street.

Reid came around the corner of the house. "Hey."

I flinched at his voice. "Did you…did you do this?"

He shrugged. "It's the least I could do."

"What? How?"

"I found your make and model online and recreated it."

"Thank you." Reid used his abilities freely. Too freely. He was either way stronger than the average Oculi, or he was burning through his reserves at a dangerous pace. I made a mental note to ask him about that.

He gave a curt nod, then jogged to his bike. A moment later, it rumbled to life. "I'll follow you to the warehouse," he yelled over the noise. He was forcing me to get back in my car. I immediately saw his ploy for what it was. It wasn't the car that I wasn't keen on, though, it was the water. Still, I could appreciate his plan. Pulling out of the driveway, I spotted Santos across the street, ready to take over watch of my house.

He'd stay there until my mom and brother came home. In only a few days, so many lives had been turned upside down because of me, because of who and what I was.

I needed to ensure those lives didn't suffer or get hurt in vain—no matter the cost or consequences for me.

Once parked inside the warehouse, I moseyed to Reid, who was bent over a table that hadn't been there just seconds before. "What are—"

I knew what it was once I drew close enough. A map, a

layout of the vice president's speech and award ceremony. He said we'd be working on logistics. "Oh."

Reid waved me over by him. "You'll be backstage." His finger landed on the large rectangle. "Santos will be here, I'll be here, and we should have two more operatives, most likely placed here and here." When his finger glided across the diagram to the various positions, I marked with my own finger where I would stand.

"Your mother will be at the back of the room, seated at this table," Reid continued. "When they call your name, you'll be signaled to walk across the stage."

I scooted my finger across the rectangle representing the stage, and Reid did the same. Our fingers bumped, and tiny tingles danced along my vertebrae.

He turned around, leaned against the table, and crossed his arms, tugging up his sleeve and revealing the tattoo Nick used to bare.

"Now let's practice like it's the real deal," he said.

I was a bit confused as to how we'd practice like it was real without breaking into the ceremony location—the hotel we'd scouted. It was probably under high surveillance due to the VP's imminent arrival. Surely the Secret Service or some kind of security would be in place. While on campaign tours or just at home, the contender for the most powerful position in the world would surely not go unguarded. "How…"

He ran a hand over his scruff. "I, uh, found a way in last night after Santos took over watch at your house, just to get a feel for the stage. Security had already closed off sections of the hotel. The room was set up, minus linens and decorations. I committed the layout to memory."

I was about to ask more questions, but something sounded behind us, catching my attention. A wallpapered room replaced the cement-block warehouse walls. A stage with heavy blue curtains behind it was the focal point.

Reid sauntered toward the stage and, over his shoulder, said, "Let's practice."

He'd just Pushed a replica of the room where the ceremony would take place for me to practice, plus he'd already Pushed a new car for me. But every Push came at a cost; he'd told me that himself. He couldn't keep using his powers so freely, not for me.

Jogging up the side stairs after Reid to follow him backstage, I hauled a door open and stepped into darkness. "Reid?"

Overhead bulbs illuminated the backstage area, and Reid squeezed his eyes tight. He blinked a couple times and said, "Okay. You'll be standing here. I'll be across from you on the opposite side of the backstage. Santos will be right in front of you, in front of the stage, on the floor. We'll both be posing as photographers—school paper and yearbook or something." He waved his hand, glossing over the details. "When the VP calls your name, you'll move through this opening straight to the podium." A wooden podium appeared, and he ambled to the front of the stage.

"Reid," I whispered again. I saw it now. The strain. The way his mouth tightened and his eyes narrowed the tiniest bit because he was in pain.

A dull ache spread in my chest.

Acting like nothing was wrong, he pointed to the back of the room, which was still the warehouse. "Your mom will be sitting at the back corner table." A large round table appeared. "One of the two Oculi from the Resistance will be sitting with your mom. Her plus-one guest will be Santos instead of your brother, for added safety. The other will be in the opposite back corner." Another table showed up, along with the back wall of the room, then the rest of the tables filled in the space between the back wall and the stage. "Secret Service will be stationed at the back wall, along with several others throughout the room. There should be two onstage, one on each side of the vice president, and the rest off to the sides."

"Reid," I said again, this time reaching for him.

"Concentrate, Josie."

Since he refused to acknowledge my concerns, I replayed what he'd said and focused my attention on the room's layout. No way in hell would I let his efforts be wasted.

He moved behind the podium and turned to me.

"Now, act like I'm the VP. You are going to walk from behind the curtain and step up to me."

"Hey, you two!" Santos called from the back of the fake room.

I waved to Santos as he weaved through the tables to the stage.

"Josie Harper," Reid said in an announcer voice.

I did as Reid instructed and stopped in front of him.

"You'll need to come in closer." I shuffled my feet forward to where I could smell his signature scent. Dear Loki.

His dark hair fell into his eyes as he shifted his arms. "He'll hand you the certificate with his left hand, and you'll accept on the opposite side of the document. Then, with your right hand, you'll shake his hand and slip the vial into his palm.

You'll pause for a photograph as you shake hands, making the exchange behind the award. Let's try it."

"Hold up," Santos said. He heaved himself onto the stage from the floor. "If you're practicing the handoff, show me where I'm supposed to be."

Reid pointed to the back corner. "The first table you passed by. Just got confirmation from Mr. Mac that you'll be sitting with Mrs. Harper."

Santos bobbed his head in understanding. "Right on."

"You set up the cameras on the buildings surrounding the Oceanside Hotel?" Reid asked.

"Not yet," Santos said. "You know that hotel backs up to a mangrove swamp, right? There's a manmade beach behind the hotel, but on either side, it's bracketed by preserves."

"You like to paddleboard," Reid said.

Santos seemed to consider that for a moment. "Working in a little fun in the sun—I like where your mind's at."

His roll-with-the-punches positivity reminded me of Hannah. The two of them really would be great together. All pom-poms and popcorn and Zen.

In a blink, he wore board shorts, sunglasses, and a white tee. Santos glanced down at himself. "Thanks, boss."

"Enjoy the beach," Reid said.

Santos slipped through the door at the back of the fake room, and the stage became brighter, pulling my attention up. More lights turned on, beaming overhead.

Reid followed my line of sight. "It will be bright and hot onstage. Okay, let's do it again at a normal pace." An empty vial appeared in my right hand.

"Okay." Stepping in to Reid, I reached my left hand toward

his hand, where a rectangular paper appeared. I clasped the edge of the document and slipped my hand into his, the vial between our hands. Pleased with the easy exchange, I peeked up to gage Reid's reaction.

A tiny amount of blood trickled from his nose.

He'd been pushing himself too hard, too fast—all for me. He was deteriorating before my eyes. I couldn't let him do this to himself. I cared about him.

Our eyes locked.

I Pushed a tissue into my left hand, replacing the fake award, and lifted it toward his face.

"I'm okay," he said.

"Just…" My right hand still in his, I tightened my hold and pulled him toward me. The space between us closed, and he bent his head to mine. I wiped the blood away.

His gaze ping-ponged around my face, finally settling on my eyes. I pushed onto my toes and ever so lightly pressed my lips to his. He didn't recoil, but he didn't kiss me back, either. His lips were like cotton candy—soft and sweet.

Flat-footed, I said, "Thank you…for this."

He slowly straightened to his full height. "Welcome." The word came out gruff.

I didn't want to care about him. I didn't want to attach emotion to the people involved in this situation, especially Reid. It would complicate things. Oculi life was already complicated enough.

Funny—complicated things usually intrigued me the most.

Reid

C'mon." I jumped off the stage and offered my hand to Josie to help her down. As soon as her hand was in mine, she Retracted the rest of the practice room, and we stood in the middle of the warehouse.

"What was that for?"

"One," she said, "because I can use the practice. And, two, because you're doing too much Pushing and Retracting. This is going to hurt you. You have to let me do more…"

I backed to the living room area, her still advancing. "Are you seriously mad at me?"

"Yes, I'm mad. You were bleeding. You shouldn't have Pushed that elaborate stage in the first place."

The backs of my legs hit the couch, and I sat. She plopped down on the couch next to me. I couldn't stop studying her lips that had just been on mine. I didn't want to like it, her little kiss, but I did, because I liked her. I had for a long time. But it was different now. I couldn't like her—I just needed to teach her and protect her.

Her hand reached toward me, slow enough that I could've withdrawn or swiped it away. But I didn't. She lifted the sleeve of my shirt and traced over the black lines of my tattoo with her index finger. "What's it mean?"

I watched her finger trail over my skin, as light and cool as a summer breeze, but it was like an electric shock I felt in my chest. "It's called a Dragon's Eye," I said. "It combines the triangle's meaning of *threat* with the letter *Y*, which means a choice of *good and evil*." I traced the inverted triangle with my own finger, then the *Y* that connected the points of the triangle. "As a whole, it stands for the balance of love, power, and wisdom. It's a symbol of protection."

Josie switched her focus to fiddling with a hole in her jeans. "If I gave it to you, why don't you just get rid of it? Retract it?"

"One, people have seen it on me. Two, I like what it symbolizes. Three, Nick was my friend. It makes me feel closer to him." I didn't tell her that I'd kept it for her.

She stared at me.

I hoped I was doing the right thing by telling her. I twisted toward her, and the inches between us shrunk. "The time he spent at the Hub…was with me. He and I trained together. Learned together. That's one of the reasons why your mom called me. I knew Nick. I know your family, uh, situation."

Josie's facial expressions didn't change. I thought for sure she'd be cursing me by now. Finally, she said, "I know. I'm glad my mom called you. You were my brother's best friend, *Cal*. I know how close the two of you were. I remember you."

It was the first time she'd called me by my given name. But Cal—the person I had been—was dead.

"Josie, I—"

Her hand skimmed over my tattoo, and my stomach clenched from her touch. I watched her ease closer, getting a better look at the ink on my upper arm, and she turned her face to mine. Her flushed cheeks begged to be touched. The air between us was heavy, making it impossible to breathe. My lungs burned, struggling to pull in oxygen.

I saw the questions in Josie's eyes, and, for once, they didn't pertain to anything Oculi. Tucking her foot farther under her, she shifted higher. It was an intentional movement, one I couldn't ignore if I wanted to. She'd purposely made a decision to move closer.

A war broke out between my head and body. I wanted to breathe her in, drink her up, feel her against me. Every cell in my body whispered her name. My brain knew better, though. If I acted on my feelings, it would make things difficult; it would change things between us. I couldn't put my wants above the Resistance, above the mission, above the greater good.

I wanted to answer the questions she held in her eyes, to confirm her hunches, to let her know how I felt about her. I wanted to press my lips to hers, but I couldn't.

I wouldn't.

Needing to put distance between her body and mine, I stood up. "Good job on the handoff. Let's get you home."

17.

JOSIE

Reid's abrupt change of mood played heavily on my mind. I knew he'd been right there with me. I'd traced the tattoo on his arm, and his eyes had darkened, his pupils widening until only a ring of blue outlined the black. His breathing had changed, and I'd counted the accelerated pulse in his neck. Then he'd pulled away.

So why did he stop?

Was it something I did? Something I'd said?

Ding. Ding. Ding.

It was like an annoying game-show buzzer sounded in my head.

I didn't like when people poked and prodded at my past, or when they asked me about topics I didn't want to discuss. Nobody really brought up Nick. Since we'd moved shortly after his death, I didn't think many people in Oceanside even knew that I'd had an older brother. But questions about my dad—yeah, those still caught me off guard.

And then I'd gone and called Reid *Cal*, reminding him of the life he'd left behind. Bringing back all the memories of him leaving everyone he knew and loved just to draw attention away from my family and me.

For both of our sakes, I needed to concentrate on the mission. Neither of us could afford distractions. Neither of us needed reminding of the pasts we couldn't change.

I burst through the door into the kitchen, my entire body tingling from adrenaline and mixed emotions. "Mom," I yelled. Every day marked a day closer to the award ceremony. Every day could be my last. I didn't want to waste that time fighting or arguing with her.

Eli ran down the stairs, his brows pulled up in concern. Mom followed behind him, not quite as fast. She glanced at my face, saw that I was upset, and said, "Go back up and play with Jeremy, Eli."

Eli, now standing in front of me, turned and gave Mom puppy dog eyes. "But Mom. Josie is sooooo much better than Jeremy at *Marvel Legos* on Xbox." He approached me again. "Come on, J. You can be part of the Fantastic Four with us."

I squatted to his eye level. "I'll play later." And I would. Time was fleeting.

"Wait right here." He dashed up the stairs, and I started unloading the dishwasher while Mom went through a stack of mail. Normal household things. Planck things. Back in record time, Eli held out a Lego to me. "Put it in your back pocket. When you sit on it, you'll remember to come play." His feet thudded up the stairs again before I had a chance to say anything.

I glanced down to the Lego. Fantastic Four's Invisible Woman. That was a pretty good pairing—she and I shared the gift of force fields. Warmth spread throughout my chest. "Love you, bud," I yelled up the stairs.

"Shut up, fart breath!" Oh, yeah. That wasn't cool for me to say in front of a friend.

I would play with him after I talked to Mom. I stuck the Invisible Woman Lego in my back pocket. Invisibility was one superpower I'd welcome now that all this Oculi crap hit the fan.

"Mom, I..." I didn't know how to apologize for my moodiness or how to go about clearing the air between us.

Mom opened the freezer behind me. "Ice cream?" She was trying to make some peace since our last talk, when I'd gone all Hulk smash.

"Yeah."

She scooped two bowls of butter pecan. I knew I'd vowed to stick to the present, to focus on the upcoming exchange, but my thoughts kept tripping back to Nick. Talking about him with Reid made me feel like my brother was still alive, like at any moment he might strut through the door, laughing, larger than life. Knowing that could never happen...

We never talked about it, after the accident. About the *actual* accident.

And, really, my brother was an Oculi. He'd trained and fought and had been able to manipulate the world with his mind. If he'd been trapped in a car, he wouldn't have freaked out like me. Nick was too smart, too strong. He would've Pushed or Retracted a solution.

Ding. Ding. Ding.

The spoon fell from my hand and clanged to the table.

"It wasn't an accident that killed Nick."

My mom pushed her bowl of ice cream aside. She didn't contradict me. But I watched her closely, the muscle moving in her jaw, the way the lines around her mouth shifted, like she was biting back words or deciding what she should or should not say.

"Don't lie to me," I said.

She sighed. "Nick started his training when he turned seventeen, much like you're doing now, only he worked with your dad instead of a trainer," she began. "He excelled in every aspect, far beyond our expectations. Due to the inoculations, like you, he was more advanced than the average Anomaly. And we felt he needed to train in the Denver Hub."

"Like there's anything average about an Anomaly in the first place."

She murmured her agreement. "After several months, we realized his abilities were far superior to anyone else's...in the world."

Mom stopped for a moment and stared into nothing. Eli's laughter broke the silence and prompted Mom to talk again. "Reid, who was training with Nick at the Hub, contacted your dad and me because he was concerned. Nick was illustrating odd behaviors, acting out of character. He became short-tempered, violent, paranoid. Then he started disappearing from the Hub, missing training sessions. He kept his whereabouts secret, then eventually shared with Reid that he didn't think the Resistance had their priorities straight. The Resistance's first priority is humanity, so something was really off. Nick left the Hub one day and didn't return. Your dad went after him, knowing he'd gone to L.A."

No. I was growing uncomfortably warm. "The Consortium," I whispered.

Mom gave an affirming sound. "The world had not seen an Anomaly of his magnitude before. If he joined the Consortium, it would've catapulted us into a war before we were ready. We—the Resistance and *humanity*—needed him to go to the Hub to train, to test, to know his abilities and limitations. He could've been instrumental in the Resistance taking down the Consortium."

I followed Mom's train of thought. I could've been wrong, but, from what I knew of war, they would need strong leaders to organize, manage, and head them into combat. "He could have been a leader."

Mom continued to play with her melting ice cream, nodding at me. "Your dad found Nick and tried to bring him back, but he was talking gibberish, going on about things not being as they seemed, people who weren't who they said they were. There was an…altercation."

Sweat covered my back, and the aftertaste of the ice cream soured in my mouth. I'd waited two years to hear more about Nick, but now I wasn't sure I wanted to.

The green in Mom's eyes shone through her tears. "Nick hurt many and killed others. He fought alongside the Consortium, Josie. He betrayed us. Everything your father and I stood for. Everything the Resistance had been created to protect."

"No. I don't believe it."

Mom's voice cracked, and she covered her mouth for a moment before composing herself enough to continue. "It was a mini-massacre. Nick did end up going over a bridge in a car after being shot in the chest. If the gunshot hadn't killed him, the drowning did."

The kitchen walls seemed to shrink in on me, and the air was too thin. I no longer felt my stomach. Who cared about a stomach when I couldn't breathe?

I refocused on my mom, sitting before me like a statue. She wiped her eyes before any tears had a chance to fall. The tears didn't count if they didn't fall, she'd told me in the past.

My dad had watched his son go rogue. He'd watched his son's execution—played a part in it, if he hadn't pulled the trigger himself. Oh God, could he have done that? No. *No.*

The question I needed to ask burned my tongue as I held it in. "Why did he go crazy?" I nervously swirled the melted ice cream in my bowl, my hands needing to move.

"In a very small percentage of Oculi, the powers... corrupt the mind. Not every person is equipped to handle the magnitude of his or her abilities. Pushing and Retracting— they contradict the doctrines that we are conditioned to believe."

What? The concept of being an Anomaly was so crazy that it drove my brother to switch sides and kill a slew of people? When Reid first described Oculi abilities, he'd mentioned that toward the end of an Oculi's energy reserve, as the abilities diminished, so too could cognitive function, resulting in neurological degeneration or death. But that wasn't what my mom was describing here. She was explaining how a small percentage "went crazy" in their prime.

"I've been conducting studies," she went on. Of course she had; Mom was a scientist, first and foremost. "Using

Oculi abilities may disrupt brain function in the frontal lobes of the brain, triggering the changes in personality and inciting adverse behaviors—"

"He's my brother, not some experiment!"

Mom's shrewd gaze absorbed my every action. Shit, did she think I'd go rogue, too? My outbursts wouldn't exactly inspire her to think otherwise.

The knowledge—no, the fear—was in her eyes. She did.

"That won't happen to you," she said in a brusque voice. As much to reassure herself as to reassure me, it seemed.

Everything around me slowed. The drum of my heart. The tick of the clock on the kitchen wall. The blink of my mother's eyes. The sliver of hope I had clung to, the hope that this would turn out all right somehow, shattered to the floor of my soul.

Something hit my leg. Mom's cane. "Josie," she snapped.

I met her gaze.

"You can't let this cripple you. Just because it happened to your brother doesn't mean it will happen to you. Your phenotypes are not the same. Your genotypes are not the same. You have different personalities, different coping mechanisms…"

I wanted to believe I was different. That I wouldn't share Nick's fate. But how could I know for sure?

"Josie, Reid is here to protect you. He is going to keep you safe."

"Safe from myself."

"He is an elite operative. He also bears a unique perspective because of his former association with our family and Nick."

I hated her. I hated how she could compartmentalize and speak so rationally when every word from her mouth cut me to the core.

"We don't have the luxury of time! You need to hold it together, Josie. Emotions have no place in this war."

My God, she was so cold.

"Train with Reid. Make the serum exchange. After the ceremony, go to the Hub. Continue your training."

"But I thought there was a leak. Isn't the Hub compromised? Isn't—"

Mom's cane tapped against the floor. "That is exactly why you and Reid need to go. If there is a leak inside the Hub and they're tipped off to your whereabouts, then—"

"Then I'd be bait. Lure them out."

She wasn't just cold—she was calculating. And I was nothing more to her than a pawn, a soldier to use in this war game.

I got it. I was a target. She'd made sure of that, with her dealings with SI and in injecting her serum in the first place. But how could she set me aside so easily? Did I matter so little to her?

The tears wouldn't come, for once, and I was grateful for it. She didn't deserve them. I understood her focus, the need to place the greater good above us, but didn't I matter at all? Didn't Dad or Nick?

"Reid is assigned to protect you, Josie. And he will. He'll train you to take your rightful place in our cause."

I didn't want to hear about her plans. "I'm going to play with Eli," I said.

"That is your choice."

Right. If it didn't pertain to the Resistance, then it probably didn't matter to her. The same way family dinners weren't important, and how, aside from our school work and whatever training she had in store to prepare us to become Oculi, family times were never high on her list, either.

I tugged my phone from my pocket and texted Reid as I left the kitchen and plodded up the stairs to Eli's room. *Talked about Nick.*

Trying to stuff the information I'd just received and my accompanying feelings about said information deep inside me, I forced my mother from my mind. I had to face the facts. No matter what way I looked at it, I probably wouldn't be around much longer. I wanted to spend time with my little brother.

My phone vibrated. Reid. *tomorrow we're taking the night off. we're going out.*

I didn't want him to go easy on me. But, seeing as I didn't know how long I had before I went crazy or got killed, I'd take going out.

18.

Reid

Mrs. Harper called and gave me an update. No wonder Josie wanted to get the hell outta Dodge.

I texted Josie to say I was on the porch. The door swung open in less than a minute and she tore out of the house past me. I followed her to my bike.

"Gah!" She kind of growled at the sky, then ran her hand through her hair. She'd left it wavy. No graphic tee tonight with her ripped jeans, but she wore more eye makeup. Striking.

She was clearly flustered but wouldn't come right out and say it. And that was okay. That wasn't how she rolled. "Let's talk about it later." I saddled up, she got on behind me, and I handed her the helmet.

"I didn't mean you needed to take me out. I meant I needed to get out of my house."

"Nah. You need to go out." I started the engine

Her left hand held on to my side as she leaned forward on

the right. "Wait. Where are we going?"

"To eat at a decent restaurant," I yelled over the roar of the bike. "Then we're doing something fun. Nothing Oculi related." *Shit. That sounds like a date.*

Her arms wound around my waist, her fingers searing my skin through my shirt. Long shadows chased us down the streets, the skies painted pink and orange with the sunset.

To give her time to relax, I took an old back road and cruised the streets running out to the orange groves. The scent of citrus hung heavy in the air. Then I angled back toward town.

We tucked into a little Mexican restaurant and talked about things that normal people talked about. Movies, books, Eli, her love of baking, and memories of our childhood she-nanigans. There was something therapeutic about it, probably because I'd laughed more in that hour than I had in the last six months combined.

When we climbed back on the bike after dinner, she leaned forward again. "Thank you. That was exactly what I needed."

"Oh, we're not done."

"What—" I wasn't going to let her protest, which was what she would've done if I'd told her my plans. She deserved to have some fun.

A few stars twinkled in the velvet black sky by the time we pulled into the warehouse. I watched Josie over my shoulder. She yanked the helmet off and stared at where the workout area usually resided. Instead, high-top tables and recycled barn-wood paneling surrounded a pool table. A jukebox sat in the corner and a rectangular billiards light illuminated the green fabric and triangle of colorful balls.

Her gaze skated to mine, a tiny line between her brows.

I held my hand out for the helmet. She placed it in my hand and hopped down, then jogged to the newly Pushed area. Her hand ran over the surface of the table as she circled it and took in the details of the new space. "What is this place?"

Crossing my arms, I leaned against one of the tall tables. "This is a replica of my favorite part of the Cavern Tavern, the Hub's premier bar and grill." I laughed. "It's brighter than it should be, though." I reached for the switch to turn down the lights.

She punched buttons on the jukebox. "The Hub has its own bar?"

"Yeah. It has everything. It's like its own little town."

Something flickered behind her eyes, and her stare fell to the tile floor as a song came on. We were talking about the Hub, where her mom wanted her to go. I shouldn't have brought it up.

Stepping in front of her, I grabbed her hand and dragged her to the bar. Pulling stools out for both of us, I sat. "If we were in the real deal, this would just be a section of the bar. We'd go through that doorway to the main restaurant."

Two frosty mugs appeared on the bar, and a little giggle escaped her. "What is it?" she chirped.

"Root beer. You want something else?"

She shook her head. "Don't you dare Push another thing," she said. "We're not even practicing anything tonight and you've used so much energy."

I'd talked to my dad about my energy stores before he went missing, and I'd watched my parents use their abilities as I grew up. I knew I had a decent supply to draw from. Not unlimited, but enough that these expenditures for Josie... they were worth it to me. Who knew, maybe that serum would be mass-produced at some point, administered to all the trainers and Oculi in the Hub. I honestly didn't know if I'd take it, even if it were available. And as far as worrying about losing my powers? Operatives at my level, out on the front lines—we were lucky to *survive* to twenty-five.

"I'm serious, Reid! No more."

"Okay." I smiled. "We haven't gotten to the best part yet."

She sipped from the mug and licked her lips. "What's that?"

Jumping off the stool, I racked the balls, placing them just so, as well as the cue ball. I plucked my preferred cue stick and chalked it. "No Pushing or Retracting," I said. Then I did my thing.

I broke and picked the balls off one at a time, calling the pockets, until only the eight ball was left. I finally peeked at Josie. Her brows drew upward, and a smile greeted me. "You call the pocket," I said, leaning on the table.

She shrugged with a laugh. "That one. The trajectory would make it nearly impossible."

"If you think in straight lines, yeah. But you have to take into account the rotation you put on both balls." I struck the cue ball, and it smacked the black ball into the designated pocket.

Josie clapped, still perched on the stool. "How'd you learn to do that?"

"Practice. The Hub can be boring for a kid. Okay, your turn."

She nearly choked on a sip of root beer. "Oh, no. I've never played pool before. And I suck at using sticks to hit any kind of ball. Like baseball or golf? Tried those. Yeah, it didn't go well."

I ambled over to her, took the mug from her grasp, and placed it on the bar, then wrapped my hand around her fingers, tugging her to the pool table. She shook her head. "I really don't know how to do this."

"I'm going to show you."

"Dear Loki."

I laughed as I seized a short cue from the wall and handed it to her. I racked and broke the balls. Then I stood next to her and leaned over the table, aiming for a ball. "Copy me. You're going to place your front hand on the table. People use all sorts of holds to guide the cue. It's really just personal preference, whatever feels like you have the most control."

She imitated my movements, knocked the ball, and it bumped two others. One crawled to the side pocket and fell in. She jumped around, squealing in excitement. Happy looked good on her.

"Okay," she said, leaning over the table, setting up her guide hand. "Let's do it again." She lined up the cue and totally missed. Standing, she frowned. "Boo. What'd I do wrong?"

"It's your back arm." I set down my cue and stood behind Josie. Stretching my arm along the length of hers, I positioned the stick over her knuckle. Then I mimicked her stance, pressing my chest into her back, then wrapped my right hand over hers on the cue. She smelled amazing. "See…you can't let your arm move." My hand slid up to her elbow. "You need to keep this closer, and…"

She turned her head. Her eyes were brilliant green as always, but, for the first time, I could see beyond them. She let me witness a part of her, a vulnerability, I wasn't sure anyone else had. And I knew what it was like trying to bury a part of yourself.

My skin buzzed where her body touched mine. And the skin that didn't touch her craved that buzz. Her lips parted, and I wanted nothing more than to taste them, to see if her mouth held that same high.

I skimmed my hand from her elbow to her hand, pulling the cue from her grasp and tossing it. It clanged to the floor, echoing through the warehouse over the music from the jukebox, but she didn't flinch. Adrenaline spiked my blood, sending my heart into spasms.

If I knocked down these boundaries, there was no repairing them. There was no turning back. For either of us. But I'd already decided.

I swept my hand over her arm and pulled her up. She turned, slow and torturous, then placed her hands on me. Tingles danced on my chest under her palms and my fingertips burned as they feathered down her back to her waist.

I backed her to the pool table, pressing out the space between us.

JOSIE

His dark lashes fanned over his sultry eyes as he blinked.

I inhaled deeply, trying to calm my nerves, but when my chest expanded against his, every sense was sent into overdrive. "I'm tired of not living," I whispered. I hadn't planned the words—they just broke out of me.

His eyes searched my face, then he dipped his head, lips

barely grazing mine. My hands traveled from his chest, up his neck, and I pulled him to me, his lips pressing against mine in a soft kiss. Pulling away, he flashed his signature half smile, larger than normal. His hands quickly ran down my sides and wrapped around the back of my legs before he picked me up, sitting me on the edge of the pool table. I let out a loud gasp.

Stepping between my legs to draw closer, he kissed me again, this time pressing my lips open. His hands wound into my hair, and I was lost in him. I had no idea how long we kissed on the pool table. Eventually, he separated from me, drawing in ragged breaths.

I was petrified he'd regret kissing me and prepared myself for when he'd go cold, thinking this was a mistake. Blaming himself for the "kissing crime" that I'd wanted him to commit. In my head, I'd already played out the scenario where he'd lecture me about how this wasn't right. And I wouldn't be able to handle that. I cared for him—I had for a long time. Right now, beside my little brother, he was the only person I felt any kind of connection to. I couldn't lose him.

His flirty smirk reappeared. "It's a school night."

"Ha." School was now a joke. It was all an act.

His hot hands rested on my thighs, burning holes to the center of me. "So…" His dark brows rose playfully. "Can we play pool again tomorrow night? I'm not quite done with our lesson."

I couldn't help laughing. "Oh, for the love of Khan."

He smiled and bit his lip. "Tomorrow it is." Then he kissed my neck.

19.

JOSIE

Hannah and I strolled through the courtyard to our cars after school, the humidity so high it was insta-sweat. The fact that I was Pushing a shield around myself and Hannah, expending crazy energy, probably didn't help. Santos or Reid was likely nearby—I didn't think I'd been left unattended since the moment they rolled into town—but I didn't see either of them. They tended to divide their time, sleeping in shifts, with Santos taking on most of the nighttime patrols so that Reid could train me during the day. Not seeing them…worried me. I glanced over my shoulder, scanned my surroundings, looking for any sign of a threat.

"What's with you, Josie?" Hannah asked. "You're going to hurt your neck if you keep whipping around like that."

Just keeping an eye out for crazy Consortium killers.

"I, uh, thought I heard someone call my name." As the award ceremony grew closer, I found myself growing more paranoid.

"I didn't hear it," Hannah said.

We continued toward the parking lot, the sun beating down mercilessly. Couple the sweltering heat with my already frazzled nerves, and it was a recipe for hot mess. Literally. My hair clung to the back of my neck and Hannah's curls were crazy. There was just enough of a breeze to make the palms sway, but not enough to provide relief.

Hannah had texted the night before, asking if we could hang out, since it was a short school week due to spring break. I hadn't spent any extensive time with her since my birthday, but with everything going on, it was hard to hang out and act normal. It wasn't that I didn't want to; I did. I was just scared. Scared of revealing my abilities. Scared of endangering Hannah.

But I realized I'd most likely be leaving in a few days after this handoff, and I didn't know when or if I'd ever see her again. I'd checked with Mom, who agreed that a visit was "acceptable." Reid said he and Santos would keep watch over the house but stay out of sight. My next "pool" lesson with Reid would have to wait.

Hannah and I crossed the parking lot.

"Josie!"

I whipped around and had to mentally stop myself from erecting a big ol' wall right in front of me. Thankfully, I didn't Push anything. Although I felt the surge in my shield, I just prayed Hannah didn't, too.

"Wait up!" Marisa skipped over, her dark ponytail swishing from side to side. "Here." She handed Hannah and me neon yellow pieces of paper. "The deets for that bonfire," she shouted over her shoulder as she ran toward other students.

Hannah giggled. "You okay?"

"Too much caffeine, I think." I lowered my shield some.

She nudged my arm. "I was thinking of asking Santos to the bonfire tomorrow night. What do you think?"

I couldn't tell her what I really thought—that I wasn't sure if he would go because he couldn't commit to any kind of relationship with a Planck.

"You should ask him. Or Ian. He'd be a good option, too." I didn't want to hurt her feelings, but I also didn't want Santos to have to reject her. She was living the life I wanted, the life I'd been working toward for the last two years. I was happy for her, but I would surely turn green from my envy. A red-headed Gamora.

"Ooooh! Forgot about Ian," she whispered. Then she hesitated for a moment next to the door of her car. "Okay, I'll be over in a few minutes. We haven't done a sleepover in forever." She slipped behind the wheel of her car, and I walked a little farther to mine, nonchalantly peeking in the backseat before getting in. If someone were waiting back there to kill me, he would've died first in the heat.

I drove home and let my mind wander. After such a crazy week, I was looking forward to a girls' night. I needed some BFF time to forget about everything, even if it was temporary. Besides, it could be my last girls' night. Ever.

Hannah bounded up the stairs, the floor creaking underfoot. "I'm here!"

Pulling in a long breath, I mentally prepared. I'd shove everything to the cobwebbed corners of my mind and pretend my life hadn't been turned into some effed-up series on the

SyFy network. Psh. No prob.

We watched the best scenes of the movies we loved and ordered pizza. Eventually, I dug out my nail polish and stretched across my bed like we'd done so many times in the last two years. In the grand scheme of things, two years ago wasn't that long, but it seemed like a lifetime after my intro into Oculi weirdness.

Things had been simpler two years ago. Heck, things had been simpler two weeks ago.

Hannah rolled a bottle of blue nail polish between her palms. "So, are you going to tell me what's going on? You've acted *odd* since your birthday, which just happens to be when Reid moved to town."

My heart stuttered and I choked on my saliva. I didn't answer. Her hazel eyes were wide and waiting.

I picked out a purple nail polish, hoping she'd change the subject.

"J? You've spent a lot of time with Reid. I'm all for helping out the new kid, and I know you guys have a mutual friend, but I think you like him."

I choked again and grabbed my water. "No," I managed to say between chugs. It was like trying to drown my secrets.

Seeing my mended stuffed puppy on the edge of my bed, I casually straightened the books on my nightstand and knocked the old toy onto the floor.

Guilt ate at me. I couldn't do this—lying to those I loved and those I loved, like my mom, lying to me. It was too much. If Hannah took one real good look at me, she'd know. She'd know I was keeping secrets, that something was wrong.

She grabbed a few tissues and started stuffing them

between her toes. "He likes you. It's so obvious." The playfulness had returned to her voice.

"Whatever."

"So?"

"So what?"

"So, do you like him back?"

"What? No. I thought we were past this. No. He's a jerk."

"Who's freaking hot."

"Yeah, he is so freaking hot."

Hannah's finger shot out at me. "Ah."

My cheeks burned. "What?" I laughed, pretending to be engrossed in the bottle of polish in my hand. "You'd have to be blind not to see that he's gorgeous."

"Gotcha." Hannah smiled with her whole face, her grin wide and infectious and kind. She was my best friend, my first true friend. And this was probably my last night with her. That realization made up my mind—I'd tell her what I could, which wasn't much, but still.

I struck the small bottle on the palm of my hand, mixing the polish. "Fine. I like him." I peeked at her again. She beamed like a proud mother, not saying a word. She knew it wasn't easy for me to talk about my feelings. I continued. "There are people who don't ask you to be something different, yet challenge you, making you a stronger person. He's that. He makes me feel alive."

"Wow. You...you *like* him like him." I shrugged and attempted to smile. "Does your mom know?" She was well aware of how overprotective my mom was.

"I'm not sure if I've left that impression or not." I shook my head, thinking about my interactions with my mother over the last week—how she kept so many secrets and now was putting me in the line of fire. "Man, my family is messed up." Hannah was the only person who knew about Nick dying and my absentee dad, so my statement wasn't untrue.

"I know. But if it makes you feel better, all families are screwed up in some way or another." She laughed, which was encouraging. She was the only child of a single dad. She didn't exactly have it easy.

"Yeah." I giggled. "You're right." I'd bet the *USS Enterprise* her family didn't have superhero powers and a legion of evil people after them. But it felt good to at least connect on that level a little.

We talked through the night about prom and plans for the summer, my computer playing music in the background. I let Hannah do most of the talking, since I wasn't making actual plans. I played along pretty well, though.

Her excitement over the possibilities of what could happen over the next several months was almost palpable. As she spoke, I saw in her a picture of the girl I had wanted to be, the life I had wanted to have. What I thought was envy growing inside me was morphing into something different. It was motivation. Inspiration. She deserved to have that life and those opportunities. I'd do this drop and whatever else was asked of me as an Oculus for her, for Eli, for the life I longed for.

I could do it, as long as Reid was there helping me.

20.

The nights were getting shorter, the days longer. That's what happened when fear clutched your heart and fate was so uncertain.

Hannah left the next day and the house was empty. Mom had probably taken Eli for lunch. She tried keeping things as routine for Eli as possible, which I supported. If Nick and I were any indication, Eli was going to be a mess later on, so he needed as much stability as possible now.

Not even five minutes after Hannah left, the doorbell rang. I peeked through the side window to see Reid pacing the porch. Swinging open the door, I said, "I want to go swimming."

About a dozen emotions crossed his face. Then he smiled fully, a real smile that reached his eyes. "Okay."

"Let me get my shoes." I ran to grab my things, thinking about the last time we were alone. Playing billiards. Kissing.

My pulse quickened remembering the moments. Would he still feel the same or would he act like it didn't happen?

He was already on his bike, watching me approach him. I was ready for a smartass remark, but it didn't come. Instead, his gaze traveled the length of my body. Nervousness swirled inside me as I climbed on behind him, more aware of his body in relationship to mine than I had been before. He handed me the helmet and I slipped it on, then placed my hands on his obliques. Leaning forward, I let my chest rest against his back and said, "Take me to the beach."

He turned his head a fraction and dipped his chin in affirmation. I was comfortable with the actual handoff. I was comfortable Pushing and Retracting. Time was running short. I needed to do something that would help me grow.

The drive was perfect—blue skies, warm sun, and a guy way too hot for me. Bypassing the busy sections of town, we headed south toward the city limits, where the coastline began to break away into a series of islands and inlets. We parked and followed a boardwalk path in silence, walking side by side. He still had barely spoken to me, but I didn't want that awkwardness between us.

The wooden walkway came to a *T*. We turned the corner, and his fingers laced in mine. I glanced up, and he was studying me.

He squinted against the sun, the midday light showcasing his light blue irises. "I admire you."

I couldn't think of a single reason someone would admire me, especially Reid.

He paused at the top of the stairs that led to the sand. "There is a lot to be said for facing a fear." Oh, that. My cheeks flamed. I wasn't looking for recognition; I just needed to do it—for me.

Reid scoped the beach. An elderly couple walked together, and three figures huddled on the coastline. Even though I didn't like being in the ocean, I enjoyed watching the waves crash against the shore and the lulling, rhythmic sound of them colliding with the sand. The vastness and openness was appealing. The salty sea breeze smelled like possibilities.

"Come on, shoes off." Reid pulled his hand away and took off his shoes, tied the laces together, and threw them over the boardwalk railing. I slipped off my flip-flops and placed them under his shoes.

It was an odd picture—his shoes and mine, like we were together, united somehow. I guessed we were. I'd never really experienced that before. Maybe with Hannah, but that was different. Or maybe *this* was different.

His warm hand enveloped mine and tugged. I trotted after him in the sand until we neared the water. Once we hit the hard-packed, wet sand, he slowed. "I'm sorry about that training session out in the cypresses."

It felt like it had been a year ago since I'd been in that drowning scenario. Truth be told, I didn't really appreciate the reminder of it.

I wondered how he knew about my fear in the first place. Had he conjured the test because he'd heard about how my brother had potentially drowned? Or had my mom informed him of my aversion after the accident, and how I hadn't gone swimming since?

"I know it isn't rational," I began. I toed a shell in the sand, and his fingers weaved in mine. His touch was timely, a reassurance that I could tell him more. "It's better than it was." I could look at a body of water without envisioning my brother trapped beneath the surface. "I threw myself into movies and books even more than I had before Nick died. I find comfort in fiction—it's safe. I can lose myself and find myself in books. It's a little ironic, actually, because now I just want to know reality."

"I get that, but…" He guided us closer to the breaking waves. "We can't always be safe. Sometimes we have to fight and sacrifice. We have to take chances."

Chance? A chance was an occurrence taking place outside of intentional design. Hmm.

"Uh-oh." He tapped my head. "The wheels are turning up there. It isn't luck or chance, Josie, although in battle, you'd be surprised how an enemy can make one wrong move—a lucky mistake or chance turn in the opposite direction—that gives you the advantage." He tilted his head to the side. "I forget sometimes how analytical your mind is." He stared past me to the water. "We make decisions, choices." His lips curved as he altered his voice to sound like mine. "'We make calculations that directly correlate with our desired projected outcome in order to enhance our probabilities of success.'"

I playfully punched his arm. "I don't talk like that."

He scoffed.

"Okay, maybe a little bit. But it isn't intentional."

"I like it. And I'll let you in on another secret. I brushed up on the latest Marvel franchises and all the Star Wars movies before I came out here."

That was thoughtful.

"You would've been proud. When I first entered the

warehouse—it was a total mess, mind you—I compared it to Dagobah, that swampy, gross planet where Luke trained in *The Empire Strikes Back.*"

I laughed. "I probably know Star Wars geography better than I know the countries on Earth." A wave hit almost to my knees. Wait. When had I moved this far into the water? "Nice strategy," I reluctantly admitted, recognizing his chatty tactic for what it had been.

"Distraction is a useful tool. You'd do well to remember that." His expression turned sheepish, like he worried about offending me by resorting to such a tactic.

"It's all good, Reid." He'd gotten me into the water. Desired projected outcome and all that, indeed.

As the wave withdrew in a bubbling whisper of foamy ripples, it left cool sand beneath my feet. His fingers gripped mine firmly, not letting me escape. The next wave crashed over my ankles and calves, sending goose bumps over my limbs.

My stomach quivered with anxiety. At this spot on the shore, the water was the depth of a baby pool. My reaction—hello, ridiculous.

"We're gonna get through this, Josie."

Did he mean my irrational fear or this war? Both? This guy, Reid—Cal—had been a fixture in my life, working behind the scenes to keep my family and me safe. What about his own life? His own wants and needs?

"You've sacrificed so much," I said, watching the water lap around my shins.

"Well," he whispered, drawing me toward his side, "some things, some *people*, are worth making sacrifices for."

I made the mistake of looking at him and taking my eyes

off the impending waves. My balance was thrown off and I swayed, almost falling over. His grip tightened and his other arm wound around me, pulling me up against him.

He bent to see my face. "You okay?"

I nodded.

"See? You're like Luke, facing something scary. And I'm Han." Humor flickered in his gaze. "I just help ya out a little."

"What?" I tore out of his hold and kicked water at him. He laughed, and it was now officially one of my favorite sounds.

He grabbed my hand again, attempted to draw me into deeper water. Nope. My limbs locked solid. I wasn't freaking out, and I took that as an accomplishment, but I wasn't going to full on take a swim, either. Not that either of us had taken the time to shuck out of our clothes.

Reid watched me intently. He inched us back toward the beach.

"You'd make an awesome Princess Leia," he said, lightening the mood.

"She's badass."

"I don't remember which movie, but in one of them she's wielding a gun and breaking Han free—all in this hot little bathing suit."

I chuckled. "Box office antics."

Reaching down to the water, he scooped a handful and splashed me.

I kicked out and shot a stream of water at him. He laughed, but from the gleam in his eye, I knew I needed to run—fast.

Reid lunged at me, and I ran for the beach. He caught up

to me quickly and wrapped his arms around my middle from behind. A thrill danced through my body when he turned me around and eyed me from under his dark lashes. His hands cupped my face, and he pressed his lips to mine, soft and slow. My eyes fluttered shut, and I reveled in this feeling. Excitement and fullness.

He deepened the kiss, and energy surged through my system. My hands twisted into his silky hair, and though there was no place to go, he somehow wrenched me closer. Electricity snapped under the surface of my skin.

He pulled his mouth away and pushed me back, his brows arched and eyes wide. "What the hell was that?"

"You felt that, too?" Heat pricked my cheeks in embarrassment. "Sorry."

"Don't apologize." He ran the pad of his thumb over my bottom lip. "Come here." He kissed me again. And again.

That was something I could get used to.

Reid

After spending a good deal of the afternoon at the beach splashing and talking, I brought Josie back to the warehouse.

We parked the bike, and she made her way backward toward the couches. I matched her step for step, like I was stalking her. She asked what I planned to do now. "Well, I could finish that billiards lesson."

Her cheeks reddened and a wicked smile slid across her face. Her legs stopped moving, but mine didn't. I scooped her up, and giggles fizzed out of her, effervescent, like a shaken can of soda.

I sat on the couch with her across my lap, leaving what would happen in her court. I wasn't going to pressure her into kissing me. As soon as she looked in my eyes, her arms tightened around my neck, and she raised her lips to mine.

I liked the ball in her court.

While catching our breath after our kiss, Josie toed the new rug in front of the couch.

"Did you buy a new rug?" she asked.

"Buy?" I considered her wording. "Uh, sure."

She tried to hide her smile. I knew she didn't want me to waste precious energy on stuff like that. "You didn't Push it, did you?"

"Yeah. I put it there for you. This is where you've been sitting. Twice now, you've touched your feet to the floor and cringed from the cold. Problem? Is red the wrong color?"

"No. That's…nice of you."

Josie slipped her foot back into the sandal, her head still down. "Hey. So, if you're my personal Yoda, can you tell me when my training is complete?"

My heart leapt into my throat.

I knew what I had to say. What I'd been reluctant to tell her. It wasn't like I could hide the truth from her indefinitely. Considering the gravity of the situation, the sooner she knew, the safer she would be.

Still…things would change after this.

"Hey," she whispered, likely sensing the shift in my mood. "What's wrong?"

I had her on my lap, and for a couple of brief seconds it

had felt like everything was right in my world. Shit, could the timing be any worse for her to bring up her training?

"Reid?"

I sighed. "The end of your training isn't something that's capped off within a set time period. Even within the Hubs, training concludes when the skillsets are mastered. Some Oculi take longer than others. It's not something that is predetermined."

"Okay. But do *I* have a lot left to learn?"

I knew from our time together that Mrs. Harper hadn't provided Josie the true scope of my role as her trainer. Nice of the lady to lump that task on me. It was a good thing Josie was sitting down.

"No, you've mastered your abilities in a fraction of the time it takes other Oculi."

She frowned. "Does that mean you won't be training me anymore?"

"No." The next stage of her training would focus on how she dealt with her abilities, the side effects of them. I cleared my throat. "So, your training, I think you're on the right track with the Star Wars analogies." I tried to draw the comparison that would best help her to understand my point. "But rather than Yoda, I'm more like Obi Wan."

"Obi Wan was great with Luke." She smiled. "You really did brush up on your sci-fi before coming to Oceanside."

"Yeah. I was thinking more along the lines of Obi Wan in *Revenge of the Sith*."

Josie didn't say anything for a moment. "Obi Wan tries to kill Anakin in that movie—that's where Anakin becomes Vader."

She gasped. Her hand covered her mouth and she shuffled off the couch. "Why didn't I put it together before?" she said, more to herself than me.

"Stay calm, Josie. It's just you and me. Nothing's changed."

A nervous laugh broke free. "Everything's changed."

"You're not going to turn out like Vader." I shoved off the couch, following her as she retreated. "And can we speak like adults minus the pop culture references?"

From her expression, that had cut her even more. Shit.

"Look, I'm gonna say it again: nothing changes. You train, we make the serum exchange, we work together to hone your abilities."

"Until I start acting a bit wacky, right? Maybe I mumble to myself or ask too many questions. Maybe I suffer a little PMS—and what then? You call my mom? You report me to the Resistance—let them do the dirty work for you?"

"Calm down." Hell, I needed to take that advice myself. "Nobody is going to hurt you—least of all me."

"Like I said, you'll have them do the dirty work for you. Like you did with Nick!"

My anger spiked so hard it was a wonder I didn't blow the roof off the warehouse. I didn't say anything, though, not a word. She couldn't have cut me deeper had she Pushed a saber and shoved it between my ribs.

Looking like she realized she'd crossed a line, Josie walked back to the couch and sat.

Neither of us spoke for a minute.

"When did you find out I'd reported his behavior?" I asked. Did it really matter? No. Still, I wanted to know.

"Mom told me a couple days ago, but I just now made the

connection that you'd have to do the same with me. I'm sorry. That was uncalled for. I know you cared about my brother. I can't imagine how difficult it must have been for you to turn him in."

"No, you can't," I snapped. "You can't begin to know how hard it was to watch my best friend change. To see him lie and hide. To know he didn't trust me. Me—who had been with him since we were toddlers! I died the day Nick drowned."

"I'm sorry—"

I know I should've accepted it. We were under a lot of stress, and the Josie I knew would never lash out at someone with the intent to cause pain. Not intentionally. "Save your apology. It doesn't change a damn thing. You like facts; you want to deal with just the information? Fine. Here goes: don't harm the innocent; don't use your abilities to hurt Plancks or other members of the Resistance; don't buy into the bullshit that the Consortium is selling—thinking that it's okay to control and manipulate people."

She didn't know how many times I'd covered for Nick, when he'd Pushed or Retracted something as a prank or when he delved into the Hub archives and went rogue investigating leads on his own. She thought I'd sold him out. Well, fine. It was better that way. Maybe she'd be more careful, thinking I was so heartless.

Josie's fingers combed through her hair.

She didn't apologize again, but when I looked into her big, sad eyes, all the fight just seeped out of me.

I wanted to know what she was thinking, but I couldn't ask. I knew I wasn't her favorite person at the moment. She shot off the couch and marched to the middle of the warehouse, then back, stopping directly in front of me, eyes narrowed. She dragged in a long breath. "Was this all part of the plan?" Her voice was quiet. "Get me to trust you, make me feel…" She paused, pressing her lips tight. What was she going to say? What did I make her feel?

She shook her head, refusing to give voice to those feelings. "Then you get close so you can monitor me, see how I mess up, and have me taken out when I least expect it. Is that how it's supposed to happen? You're the judge and the jury, then you'd send for my executioner."

I swept my hands in front of me like I was calling someone safe at home plate. "No. It's not like that."

"What's it like?"

"It isn't that simple, Josie. Just calm down. Please. You can trust me." I didn't break eye contact. I couldn't lose all the ground I'd gained over the last few days. And I also couldn't let her hate me.

Josie began to turn away. I grabbed her arm and wrenched her into me, throwing off her balance. She fell forward, her hand landing on my chest to steady herself, and her body smashed up against mine. Her breath was on my neck, I could barely think with her so close. "Don't go off the deep end and you'll be fine," I said.

She thought I'd betrayed her. And maybe I had. I'd definitely betrayed the Resistance by not telling them how I felt about her before becoming her trainer, becoming her protector, becoming her friend.

In a way, I'd betrayed myself.

She raised her chin and looked me square in the eyes.

Josie pulled her arm out of my grasp and stumbled

backward over the new rug. I stepped toward her to grab one of her flailing arms, wrapping my other arm around her waist. My toe hit her foot, throwing my balance forward. We stumbled toward the floor. I Pushed a beanbag chair just before we hit the cement floor to break our fall, and then spun so I took the brunt of it. We landed in an embrace.

My body melded into hers, and for a second I let everything fall away. It was just Josie and me, lying heart to heart, forced to look each other in the eyes. Every place we touched—our chests, our stomachs, our arms winding around each other—buzzed with energy. I'd never felt this before. Did she feel it, too?

Her lips parted a fraction as her chest expanded against mine. And there it was, in her eyes, in her face, the thing that hadn't been there before, the thing she wouldn't let herself feel. A desire, a need.

"No," she whispered.

I pulled my hand out from behind her back and shoved myself up to a standing position. My body chilled without her close. I offered Josie my hand, and she examined it like she didn't know me, like the last few days, or even the years of growing up together, hadn't happened. Like every kiss we'd shared had been a lie. My stomach dropped.

But then her soft, warm hand took mine, I pulled, and with one fluid motion, she stood and paused in front of me.

I had to be truthful. She had to know everything, and then maybe she'd understand.

"I took this job because I couldn't let anyone else have it. If your trainer found a reason to report you…I'd kill him. I can watch you and help keep you safe. I won't let you do anything that would jeopardize yourself." I didn't say, *I won't let you turn out like Nick.*

But the sentiment hung unspoken between us.

The walls she was so good at putting up to keep others out were back in place.

"I care for you, Josie. I have for a long time."

"Reid…" Her voice was barely above a whisper. "I need to go."

She ran out the door.

I wanted to know what caused the fear in her eyes and what she was thinking about everything. About me.

I followed her home and watched her climb the stairs to her front door. She glanced over her shoulder at me.

Every fiber of my being screamed for her, but I didn't say a word.

JOSIE

Two very profound things had been pointed out to me in that warehouse. One: Reid was my trainer *and* my prosecutor. And two: It had been my mother who sent for him.

Did I resent Reid for doing his job? Not really. I would've preferred to know this crucial tidbit of information from the start, but, if I had, would I have grown to trust him at all? Likely not. It angered me to recognize that he'd played me. And, if I was really honest with myself, Reid playing me hit on a far more emotional level than I wanted to admit. Tate dumping me? Psh, that was so completely, utterly painless in comparison to this. To this…*hurt*.

But what cut deeper, what left me bleeding inside and longing for numbness, was my mom's decision. She had specifically called for Reid. She'd placed me under his tutelage with the full knowledge of what he'd be tasked to do. What game was she playing at? Mom was like me—*where do you think I learned to assess and calculate?*—she would've considered Reid's training results with my brother. She knew that he'd blown the whistle on my brother. Right or wrong, Nick didn't deserve to die.

Someone should've saved Nick. Surely there was some prescription, some remedial action that could've been taken to spare him.

I glanced around, recognizing the familiar sights and scents of my kitchen. Holy shitballs, I must've been numb, because the drive home was forgotten, and I had zero recollection of opening the door, shucking my shoes, or plodding through the family room.

Mom stood at the kitchen island cutting an apple for Eli. With her analyzing eyes on me, she said, "Eli, why don't you take this snack to your room while you do your homework?"

He gave a fist pump. "Yes!" Eli didn't usually get to take food to his room. His excitement was a stark reminder of what I was supposed to help preserve—the normal Planck world. Eli most likely wouldn't be a Planck forever, but he was for now. His behavior didn't diffuse my anger with my mom, though.

I caught him in a hug before he ran out of the room. I squeezed him until he wriggled to be set free.

"Josie," he whined. Already he was approaching the age

where PDA made him uncomfortable. God, so many things were changing.

"Sorry, bud."

Eli hightailed it upstairs with his after-school snack in hand, and when I heard his door shut, I moved in front of my mother. Her face was guarded, emotionless, which stoked the red-hot embers of my rage.

I laced my fingers together to still my shaking fingers. "Why did you ask Reid here when you knew he could also end up determining my fate?"

She pulled a stool out and sat, leaning her cane against the cupboard. "That is one of the jobs of a trainer. You'll be fine."

"I'll be *fine*?" I shook my head as I tried making sense of her indifferent take on the situation.

"Reid is one of the most gifted Anomalies in the world. He won't let you do anything that would require him to report you."

Like he'd protected Nick? I wouldn't go there.

"Obey the Resistance rules—"

"Do you hear yourself?" Heat, pain, nausea, but not near the level it had been at the beginning of the week. A small trophy with a gold star balancing on top appeared on the island between us. My mom eyed the award and asked, "What is it?"

"That's your Mom of the Year Award. Calling your daughter's judge and jury. That's dedication."

"It's more complicated than that, and you know it." Her voice had elevated in pitch; there was more emotion in that sentence than I'd heard in a long time. And that pissed me off. Because the emotion wasn't in defense of Eli or me. She was talking about this big, jacked-up world. "If you or any other Resistance member put us or our cause in danger, then you will face consequences. Keeping the Resistance safe is of the utmost importance—we are fighting for ourselves and all humankind. The Consortium will grow too powerful if we don't. The greater good outweighs the acts of one traitor who could ruin it all."

My stomach roiled, and a bitter taste filled my mouth. I wrapped my arms around my middle, trying to hold myself together, because her sharp words slashed into the center of me. The greater good was more important than me, her daughter. I was alone in this, in everything.

Tears stung at the backs of my eyes.

Mom's cold index finger on my chin startled me. Hunching over on the stool, she tried to look at my face, throwing herself off balance. She clasped onto my forearm, and I helped her balance on the stool.

I stared at my mom, deteriorating and weak. She'd given her life, her physical and mental self, to the cause. She wasn't looking for accolades or recognition. My parents just wanted to do what was right—I could comprehend that. I could even respect it. What I couldn't understand was putting your own child in the line of fire and welcoming her prosecutor with open arms. That was not love.

"Look—" Whatever emotion she'd accidentally let slip through was gone. Her cold exterior slid back in place. She reached for my arm.

"*Noooo!*" I Pushed handcuffs and chained her to the countertop, preventing her from touching me. "*You* look. You have two kids here you've ignored for years, so don't pretend like you care now. I've been more of a mother to Eli than you have." Something behind her eyes flashed—hurt, maybe, or surprise—but I continued. A couple of sparks of emotion after years of neglect wasn't going to lessen my pain. "I will do this drop, but not for you. For Eli and every other kid who is oblivious and innocent."

I Retracted the cuffs but left the trophy.

Stepping away from her, I eased toward the stairs. "Neither Eli nor I will ever replace Nick, but we're alive. Act like it."

I turned away before seeing a confirmation, but it wasn't up for discussion. On the way to my room, my phone vibrated, indicating a text. Reid.

U ok?

I peeked out my blinds and found him in my yard below, staring up at my window. My heart faltered.

That was a loaded question. Was I okay? No. On top of stuff with my parents and my role, Reid had basically admitted he had feelings for me. Reid, who was really Cal, my brother's longtime friend and my first true crush.

Reid, my potential whistle-blower. Who would bring upon my execution if I went crazy.

21.

Josie needed a short crash course in weapons training. With the Consortium after her and the possibility of an attack at the award ceremony the following day, it was better to be prepared. She had to know how the weapons looked and felt, as well as the ammunition, if she wanted to Push them.

Santos took over my watch halfway through the night and followed Josie to the warehouse in the morning. Santos was one hell of a wingman, and he'd done his best to diffuse the situation, explaining to Josie how we'd successfully trained fifteen Oculi and how we weren't in the habit of causing anyone suffering, least of all the recruits left in our care. According to Santos's last text, Josie was cool. She was keeping it "strictly business."

If I was smart, I'd do the same.

The door swung open with an abruptness only a kick could deliver. Josie's head peered through the opening. She looked over her shoulder back to the parking lot, examined the floor, and shut the door. She was getting the hang of all this.

"We aren't doing any attack training today," I said.

She crossed the warehouse and came over to check out the collection.

Josie held her hands together as if afraid to accidentally touch something. Looked like her initial excitement was replaced with hesitancy. I could fix that. Once she was educated on the weapons, she'd feel more comfortable.

"Pretty awesome, huh?" Santos entered behind her.

Josie tilted her head from side to side, as if she couldn't decide, as she considered the table of destructive tools. Santos and I had discussed being on our best behavior, especially since Josie had so many weapons at her disposal. There was a joke in there somewhere, I was sure, but under the circumstances, I didn't have much to laugh about. I approached her from behind, announcing my nearness by clearing my throat.

I needed to smooth things over between us, and I knew it wasn't going to be easy. "Welcome to Weaponmart. May I help you find something? A pair of brass knuckles would complement your outfit." She rolled said eyes and gave me the Vulcan hand gesture.

"I think your Vulcan salute is backward. I thought you'd know that, nerd," I said, trying to keep it light.

She turned her hand the correct way, the palm facing me. "No, this is what Vulcans like Spock use, which means 'live long and prosper.'" Then she flipped her hand so the backside faced me. "I'm using it backward, which means the opposite. 'Die and languish.'" She flashed a fake smile.

Yeah, things still definitely needed smoothing out.

"Santos, customer!" I yelled. He jogged to her side with all the enthusiasm of a Walmart greeter.

"You ready?" I asked. "All you have to do is learn about them, how they work, what they look like. Then you'll be able to Push each of the weapons if and when you need them. If you don't know what you're trying to observe into existence, you won't be able to make it materialize."

Santos continued where I left off. "This handgun has six rounds, but others have a detachable magazine with twelve or more. Some assault rifles, like the classic M16, have forty-five to sixty rounds, depending on the clip. You need to know how much ammunition each weapon holds and what it sounds like when it runs out of rounds, so you can mentally refill it when you need to. Pushing a constant stream of endless ammo is possible, as long as you're cognizant of it. But if you have people trying to kill you, sometimes endless rounds are tough."

Josie eyed the six-chamber in Santos's hand. "Why would I need to know the sound it makes when it's out of ammo?" Her eyes flitted to my face for a moment and then back to Santos.

Santos, being a bit of a weapons nerd, was eating this up. And Josie was taking instruction from him better than she'd probably take it from me at this point. "Say an armed person is chasing you," he said, "and your mind blanks on what weapon to Push into your hand. You come across a dude lying dead on the ground, a handgun in his hand."

Santos stepped away from Josie. "You grab it and point it at an armed person chasing you, and it makes this sound." Santos pointed the gun down at the floor. He pulled the trigger. A *ch-ch* sound echoed off the warehouse walls. "You hear that? It's out of ammunition. You need to know to Push more ammo. The first time that happens, your instinct will be to drop the weapon, but that leaves you vulnerable. All you have to do is observe the bullets coming out and they will. It just takes practice."

Josie's ponytail bobbed. Her head was saying yes, but her eyes said something else. Santos handed her the gun and she mimicked his hand position, turned in an about-face, and pointed it at the life-size mannequin at the end of the training area.

"Reid," Santos said. "Why don't you go hang this outside?"

"Hang what?"

A moment later, a six-by-ten wooden sign dropped at my feet: SAMMY'S SHOOTING RANGE.

When had I become the errand boy? And the warehouse was already insulated with soundproofing—we'd made sure of that when we first moved in. I listened intently to Santos's instructions and how he helped Josie to acquaint herself with the weapon. He didn't do a damn thing untoward, but that didn't quell the urge to punch him. Before I gave in to the notion, I hefted the sign onto a dolly and rolled it toward the front of the warehouse.

A couple of Pushes and it was hanging in place.

When I returned to the warehouse, Santos had stepped beside Josie and was busy repositioning her supporting hand. "Now," Santos said. "This reaction needs to be automatic, like what Reid has taught you about being aware of your environment, the quick thinking, the close-combat skills. They all need to be habits. An immediate reaction. Most of us train for months—years. You're getting the crash course."

"Santos," I warned.

He shook his head. "She deserves the full truth, Reid. She can handle it." He glanced back at her. "You know, Josie, on the bright side, you haven't had to train as hard. You really are a natural. And talent trumps training when it comes to being an Anomaly. Understand?"

She nodded.

Yep, that jealousy reared its ugly head again.

Santos Pushed ear and eye protection on the three of us. He gestured toward the mannequin. "Brace yourself and fire."

Josie fired and missed the dummy entirely. She tried again and got off a couple shots in the legs.

She was dropping her hand, anticipating the kickback. "Hang on," I said. "Adjust your hand. Wrap it closer."

"Huh?"

I glanced at Santos. His eyes twinkled—yes, twinkled. "Maybe you should show her what you mean, Reid."

Could he be any more of an adolescent?

I approached Josie cautiously, and she awaited my instruction.

"Play nice, kids," Santos said. "I'm out."

He whistled as he strolled toward his room.

Josie's hand dropped to her side, her knuckles white-gripping the gun, her brows furrowed.

"Here, let me." I shifted her hands on the weapon and stood behind her to absorb some of the recoil. "Try it now."

Her breathing changed a bit.

"You have to aim higher, to account for the distance and velocity." Bullet trajectories, speed, accounting for gravity, all of those details should be right in her wheelhouse. I wrapped my arms around hers and raised her hands into the proper position. She shuddered.

I didn't let go. I didn't back away. "Josie."

She leaned on me, just the barest of movements, but there was trust in that gesture. She would never forget or forgive me for what happened with Nick. I didn't expect her to. But there was a measure of acceptance in how she allowed me to touch her. My lips brushed the top of her head too gently for her to feel.

"Ready?"

She nodded. We emptied that six-shooter, and then I instructed her to Push bullets into the chamber. She did. Seamlessly. As for her aim—decent. Maybe 70 percent accuracy, and for someone who'd never practiced with a gun before, that was considerable.

"Acquaint yourself with the rest."

She walked to the table, putting the six-chamber next to an AK47. I watched her reach out and touch the automatic weapon, as if checking to see if it was real.

Rather than select the one from the table, she Pushed an AK47 into her hand. She examined it from all angles, then placed the weapon down on the table beside the original. "Reid, if...if I do lose my mind, if I turn..." Horror clouded her features. "You know what I'm capable of."

"That won't happen." No way. No how.

"Promise me," she said.

I knew what she was asking of me. Would I turn her in if she became a threat to innocent people? I'd like to think I could give her a yes, but the truth was, I couldn't. I cared for her in a different capacity than I'd cared for Nick. I wouldn't let it get to that point. Period.

"Won't. Happen. You hear me? I won't let it."

"Okay," she whispered, claiming the assault rifle and stepping up to the firing range.

My pep talk seemed to have helped, but things remained strained between us. I didn't expect anything less.

We worked our way down the table through the various weapons. She held a grenade, crossbow, flamethrower, shotgun, standard-issue Glock, AK47, and everything in between. Over the course of the next couple of hours, she learned the basics of operating each, and how to reload or recharge the weapon as needed.

Josie examined the last weapon, a Taser, with a smile plastered on her face.

"Your excitement for the Taser worries me a little."

An honest laugh burst out of her as she placed it back on the table.

I stepped in front of her, making her look at me. "Seriously, though…" I didn't want to stop her laughter, but she had to know the reality of warfare. Her penchant for the Taser reminded me of the first attack in the park, less than a week ago. She'd felt sorry for her attacker. That sentiment would be her downfall. "If you're ever in a situation where someone is after you, don't Push one of these." I held up the Taser. "Push something that will do the trick. Push something that will kill the person after you. And, Josie, don't hesitate to pull the trigger."

JOSIE

Well, I was supposed to continue with my previously planned week, so to the bonfire we went…with the guys in tow. Hannah was more than enthusiastic, excited about the chance to hang with Santos.

We rode in Hannah's car, the guys in the back. We talked and laughed and listened to music like normal people our age. I wondered if this was what a real double-date thingy would feel like. I stuck my hand out the window and played with the flow velocity. The force of air tickled my palm and my body relaxed for the first time since learning Reid had orders to report me if I went berserk.

We pulled up to the beach lot. Hannah looped her arm through mine as we walked through the cars and bikes to the beach. I spotted a roaring fire.

Hannah pulled me a little closer and tilted her head toward me. The guys followed about ten feet behind us. She whispered, "He's so into you."

I shrugged. I mean, I couldn't tell her our freaking confusing situation, that someone who I'd made out with and liked—and who liked me back, I thought—was also supposed to report me if I stepped out of line, which could result in my death. "We'll see what happens."

I inhaled the smell of the refreshing, salty ocean mixed with the earthy scent of the fire. Hope and energy rolled together. It was invigorating.

She totally side-eyed me. "What do you mean, 'see what happens'? Make it happen. It's in your ability to make anything happen." I was dying inside at the irony of her statement. "Just sayin'."

It was as if gravity increased. Hannah's words weighted my body to the ground, making it difficult to pick my feet up and move them forward.

It's in your ability to make anything happen.

That was one of the scariest statements I'd heard in my life. But also the most liberating.

We crossed the dunes onto the beach, kicking up sand behind us as we stepped. The cool ocean breeze lifted my hair and zapped across my skin like I was magnetized and my body was conducting a charge.

Hannah stayed close. "You should…" Santos ran up from behind us, roaring, his arms closed around Hannah, picking her up and whirling her around and around. They tumbled to the ground in a heap of tangled limbs and laughter.

Reid ambled up to my side and shouted at them. "You guys want some privacy?"

Santos looked up. "Yeah, go away."

Reid shook his head. "Let's go eat some s'mores." He walked ahead of me.

"How do you know they have s'mo—" A plastic grocery bag appeared in his hand. I still wasn't used to that, even after all I'd seen and done in the last few days. He glanced over his shoulder to me and grinned. I ran to catch up.

I Pushed long, cut twigs into my hand for the marshmallows before we reached the crowd around the bonfire.

Charles and Lauren waved. I was really going to miss my lunch mates.

I sat on a big log close to the fire, and Reid did the same. He pulled the s'mores sticks from my hand and placed them in the grocery bag next to him.

Reid stared into the fire, the light dancing in his clear eyes. That look—it was Cal, the Cal I remembered.

My hands were stuffed in my pockets—to avoid the chilly air, but also because I didn't know what else to do with them, I had so many conflicting feelings for him. I knocked his knee with mine. He turned to me, and my words toppled out, unplanned. "I'm scared."

He swung one of his legs around to straddle the log and faced me head-on. He nestled the bag of marshmallows between us. "I am, too."

"You are?"

"Of course. But I also know it will be okay."

"How do you know? What evidence suggests that? There are so many variables."

He chuckled. "I feel it. In here." He touched his stomach. "And in here." His hand slid up to his chest. "And I think it in here." He tapped a finger to his temple.

He shrugged and gave me a genuine smile.

Lauren and Charles came over to where we were sitting. Lauren held a s'mores to Reid. Guess we weren't the only ones craving them tonight. "I've eaten so many, I'm going to be sick. You can share with Josie." Lauren peeked over her shoulder to me, smiling, and Charles pointed between Reid and me. Yeah, that was subtle.

I gave them a "did you really just do that?" look and they skittered away, giggling.

He eyed the treat in his hands for a second, then held the s'more toward me.

I laughed and grabbed it, placing my fingers over his

and took a bite. So yum. He leaned forward and took a bite from the opposite side, my fingers still on his, only a graham cracker separating us. And, per usual, his eyes didn't leave mine. Despite the cool breeze blowing off the Gulf, I thought I'd burst into flames.

We took turns eating the gooey treat until it was gone and our hands dropped away from each other. The corner of his mouth pulled up in a naughty grin. "You have a little chocolate…" he whispered. His hand came toward my face and his eyes fell to my mouth. The pad of his thumb landed on the corner of my lower lip and smoothed across. Feelings I couldn't identify swirled around inside me. Strong feelings. Conflicting feelings.

Someone screamed.

I Pushed my shield. "Ow!" Reid yelped.

I didn't know where my attention was needed. Reid seemed fine other than a funny, pained look on his face. The two girls who had screamed were on the opposite side of the fire. They screamed again a few times, pointing and squealing at a guy showing them something on his phone. I checked the tree line and glanced down the beach. Everything was fine. Obnoxious, but fine.

"Josie? Was that your shield?" Reid asked in a low voice. I nodded. "Y-you shocked me or something." His face darkened, and he looked down at the log we were sitting on. I guess he hadn't ever been close to me when I'd Pushed my shield before. I'd Pushed it with Hannah, and she hadn't been zapped. I didn't like Reid's reaction. I hadn't meant to hurt him.

Someone threw a bottle into the fire and flames blazed

with a vigorous energy. Hollers and whoops followed.

Santos called out to us. "Reid. Take a walk along the water?"

Reid glanced at me to decide.

"Okay."

He stood and helped me step over the log. I strode through the sand after Reid, toward the darkness, where the moon reflected over the surface of the ocean and the waves crashed against the shore. Santos and Hannah goofed around at the water's edge, their dark figures just visible. I was almost to Reid when he stumbled and fell. He landed on his back in the sand and yelled, "Santos, you dick."

Oculi games. Pushing and Retracting in the dark, close to Plancks. I didn't know how I felt about that.

I approached Reid, offering him a hand up. I tripped on something—something that hadn't been there moments before—and I fell.

I saw a flash of Reid's hands out to catch me, but it all happened too fast. The next moment I was facedown, on top of him.

Giggles erupted from the beach. Santos and Hannah. "Santos," I yelled into Reid's shoulder. "You dick."

Attempting to pull my trapped arm from between my body and Reid's, I tried placing a knee on the ground to stabilize myself.

"Watch the knee." Reid winced, shifting his hands to my arms and moving a leg underneath me to protect himself.

"Sorry." I laughed into Reid's shoulder. My face burned from embarrassment. I tried to breathe through it and ended up inhaling a lustful smell. Reid's signature scent. I couldn't get enough.

My cheek brushed his as I pulled my head off his shoulder, and I paused when my mouth hovered over his. His stare was like an entirely different universe, light-years away from our world—a safe place. I shook myself out of his trance.

In one fluid motion, Reid pushed my torso up and I slid my legs to one side of his body. My knees hit the sand and I sat back on my heels, thrusting my now-free hand out to Reid. He took it, anchored his feet in the sand, and we both pulled, using each other's weight to help each other off the ground. Every movement in sync.

We stood face-to-face.

"Let's go for that walk," Reid said. As soon as we turned, Santos took a nosedive into the waves lapping up onto the shore. A string of inventive curses rushed out as he hoisted himself out of the water, soaked.

"Karma, man." Reid headed for the hard-packed sand closer to the water, making it easier to walk. Santos and Hannah trailed close behind. Reid and I walked in a comfortable silence next to each other.

Santos jogged up behind us. "I need to change clothes, bro. You want us to go and come back?" I'd forgotten he couldn't Push anything in front of Hannah.

Reid looked to me for an answer. "No. I think I'm ready to go home, actually." Even though I didn't want to say good-bye to Hannah, I needed to mentally prepare for the next day.

We piled back into the car, Santos shamelessly shucking his clothes in the parking lot and swapping into a fresh pair of shorts and a shirt, which he'd packed in a bag that Hannah "must not have noticed when he got into the car." If she'd pondered that for more than a moment, the thought fled her mind once he dropped his jeans.

The drive back to Hannah's house was the best fifteen minutes I could call to memory. Music, laughing. Sitting in the backseat with my head resting on Reid's shoulder.

Reid was going to take me home. Hannah asked Santos to stay and hang out a while, but he used the wet clothes as his excuse to get home. They couldn't start something even if Santos wanted to.

Hannah started for her door, completely unaware that I'd most likely leave town the next day. "Hey!" I ran across the yard, up the front stairs, and flung my arms around her.

"Aw. See you Monday. Good luck tomorrow." She pulled back to see my face. "I'm so proud of you! Oh—and good luck tonight!" She wriggled her eyebrows.

My sinuses burned, holding back tears. "Thank you. For being my friend." *My only real friend.* I let go of her before I lost it and hopped onto the bike behind Reid.

I'd just said good-bye, and she didn't even know it.

22.

Reid

I walked her to the door. "Mom," she yelled as she stepped into the entryway. No answer.

I closed the door behind us. "If she's not home, I need to sweep the house. Understand?" She Pushed her shield. I stood close enough that I could feel it sting my skin. "Good call." I Pushed my shield and Glock into my hand. "Ready?"

Josie nodded and followed me into the living room. Nothing appeared amiss. But the house was eerily silent. The alarm hadn't sounded when we entered—standard operating protocol was for Mrs. Harper to keep her high-tech security system armed at all times. I prayed the Consortium hadn't breached this house. One glance at Josie and I saw my worry mirrored—and multiplied—on her face.

We swept through the hallway. I kept her behind me, clearing the rooms and aiming into the blind areas with the precision that had been hammered into me by countless drills and training exercises in the Hub. Cut, turn, sweep. I angled my gun up the main stairwell. Held Josie back when I took the corners.

Our last training exercise had suited her. When I glanced back at her again, she was suited in a Kevlar vest—which she also had Pushed on me at the first sign of danger—and armed to the gills. Assault rifle slung over a shoulder and .38 Special clasped in her hands.

As I checked the kitchen, laundry room, and bathroom, she pivoted, watching our flanks. Hell yeah. If I hadn't already fallen for this girl, seeing her like this would've shot me straight over the edge.

We crept into the decoy lab.

"Reid!"

Her stare pinballed around the room. It had been ransacked. She didn't touch anything or speak. Instead, she did a 180 and sprinted through the family room toward the stairs. I caught her around the waist.

"On my lead," I hissed.

I took the stairs quickly, knowing if I didn't, she'd bolt past me into whatever danger might lurk above. I would've argued for her to stay downstairs or to go outside, but I knew she wouldn't listen. And I couldn't afford to leave her alone until I knew what we were up against. I should've shuffled her into that damn panic room and locked it down. Though she probably would've fought me on that, too.

Even if I could convince her to wait in her mom's subterranean room, I didn't like the idea of her being unguarded, no matter how secure that lab was purported to be. So for now, I'd keep her at my back, and I'd keep her safe.

I Pushed on my infrared goggles. No movement on the upper floor. That was good news for the likelihood of bad guys; not so good news for discovering her brother or mother. Even the dead gave off a heat signature, at least for a couple of hours.

Josie stopped when I kicked the door to Eli's bedroom. In three seconds flat, I'd cleared the room, checking beneath the bed and inside the closet. She rushed past me and touched Eli's bed.

"What?"

"His pillow and stuffed animal are gone."

"Maybe he's at a sleepover."

"We don't do sleepovers." She opened and closed drawers. Then she pivoted, shoved past me, and ran into her mom's room.

"Damn it, Josie!"

When I reached the doorway, I paused. She was sweeping through the room like a hurricane, tearing open drawers, ripping through the closet, rifling through the items on the small corner desk. Without a word, she ducked under my arm and darted down the stairs. I trailed her as she opened the closet door and worked the security lock for the lab. No signs of forced entry on the hidden panel. That was good.

I peeked into the garage. Empty.

The security keypad beeped, signaling a successful entry. Pulling the door back, she slipped in, and I shut the closet door and followed. She lashed out blindly, banging into the walls. I still had on the goggles, so I grabbed her hand and took the lead.

"Easy," I whispered.

Her fingers clamped down on my wrist and didn't relent.

I guided us to the end of the pitch-black hall. We dropped to our knees. She fumbled for a second to engage the panel, and the moment it slid back, she slapped her hand over the blue screen. We entered the elevator without speaking.

The door to the lab opened with a hiss.

I followed her into the room. No Eli. No Mrs. Harper.

No signs that either of them had passed through the escape tunnels. There were no signs of destruction or that this hidden room had been discovered.

Josie inched her way across the lab and then froze. She stood before the lab table like it was an altar, regarding it with quiet respect. I approached her from behind. "Josie?"

She didn't acknowledge me.

Taking a couple more steps, I looked over her head. The vial lay in the middle of the table on top of a yellow sticky note that read, *You can do this.*

My gaze immediately jumped to Josie's face. Tears stained her cheeks.

She wouldn't make eye contract. "I have to do this on my own." The hurt in her soft voice ran deep. "No one took them. They…they left me."

She melted to the floor. Her body rocked with sobs, but no sound came.

I folded myself around her, pulling her into me, holding her. I wanted to take the pain away, but I didn't know how. After the serum handoff, I'd be there, for however long it took to help her heal—as long as she wanted me.

Eventually, she fell asleep in my lap, and I swept her into my arms. Climbing the stairs to her room, I laid her in her bed, slipped off her shoes, and covered her. I pulled her chair over by the head of her bed and watched her sleep, smoothing her hair.

She was the only beauty in this mess.

JOSIE

I woke with a jolt, the room dark. Then it all came crashing down around me. My mother had left me. She'd abandoned me. She'd taken Eli. I didn't get to hug him one last time. I didn't get to tell him I loved him or say good-bye.

The agony and despair bored an non-repairable hole in my heart. There was no filling it.

Then my gaze darted around me, to the closet door, to my blanket. My bedroom. I was in my bedroom. I rolled over and found Reid asleep in my chair, leaning on my nightstand, about to fall on the floor.

Pushing the blanket back, I pulled his arm. He startled awake, sucking in a quick breath. "Hold me."

He didn't hesitate. He climbed into bed, pulled the covers over us, and circled his arms around me.

23.

JOSIE

I arrived at the back check-in area of Del Mar Hotel, Reid not far behind but not looking as though we were together. I responded to Hannah's text wishing me good luck and told her I'd call her later. I gave my name and was promptly escorted to the identification station. The security attendants asked for the letter sent from the vice president's office, my birth certificate, driver's license, and social security card. My fingerprint was scanned and checked against the fingerprint that had been taken several weeks ago.

I was escorted backstage and snagged a tissue once I found my place, since we weren't allowed to bring anything with us. The awards would be presented before the campaign speech, thank Thor. A kid, about Eli's age, stood in front of me. Oh, man. This needed to go right. Innocent people were here — kids.

The vice president addressed his hometown and received

hoots and applause. He went on to talk about the importance of "our youth" as he prepared to present the science awards. I tuned out most of what he'd said. Not because the politics didn't interest me, but because I needed to focus.

I catalogued the people around me. The positions of the security personnel. The exits and entrances to this backstage area. I Pushed my shield, so that it tingled just along the surface of my skin.

A name was called, the crowd clapped, and the kid in front of me moved in front of the curtain. Huh? It was happening.

"Are you ready?" the event coordinator asked. The tall woman smiled around the ear-microphone combination that blocked her mouth.

"It's an honor," I managed.

I grinned, but my smile was a contradiction to the way I felt. I could die at any moment. Any breath could be my last. My heart kicked like a bronco.

I Pushed my shield wider, turned away from the people backstage like I was blowing my nose, and grabbed the vial from my bra. I wrapped it in the tissue, holding it comfortably in my hand.

Someone cleared her throat directly behind me, giving my heart palpitations. I swung around, and my lungs seized. Mom's green eyes stared back at me.

I let my shield fade and threw myself at her, and now I could breathe again. I didn't think she'd leave without saying good-bye. She wouldn't do that. Eli was too young.

I drew myself out of her grasp. "What…?"

"I had to make it look like it was me. Needed to be a decoy. I can take it now," she whispered.

She was taking back the responsibility? Oh.

"It was wrong of me to put this task on your shoulders. I'll meet with the VP." She leaned forward to kiss the top of my head. "You've been through so much, Josie. Too much."

The boy who stood in front of me pranced around the corner, past Mom and me. Did she think I would fail? I wouldn't let her down. I could do this.

"Josie Harper." My name was announced. I had to go. I pressed the vial into Mom's hand and turned. I stepped in front of the curtain from the side of the stage, and the crowd roared.

Glancing across the stage, I saw Reid, dressed in black pants and a button-up with a camera in his hand, posing as someone from the school newspaper. Behind him, men and women in suits and gowns clustered at round tables, enjoying a dinner that I'd heard cost fifteen hundred dollars a plate. The VP might not Push money, but he had no trouble raising it.

I immediately found Mr. Mac in the back of the room and a man standing beside him, guarding the doors, as I peered out over the crowd. Mr. Mac said something to the man, who I realized had to be one of the undercover Resistance operatives, before he slipped out of the room. Then the spotlight hit me, and it was hard to see beyond the stage.

If the Consortium knew about me, would they target me now? I concentrated on my shield and on placing one foot in front of the other.

I sucked in a deep breath when I approached the podium, my lungs having forgotten how to breathe. To any onlookers, they would've thought my gasp—which echoed over the podium microphone—one of delight at coming face-to-face with the soon-to-be commander in chief. When Vice President Brown shook my hand, he said, "Congratulations on your achievement, Miss Harper." I smiled at him. He looked like such a kind man, with his wide green eyes and clean-cut face. I glanced over my shoulder at my mom.

She had her back to me, shuffling away from the stage, leaning on her cane. Which was in the wrong hand.

My heart hesitated.

The world seemed to slow down as my mind worked in fast forward. That wasn't my mom. And the realization must've shown on my face, because in that one instant when she glimpsed over her shoulder, she dropped the facade entirely and jogged away, carrying the cane.

The VP pulled his hand out of mine, taking the real vial of serum with him.

"You honor your family and our cause," he said.

I turned, with my award in hand, and caught the back view of my mother fleeing around the corner. I moved as quickly as I dared off the stage. *Never reveal abilities to Plancks*.

I wanted to run. To Push shackles around the imposter and bring her to her knees. Once beyond the curtains, I sprinted through the backstage area. I followed the stage back to one of the main halls and I saw her face—and Mr. Mac's—an instant before the elevator doors closed. I ran to the elevator and watched where it stopped, pounding on the door. Reid ran up behind me—I didn't know how he made it past security, and I didn't care.

"What's going on?" he asked.

I told him about my mother, or whoever was pretending

to be my mom, and how my physics teacher was in cahoots with her. I watched where the elevator stopped. Top floor.

We took the slowest elevator on the face of the earth to the top floor, ready to find whoever took the fake vial. The doors opened to a sign with an arrow and fancy script that said: ROOFTOP ACCESS. I followed the arrow around the corner, but Reid shoved past me and Pushed the roof door open, waiting a few seconds before crossing the threshold. My heart jumped around in my chest like a bouncing electron as I surveyed my surroundings. Thick air clung to my body and a warm wind blew wisps of hair free from my ponytail.

I searched the rooftop for movement. Nothing. On one side of the hotel were the city lights, sprawled along the coast. The Gulf thrived on the other side. Twinkling stars dotted the darkening sky above, but a storm brewed out at sea. Big mechanical boxes sat randomly around the roof, housing exhaust and air-conditioning type things…and possibly hiding someone.

Reid leaned toward my ear. "Stay here but be ready."

He crept around a corner, and something creaked behind me. I spun, hands up, ready for an attack. Nothing there. *Where did that noise come from?* I wedged myself into a corner and Pushed a mirror into my hand. Using the mirror, I peeked around the other side of the wall. Clear.

I dropped the mirror, and a blonde in shorts and a tank pointed a gun at my head.

I blinked and a brick wall, eight feet tall, erected a foot between us. It didn't promptly disappear, so the girl, who I guessed to be a Consortium chick, just let me know she couldn't Retract. She rounded the corner of the wall I'd just

Pushed and sprinted at me. She looked so much like every other girl from my high school that I almost expected her to ask me for my physics notes.

I widened my stance and braced as she dove at me. Her hands went for my neck and we crashed to the rooftop floor. I looped my hands between her arms, swept them out and down as quickly as I could, then reared back and slammed my head into her face. The girl groaned and went slightly limp. I rolled her off me while keeping hold of her arms. I straddled her body and crashed my knuckles into her cheekbone. One, two punches, and her head rolled to the side. She laid there, breathing but not moving, her eyes closed.

I stood, my legs trembling under me, and Pushed rope around her wrists, ankles, knees. That might keep her for a minute. I backed away, keeping my eyes on her, my breath shaking in my chest. I needed to find the person who looked like my mom. Or Reid. I hit something behind me.

Turning, I found a dude who could grapple with The Rock and was at least six and a half feet tall. Judging by the maniacal gleam in his eyes and the tattoo of *Your Pain, My Gain* on his forearm, it was safe to assume he ate nails for breakfast and played with scorpions because they tickled.

His eyebrows furrowed as he looked over my shoulder. The girl I thought was unconscious stood with blood dripping from her nose. She looked pissed. She released an anguished scream as Mr. Mac slammed into her. They tumbled to the ground. My teacher was fighting against the Consortium. He was one of us. Thank Thor.

I stepped sideways away from both of them, but the guy's enormous hand clutched my wrist and reeled me back to him.

I Pushed my shield a second too late, since he already had a grip on me. So I Pushed a KA-BAR knife in my hand, the one Reid and some Marines preferred, at the distance from his body where it'd have enough momentum to plunge into his gut.

It disappeared. The thug smiled. He'd Retracted the knife. Good to know.

He wrapped both hands around me in a hug, pinning my arms down at my sides.

As he held me against his chest, the air squeezed out of my lungs and my back cracked. This would've been a great time to be able to Push living things, like vicious animals.

Reid's voice echoed in my head again: *Think quick.* I took in my surroundings. I was close—unusually close—to the person trying to kill me. My arms were still pinned to my sides and I couldn't maneuver my feet due to the strength of the guy, but I could move my wrists just enough.

The man holding me squeezed harder. Pain shot through my chest like nothing I had ever felt before. My ribs were close to their breaking point. I Pushed and Tasered the guy's crotch within the same two seconds. He dropped to the rooftop, and I wasn't sticking around to see if he'd get up.

Damn it, I knew not to Push a Taser. But I'd panicked.

I ran for the door, but the chick came at me. Behind her, I saw my physics teacher on the ground, his eyes open, glazed with death. She killed him? I wanted to cry, to run to him, but I couldn't wholly process his death.

I'd caused this. I'd spared her life and, in turn, she'd taken Mr. Mac's.

He was dead because of me.

No.

Reid was right. I'd have to kill to defend myself and others. I had to step it up whether I wanted to or not.

An image slipped through my mind, and in the next moment, her hair went up in flames. I Pushed freaking fire? This was a new development. Her shrill screams cut through the night air, but I only had a second before she'd Push something to extinguish the blaze. I Pushed a handful of knives and chucked three of them at an attacker approaching from my left, one of them sticking in his gut and another in his leg. I threw two at the girl on fire, one hitting her side and another in her chest.

I Pushed, and Kevlar wrapped around my chest. An assault rifle clanged against my back. I clasped a gun in my hand.

I was able to make it to the rooftop door without any more Consortium crazies getting in my way. The door opened and a cute bellboy about my age walked out onto the rooftop. I hoped he wouldn't be able to see the bodies behind me. I shoved the hand with the Glock behind my back. "I was just leaving," I said as I sidestepped him.

He moved in front of me, blocking my way. "I don't think so."

Are you effing kidding me?

The next thing I knew, I was on my back, looking up at the dark clouds skulking in from the Gulf, hiding the stars. The back of my head throbbed. Damn. I needed to remember my stupid shield.

The bellboy sat on my hips. He Retracted all of my weapons. I half sat up, grabbing for his skull to head butt, but he caught my hands and forced them to the concrete. I wasn't moving as fast as I usually could after that blow to my head. Everything seemed disjointed. His eyes narrowed, and he said, "This won't hurt…for long."

I kicked my legs and attempted to move my arms in every direction to no avail. He must've sensed my movement because his head swung around, and a second later, my ankles were strapped together and anchored to the rooftop. The bellhop smiled. I dragged in a breath, knowing it would probably be my last. His hand covered my mouth.

Reid was going to be so pissed. Someone would get his head bashed in.

I tried to Retract my restraints and managed to free my feet. But with his hand covering my nose and mouth, it was hard to focus on anything other than breathing. I bit at the hand constraining me.

The clouds moved fast above me, and they gave me an idea. Not knowing if it would work, I Pushed anyway.

A full-throttle migraine exploded in my brain, pulsing against my eyes. But instead of nausea, everything was clearer and the scent of my surroundings overwhelmed me. Salt, my perfume, the deodorant of the guy on top of me.

Lightning struck nearby. Wind howled. Rain was on the way.

The guy looked to the sky above us. *Thwack. Snap*. His head jutted forward and he collapsed on top of me. Pushing away his limp body, I sat up. An industrial shovel lay at my side, the one I'd used to hit the guy on the back of the head. The undercover Resistance guy who'd stood beside Mr. Mac at the back of the room during the award ceremony was running toward the huge guy to make sure he was dead. Probably a good call.

He hauled me to my feet before bending to deal with this attacker. "You need to evacuate the premises, Miss Harper."

No kidding. But I wasn't leaving without Reid.

Utter chaos had broken out.

Clouds swirled around the rooftop and thunder shook through the building below. I couldn't believe it. I'd Pushed a tropical storm. Wind whipped through my hair and took my breath away. A familiar electricity skidded over my skin. Lightning flashed, brightening the figures fighting around me. A face I recognized flickered in the light.

Reid. Relief and guilt hit me at the same time. His fist connected with a guy's face, in a crunch of bone and spurt of blood. The Consortium dude pulled a gun of some sort, but it disappeared immediately. Shiny metal objects released from Reid's hands but dropped short of the guy. He'd Pushed his shield.

The undercover Resistance guard fired three times to my right. The blond girl's body shuddered and tumbled to the rooftop.

Someone grabbed my ankle and yanked my leg backward. I pitched forward and Pushed a thick pillow under me a second before my face hit the cement. It buffered the impact, but my head still ached.

I turned my face and saw Mr. Mac's lifeless body across the distance again. I wouldn't let him die in vain.

I couldn't hold back. Not anymore.

24.

Playtime is over, fellas.

The Consortium dude I'd been fighting was an Anomaly, which meant we were in an endless game of Push and Retract and Shield. It could go on forever. Or until one of us slipped up, anyway.

The guy's eyes narrowed as he Pushed stairs up toward the sky, one appearing under his foot as he stepped. I wasn't sure where he thought he was going, but it wouldn't be far. I Pushed a ramp, a section at a time, manifesting under me as I stepped closer to this d-bag. We were on a collision course.

I Pushed a spear into my hand, and it arched gracefully through the air until it hit his shield. I picked up my pace, and as soon as I was about to crash into him, he dropped out of my line of sight. I glanced down. He'd landed on top of a rooftop exhaust unit. I Retracted my makeshift bridge, ran along the ramp I'd erected, back to the rooftop before Retracting that, too. The sky spit large drops as I sailed through the air, my eyes trained on the Consortium guy.

My feet hit the hotel rooftop and I paused to breathe. A bolt of lightning hit something close on the beach side of the hotel. I'd lost the Consortium goon, but the quick glow from the lightning illuminated the scene like it was momentarily daylight. Bodies lay around the rooftop. The blonde, the big guy. At least one undercover Resistance. Mr. McIntosh. Josie was standing, bracing herself against the short wall that ran the perimeter of the rooftop.

Santos ran toward her. Thank God.

But Santos wasn't slowing. If he continued at that speed, he'd shove her over…

JOSIE

I turned just as Santos crashed into me, his weight slamming into my chest. A body in motion stays in motion in the same straight line unless acted upon by an external force. Simple physics.

I fell over the edge of the ten-story hotel, head first. Adrenaline surged through me. For a split second, I thought about Pushing a chute, but with the high wind, that wasn't a good option. I wasn't sure if I knew how to control the wind or the chute. Instead, I Pushed an inflatable bounce house directly under me and fell into the softness on my back, arms crossed over my chest. I Retracted it the moment I pushed to my feet, not sure of Santos's location after he'd tackled me off the roof.

My mother stood before me.

In the next blink, it was Santos. *Oh no.*

Santos worked for the Consortium, and he'd learned so much about the Resistance over the last week. He'd tried to get the serum—he thought he had the serum now.

"It's nothing personal, Josie."

Um, I was pretty sure he'd just tried to kill me. I didn't think it got any more personal.

He laughed and stalked toward me.

I Pushed my shield and ran toward the beach, away from Planck eyes, closer to the crashing waves.

I spun and stopped. He didn't appear to be in any hurry. Walking backward, headed south along the water, I kept my eyes on him. I wouldn't turn my back.

Every nerve in my body was awake and each sense was intensified. My shield seemed almost tangible. "Why, Santos? Why do you want the serum?"

"You need to listen to me, Josie." His voice was steady and his face just as welcoming as usual. "Things aren't what they seem." What did that mean? "I needed to stop that handoff from happening. The VP couldn't get his hands on the serum."

I wasn't going to tell him that I delivered the real vial. I Retracted the sand under his feet, he vanished, and I filled it, burying him. I still only had seconds, though. I sprinted toward the naked expanse of the beach. I concentrated so hard I thought my insides would tumble out of me. A section of tropic jungle I'd visited with my family in Hawaii before Nick died manifested in front of me, blending flawlessly with the surrounding mangroves.

I stumbled in the sand, spinning around. Santos was out of the hole, racing toward me. Good. That's what I was banking on.

I'd matched the shoreline of my Pushed environment with the real shore. The soil significantly changed under my feet. I dashed backward behind a plant, the giant fronds camouflaging me from Santos. The rain was now coming down in a steady shower. I'd wanted the storm as distraction on the rooftop, but I no longer needed it. The rain made it hard to see, but maybe that meant that Santos couldn't see me.

Moving deeper into the slice of tropical forest I'd Pushed, I snapped the leaves on purpose, causing more noise than necessary, but I needed him to follow me. And he did.

I didn't want to kill him, but if I didn't, he'd kill me. Or he'd injure me enough to take me hostage, to hand me over to the Consortium. I didn't know which thought terrified me more.

I still couldn't believe he'd betray us. Laughing, joking, affectionate Santos.

But the words he'd uttered bore a striking similarity to how Nick was described in his last days. Maybe Santos suffered from the same affliction?

Under the canopy, darkness clung like a sticky blanket. If it weren't for the moon, it would've been impossible for him to follow. He Pushed a falling tree inches in front of me. Jumping out of the way, I Retracted it before it hit the ground. Too close.

"You know…" Santos yelled. "The Resistance isn't all it's

supposed to be, Josie."

I didn't know what he was talking about, but I wasn't going to ask questions.

A branch snapped. "Santos," Reid called.

"Ah, the Boy Scout." Santos paused like he might pursue Reid instead.

I couldn't let that happen. "What are you talking about?" I said, drawing his attention back to me. The words were rushed. I took my first real breath since falling over the ledge.

Keeping low to the ground, I passed a flowering bush, continuing to where I needed to guide Santos.

I stooped behind a large tree trunk and nestled between its thick roots. He should've been behind me, coming past the bush. I peeked around the tree. Nothing but the sound of local frogs and insects in the distance, already infiltrating the new landscape I'd introduced to them.

Pop. Something moved.

My head wheeled, searching for the cause of the sound. Found it. A grenade landed ten feet to my left. I Pushed my shield wider, stronger, the movement as instinctual as blinking. The explosion ripped apart several trees, branches and foliage rained down, leaving me without a hiding spot. I prayed someone would hear the grenade, that help would be forthcoming. But even if the Secret Service or local PD arrived, it wouldn't be in time to save me.

Thunder rumbled overhead, the storm taking on a life of its own. I turned to move behind the trees, and something sliced the air next to my ear. I dropped to the ground.

I'd become the hunted. But Reid was hunting Santos.

I Pushed infrared binoculars—as I'd seen Reid do—while

on my hands and knees. I moved deeper into the jungle, quickly but as quietly as possible. I picked out a lone human-shaped heat source tucked beside a shrub only fifteen feet away.

I backed away from Santos, keeping my sights on him, while I moved in the direction of high ground. The map of tropical forest was etched into my brain. Between moves we'd stayed in a beach house, and this bit of the jungle hugging the beach had been ours temporarily.

"If you join the Consortium without force, you won't be hurt." His voice clashed against the serenity of the trees. "If you don't come, you will be considered a threat." He sounded closer. Where was Reid?

I crouched behind a boulder and Pushed a Beretta, the metal cool against my hot skin. I hated how comfortable it felt in my hand. My heartbeat pounded through my skull and I sucked in a breath to calm myself. The smell of mildew and vegetation was overwhelming. The ocean breeze blew through the trees, making palm fronds dance above us.

I could only make out Santos's silhouette, but he turned in both directions, searching. He ran a hand over his face. "You don't want to end up like Nick. A victim. The Resistance killed him, Josie. They killed your brother. We could work together to finally end all this madness."

Hearing my brother's name come out of Santos's mouth sent bile up the back of my throat. I bit the inside of my lip to keep from screaming at him. I sat behind mossy rocks and watched. The moonlight reflected off something shiny in his hand that hadn't been there moments before. He turned again. A massive knife. Wind gushed past me, electricity crackled in the clouds above us. His other hand shot out at the moving vegetation, a gun appeared, pointing at nothing and everything. The rain pattered out a steady rhythm as the drops collided with the earth.

"Why are you doing this, Santos?" I yelled.

My wet fingers slid around my gun. I Retracted the water and gripped tighter. *Deep inhale. Slow and steady exhale.* A new drop of sweat rolled down my chest.

He made another turn, gun raised. I stood and moved out from the cover of the rocks, bracing myself. His eyes locked with mine. Simultaneously, he flung the knife and shot the gun. I Retracted them from his hands and Pushed like I never had before. My shield radiated out from my body with a swell of energy that spilled from the center of me. Electricity crackled and scorched the plants around me.

Santos's body flew backward through the air like he'd been hit with a shock wave.

What the hell did I do?

I leaned back against the boulder to regain my equilibrium and watched him.

After a moment of no movement, Santos rolled over, groaning. He cringed as he sat up, looking at the scorched earth in front of him. "You've got some skills. Just as good as Nick, from what I saw." What? He knew Nick?

Santos stood. "Your dad would be interested in your progress."

"*NO!*" Reid yelled. He came into view not far from Santos, the moonlight reflecting off his sweaty face. "Don't talk to her. Talk to me." His eyes focused on Santos. "Why? Why are you doing this?"

Santos barked a sarcastic laugh. "Do you have any idea how annoying it's been to watch you these last years? To see you squander your powers? It's not fair that you Anomalies have all the power. Can't you see that? The serum would allow me, and any other Pusher or Retractor, to be just as strong as you. Besides, your precious Resistance isn't exactly who they claim to be. You need to reevaluate—"

"*No,*" Reid boomed. "*You* need to reevaluate your beliefs." Reid's body shook with anger. "You hurt innocent people. You're willing to put Josie in danger. You are a disgrace and a traitor and—"

"*I'm* a traitor?" Santos cackled. "Don't talk to me about loyalty, Reid. You don't even know what that is." He turned to me. "Josie, why don't you ask Reid about betrayal? He's an expert. Have him tell you about the time he shot his best friend dead."

My gaze shifted to Reid. What was Santos eluding to? Reid didn't respond. He'd frozen, staring blankly at Santos. "Reid?" The word came out a whisper but he turned to me, the moonlight highlighting his sorrowful eyes.

No, no, no.

He killed him. Reid *killed my brother.*

They'd let me think Nick was crazy, that the Resistance had acted out of mercy, for the greater good. And maybe they had. But Reid—Cal, my brother's best friend—he had been the one to pull the trigger.

I fell to my knees, my lungs burning and heart aching. What had begun as a crack in my soul spread into a gaping fissure.

My brother died. Okay.

My dad was gone. Okay.

My mom put me in harm's way and abandoned me. Okay.

But the only person I let make me feel…no.

Reid was the one who was real. Reid was the only one who anchored me to reality, and now I didn't have that. There was no moving forward from this spot. No matter what I did, there was no winning. I'd lost everyone.

"Josie." I usually liked the timbre of Reid's voice, but right now, he might as well spit venom at me.

The tears streamed out, scorching my cheeks. *"DON'T!"* It was a primal scream.

"I didn't mean to kill him, Josie. And there hasn't been a day that I don't hate myself and regret it. If I could undo it, I would. I was waiting for the right time to—"

Two bullets tagged the rocks next to me, just outside my shield. Santos scurried away, his back to me.

Reid fired off a slew of bullets, but they didn't penetrate Santos's shield.

So I Pushed my shield again, sending out another shock wave, and he fell face-first to the tropical forest floor.

For some reason, I could feel his hold slipping on his shield. I sensed the energy he was using, the molecules around him. The molecules in everything.

Three. His shield was shrinking. *Two*. It was just outside his body. *One*.

Knowing Santos couldn't Retract, I Pushed hundreds of pounds of chains around him. I Retracted the ground beneath him, causing the forest floor to disappear at the same moment. But in the same moment, Reid launched himself at Santos and Santos Pushed the same chains around Reid. Reid's body, weighting down by the chains, fell short of

Santos, inches from the edge of the forest floor. I Retracted Reid's chains, but they reappeared the second before both bodies hit the water, still bound.

I Pushed.

A bolt of lightning hit Santos.

Both bodies sank under the surface.

Reid.

I ran, sucked in as much air as I could fit in my lungs, and dove off the edge into the ocean.

The cold water bit at my face and swept over my body like shards of glass. Sweeping my arms behind me and kicking, I propelled myself down and forward. Reid. But I couldn't see. I Pushed. My air was running out and therefore my energy. I Pushed flippers, a scuba tank, and the accompanying mouthpiece outfitted with a light.

I found both Reid and Santos unconscious and sinking.

As soon as Reid's body came into view, I Retracted the chains, Pushed scuba gear onto him. Wrapping my arms around him, I held his unresponsive body close and Pushed a raft under us. I didn't care at that point if someone could see us emerge from the Gulf—I just needed to get him out safely.

We broke the surface, and a wave toppled us from the raft. I Retracted my air tank and mask, the waves crashing over my head. One moment he was next to me and the next, the waves carried him away. "Reid!"

I couldn't see him. My skull throbbed unbearably. My limbs weakened, I sensed my body shutting down, becoming lethargic, my energy depleted. "Reid!" I cried.

I rode the waves into shore and slowly made it to my feet.

I Pushed the infrared glasses on my face again. "Reid," I

screamed with no response. Nothing showed up through the glasses.

I'd just killed Santos with a bolt of lightning. And if that didn't do the trick, drowning while unconscious would. Plus, now, I didn't know if Reid had made it—if he was alive. My stomach lurched and my heart physically ached. The hurt from taking someone's life, the hurt from losing someone I cared about—it was too much.

No. No. No.

I needed to find Reid. I wouldn't stop until I found him.

I ran along the shoreline back to the resort, scanning the water for Reid. No cops cluttered along the shore. No Secret Service or Special Ops or any other covert group—Oculi or Planck— stirred beyond the mangroves. If the gunfire or grenades had drawn attention, the storm raging above in a cacophony of thunder and lightning must have obscured it. I heard a helicopter in the distance and distinguished its flickering lights reflecting off the water as it flew in low and fast.

The black chopper hovered over the water for a few moments, the Consortium assassin Reid had fought visible from the side. They either didn't see me or didn't care. Then it flew north. I stayed there in the open, as the heavens opened up and rain poured down on me, scanning the beach, searching for Reid.

I consciously wished the rain would stop, and the water tapered to a drizzle before it ceased altogether. Only a few dark clouds remained. The remnants of the storm, of the electrical energy in it, hummed along my skin. The sharp smell of ozone lingered in the air. My abilities were more powerful than I knew possible. And I was sure they'd only grow stronger as I mastered and explored my abilities.

I staggered along the beach, searching for Reid. I had to find him.

25.

JOSIE

When I'd jumped in the ocean, I didn't know if I'd live. And if I did live, I didn't know if Reid would. And that mattered more than I ever imagined.

I heard my name over the waves. I spun and almost collapsed when I saw him standing. Was I hallucinating? I couldn't breathe—and I wouldn't breathe until I touched him.

I pushed my toes into the sand, propelling myself forward. As I ran, I decided I didn't care what I'd said, what he'd said, what was expected or not expected of us. I needed him. In what way? I didn't know. But I needed him.

My legs burned, my ribs hurt, and my chest heaved, but I ran as hard as my body allowed. I jumped into him, throwing my arms around his neck. His body collided with mine and he swept me up into his arms. He was real.

His head landed in the crook of my neck. "Josie," he mumbled against my skin. "Josie." His lips grazed my neck,

setting fire to my body. His mouth brushed along my collar-
bone and back up my neck. His touch was like air — I needed
it to survive.

I pulled my head back to see his face, to make sure he
was all right. He let me slip through his arms, my body sliding
against his, until my feet hit the ground.

I filled my lungs with the salty ocean breeze and let out a
long sigh. Allowing my head to fall against Reid's chest, the
tension fell from my muscles. I steadied myself by placing my
hands on his chest. One of his hands landed on the small of
my back and the other brushed my jawline, pulling my gaze
back to his face.

"Josie, I'm sorry. I didn't want to do it. I didn't want to
shoot Nick, but he'd murdered people, was ready to expose
us. You have to believe me…when I killed him, I killed a
piece of myself, too. A piece I'll never get back."

His gaze slid to the right of my face.

"And I don't know how I didn't realize Santos was playing
me. I led him straight to you. I put you in danger. I…How
could I have missed it?" His head shook in disbelief. "He
was my friend. The only friend I allowed myself after what
happened with Nick and…I don't…" His voice cracked.

I knew the pain in his eyes. I knew it intimately. It was the
kind of hurt you felt in your bones.

Tears streamed down my cheeks. I knew he was telling
me the truth. He was a good guy. How many times had he
saved me in a week's time? Every one of his movements and
decisions were thoughtful. He didn't take any of this lightly.
And he'd been willing to die for me.

His eyes held mine as he wiped away my tears with his

thumb. "Forgive me."

I couldn't speak. I had so much going on in my head, so much to process. I just nodded.

Both of his hands held my face, and he dipped his head to mine cautiously, like he was measuring to see what was acceptable or not. His soft lips pressed to mine, and my eyes closed against my will. He gave me a gentle, sweet kiss.

Resting his forehead against mine, he moved his hands to my back, helping hold up my weary body. "I thought I'd lost you." His voice was velvety. "And I can't lose you."

I cleared my throat and nodded. "I'm too important to the Resistance."

His brows knitted together, then a ghost of a smile tugged at his lips. "No. You're too important to me."

I smiled. But it quickly faded. "Reid…something's happening to me."

Then the world tilted and I felt myself falling, slipping into darkness.

Reid

One second Josie was on the verge of smiling, and the next she'd crumpled to the ground. I caught her head, keeping it from striking the sand. "Josie? Josie?" This happened to Nick a few times after excessive Pushing and Retracting. Between the storm—which I was fairly certain she conjured—and the forest, she'd overexerted herself.

She made a sound in the back of her throat and moved

her head but didn't open her eyes. She should be okay after some rest, but I still didn't like it.

I carried Josie farther along the beach to the winding path that cut through the mangroves and back to the main roads. We exited to a silent street. A handful of cars were parked in metered spots beneath the streetlights. I Pushed an older model Mercedes. The better to blend in with the campaign fundraiser/award ceremony attendants. I jogged to the car and set Josie on her feet, leaning on me. She slumped against my side. I settled her across the backseat, then climbed in the driver's side and started toward the tiny hole-in-the-wall motel I'd checked out when we first came to town.

We pulled up to the motel, off Highway 75, hidden behind several larger buildings and surrounded by pines. The *L* flickered on and off. The *MOTE* had seen better days. Like maybe in the sixties. A single light highlighted each grungy red door, except the one on the far end. In a movie, someone would probably die in a motel like this.

I parked in the stall directly in front of the lobby window, so I could keep an eye on the car while I booked us a room. I Pushed a blanket to cover Josie in the backseat. We couldn't take a chance that anyone would see her.

The old lady behind the check-in desk looked cozy, with her nose buried in a romance novel and her feet slung across a stained recliner. I checked in and swung back to Josie in less than three minutes. I moved the car down in front of our room—the one missing the overhead light on the end. A banyan tree blocked the view of the car from the main road. To be safe, I Pushed the exterior of the car to match a beat-up Taurus.

I bent into the backseat to pick up Josie, letting the blanket fall away. Placing my head by her face, I waited for her breath on my cheek and watched her chest rise and fall. The movement was slight, but it was there. I placed my fingers on her neck and found a pulse. Like a drained battery, she'd be out of commission until she recharged.

I carefully scooped her into my arms, checked the area for anyone watching, and carried her into the room. I Pushed an entirely new bed, including *Avenger* sheets like Josie's.

I sat next to her on the bed, one dim table lamp illuminating her face. I didn't know how long I stared at her, memorizing her face as if it wasn't already imprinted onto my brain. Eventually, she stirred, and I stretched out so my face was in front of hers. "Josie?"

Her eyes blinked open and she grabbed her head. "What happened? Where are we?"

"You fainted—I think you've used a lot of energy today. We're in a motel."

She shifted up to a seated position.

"Go slow," I cautioned. "How do you feel physically?"

She shook her head. "I feel...okay." Her gaze fell to the bed and her fingertips traced the outline of Thor printed on the sheets.

Not wanting to rush her, I waited for her to talk. After a few minutes, she finally cleared her throat but continued to study the bed sheets. "I killed people," she said quietly. "Well, I killed Santos for sure." Her head shook. I understood the overwhelming feelings that came with taking a life. It would require time to process this, to move past it. If I were being honest, most people never did. Killing...stayed with a person.

And in this war, I suspected there would be many casualties before the end.

She lifted her face to mine. "I'm sorry I killed him. I didn't want to hurt him. I really...I don't want to be vengeful." Her face dropped to the bed again. "How could I end a life? That's..."

"Hey," I said, pulling her chin up. "Don't you dare apologize. You were protecting yourself against someone who intended to harm you. Besides, he wasn't my friend—it was an act."

I needed to get her mind off Santos's death and, thankfully, I had something that might do just that.

I dug in my pocket, held my hand out to Josie, and she automatically opened her hand under mine. "This was left for you." I let the tiny memory card fall into her hand. "By your mom.

"Here." I pulled out my phone. "You can use it in here." She silently offered the rectangle back to me and watched as I inserted the memory card and accessed the storage. "There's only one thing on here. A video." I got it set to play, then handed Josie my phone.

This message was personal—I didn't need to hear it. "I'll step outside the door and give you—"

"No!" Her hand clasped around my forearm. "Don't. Don't leave," she pleaded, the fear in her voice thick.

"'Kay."

Her finger hit the triangle, and her mother came onto the screen. It appeared as if she'd videoed herself with a phone.

Mrs. Harper cleared her throat and began. "Josie, we received intel that the mission had been compromised. Your brother was sent to a safe place, and I left town as a decoy. We'd hoped the operatives would advance on me."

A deep crease formed between Josie's brows.

"As of right now," the video continued, "I don't know how this will turn out, but you must know that I asked you to do this not because I wanted to put you in danger, but because you are the only person in this world I trust. You are a good person—so good and bright and caring. I knew you could complete the mission. I had every faith in you." A tear rolled down Mrs. Harper's cheek and dropped off her face.

"You are one of my best accomplishments in life, alongside your brothers. I know I don't always show it and I'm sorry for that. Just know…I love you more than any serum or cause. I love you more than life. I'm so proud of you."

Rivers of emotion fell from Josie's eyes. She cried, yet the corners of her lips turned upward in the smallest smile. I gently rubbed her shoulder. I didn't know what kind of comfort or support to give in this situation. I shot off the bed to retrieve the box of tissues and stuffed one in Josie's free hand.

Mrs. Harper continued on the video. "The Hub is expecting you, but they do not know that you'll be trying to identify the leak, that you'll be on your own mission. If you decide not to do this, I understand. It is asking a lot of you. Either way, I'll be in touch with you soon." Mrs. Harper wiped the tears from her cheeks. "I love you, Josie." Her mom ended with a smile.

Josie grinned at the video through pools of tears. I'd never realized how much someone else's hurt and healing could affect my own—until now.

Josie set the phone on the nightstand next to the lamp,

and I shoved more tissues into her hands. "You wanna talk?"
I asked.

Her head shook. "About Mom? Eventually, but not yet.
Thank you. Will…will you hold me again?"

I smiled. "As long as you want me to." Josie's head rested
on my chest, and I wrapped my arms around her. I Pushed the
lamp off and we laid together in the dark.

"This is so screwed up," she said after a couple of minutes.
"Do you think we'll survive?"

"It is. Everything happens for a reason, though. We have
to believe that or there is no hope. But you don't have to go
to the Hub. You have a choice. You can go into the Hub with
me or you can go into hiding. Or do whatever you want. With
or without me." I'd never willingly leave her, but I didn't have
to be next to her at all times to keep her safe.

Did I want her to tell me to leave her? Did I want her
to choose to do something without me? If I was honest with
myself, no. I was a selfish bastard. I wanted to be with her, no
matter what she wanted to do. But the choice was hers, not
mine.

Silence filled the air. "Josie?"

"I'm going to the Hub. With you. That's my choice."

I pulled her tighter.

"Reid?"

"Yeah?"

"This is just the beginning, isn't it?"

"Yeah. Santos isn't the only Oculi who wants the serum.
Now that it's out in the world, in the VP's hands, there are
going to be others dying for it. This is war."

Josie

We rumbled down the road, the sun not above the rooftops yet, the sky painted pink.

I wasn't sure I'd ever sleep again after personally taking someone's life. Visions of a figure bound in chains, falling into the ocean, haunted my slumber. The same dream played on repeat but in the last one, the dream before I woke, I could see the person thrashing underwater. Then, like the camera zoomed in, I saw the person's face. And it wasn't Santos. It was me.

I wanted to talk to Reid about it, but I couldn't yet.

"Can we swing by the school on our way out of town?" I yelled into his ear.

He laughed. "Only you would want to blow kisses good-bye to your school." I pulled my hand off my thigh and put it in his peripheral, then gave him the backward Vulcan salute. "You're not supposed to distract the driver," he shouted over the engine.

We pulled up to the main entrance of the school, Stingy the Sting Ray statue greeting us. Reid gave me his cocky half smile. "I'll give you two a moment alone."

I rolled my eyes at his smartass comment and left him on the idling bike.

I slid my hand over what had become my usual lunch table. All I'd wanted was my own life when I thought everything was going against me. But it was in me all along. The ability to create my own reality.

I slapped the concrete table.

Reid watched me quietly and didn't make any wisecracks when I jogged back to him. We took off on the bike again, and I glanced over my shoulder to watch my school shrink to a dot on the horizon. *Good-bye, Planck life.*

Ten minutes later, Reid and I were one stoplight away from the onramp for the interstate highway.

Leaving everything I knew behind me, I traveled in the direction of uncertainty. Though I didn't know what the future held, I knew I'd have more choices presented to me. And it was what I did with those choices that would make all the difference.

ACKNOWLEDGMENTS

First, I thank God for a world full of possibilities. Then I must thank you, readers, for taking a chance and picking up this book.

A heartfelt thank-you to Liz Pelletier, my editor and publisher, for giving me the opportunity to turn my dreams into reality. Mountains of gratitude and rivers of gold wouldn't be enough to express my appreciation and love for my friend and agent, Nicole Resciniti. Thank you, Nic. Stacy Abrams (who is made of pure awesome), Meredith Johnson, Robin Haseltine, and Tiffany Inman, thank you for being editing ninjas. Debbie Suzuki, Heather Riccio, and Deb Shapiro, thank you for your guidance and publicity work.

Thank you to: Marisa Cleveland, you got this party started and I wouldn't be where I am without you; Eliza Tilton, Laura Stanford, Lisa Burstein, for your crits over the years; amazing authors who've provided writer love and friendship—Cecy Robson, Kate SeRine, Jessica Lemmon, Elizabeth Eulberg, Dawn Chartier, Lydia Kang, Danielle Young, Mary Weber, Brenna Ehrlich, and Cole Gibsen; Kate Brauning and Lynne

Matson (my personal Yodas) for taking "crit partner" to a different level. Love you, ladies. To my local Starbucks baristas, you guys rock.

To my dear friends, Courtney Suarez, Claudia Lokamas, and Debi Auch Moedy, who've cheered me on since day one, you have no idea what that means to me. Your friendship is priceless. Thanks to the Kuper family for your ongoing support—I'm so fortunate to have the cool in-laws. Mom (Mary Youngblood), Dad (Dean Youngblood), and Deanna Trout (my rad sister), along with her fam, Brian, Toby, and Cheyenne, your enthusiasm and encouragement has filled my heart—thank you. Fletcher and Sullivan, thank you for sharing me with my characters and being the best part of my reality. Your compassion and silliness is what inspires me. Chaz, this book wouldn't exist without you. You've made sacrifices and given more than you had, just to see my goals realized. You believed in me even when I didn't. I'll never be able to thank you enough, but I'll spend the rest of my life trying. My three boys, you are my everything—I love you.

What would you kill for?

After a brutal nuclear war, the United States was left decimated. A small group of survivors eventually banded together, but only after more conflict over which family would govern the new nation. The Westfalls lost. Fifty years later, peace and control are maintained by marrying the daughters of the losing side to the sons of the winning group in a yearly ritual.

This year, it is my turn.

My name is Ivy Westfall, and my mission is simple: to kill the president's son—my soon-to-be husband—and return the Westfall family to power.

But Bishop Lattimer is either a very skilled actor or he's not the cruel, heartless boy my family warned me to expect. He might even be the one person in this world who truly understands me. But there is no escape from my fate. I am the only one who can restore the Westfall legacy.

Because Bishop *must* die. And I must be the one to kill him…

From Chapter 1

"And today, for the first time, we have a marriage between a Lattimer and a Westfall," President Lattimer says with a smile. It looks genuine to me, and maybe it is. But I also know what this marriage means to him. It's another way to cement his power, which is what he is really happy about. After my father, there will be no more Westfalls. It's not enough for President Lattimer that the Westfall line has run out—he has to turn my children into Lattimers, too.

"Up until now, neither one of our families has been very good at producing girls," President Lattimer continues. There is a rumble of laughter from the crowd, but I can't bring myself to join in, even though I know I should. When the chuckles die down, President Lattimer holds up the envelope for everyone to see. "The president's son and the founder's daughter," he calls.

My father was not the founder, of course. It was his father who founded this town and was then usurped by Alexander Lattimer and his followers. But it was established early on that the original founder's descendant would take on the title of founder, the same way Alexander Lattimer's descendant is called president. It's a meaningless title. The founder has no say in how the nation is run. He's only a ceremonial figurehead, trotted out to prove how peaceful we are. How well our system of government works. The title of founder is like giving a beautifully wrapped present with nothing inside. They hope we'll be so distracted by the shiny outside, we won't notice the box is empty.

"Bishop Lattimer," the president calls out in a clear, ringing voice. The sound of the envelope, the paper tearing, seems as loud as a scream to my ears. I can feel hundreds of eyes on me and I hold my head high. President Lattimer draws the paper out with a flourish and smiles in my direction. He mouths my name, *Ivy Westfall*, but I can't hear him over the ringing in my ears and the pounding of my heart.

I take a final deep breath, trying to draw courage into my lungs like air. Trying to stomp down the anger that buzzes through my veins like poison. I stand, my legs steadier than I thought they would be. My heels click on the tile floor as I make my way to the stairs. Behind me, the crowd claps and shouts, a few irreverent whistles punctuating the chaos. As I start up the stairs, President Lattimer reaches down and takes my elbow.

"Ivy," he says. "We're glad you're joining our family." His eyes are warm. I feel betrayed by them. They should be icy and indifferent, to match the rest of him.

"Thank you," I say, with a steady voice that doesn't sound like my own. "I'm glad, too."

Once I'm onstage, the other couples move even closer to the edge so that I can make my way to the center, where Bishop Lattimer waits for me. I hold his unwavering gaze. He is even taller than I thought, but I am tall, too, and for once my height is a blessing. I would not want this boy to dwarf me. I feel powerless enough already.

He has dark hair, like his father. Although up close, I can see lighter streaks in among the coffee brown strands, as if he's spent a lot of time outdoors, under the sun. That makes sense given the rumors I've heard about him over the years: that he prefers to be outdoors rather than in, that his father has to force him to attend council meetings, and that he's more often found rafting on the river than inside City Hall.

His eyes are a cool, clear green, and they study me with an intensity that makes my stomach cramp. His gaze is neither hostile nor welcoming but appraising, like I am a problem he is figuring out how to solve. He doesn't come toward me, but when I get close enough to hold out a hand, as I've been coached to do, he takes it in his. His fingers are warm and strong when they close over mine. He squeezes my hand briefly, which startles the breath in my throat. Was he trying to be kind? Reassure me? I don't know, because when I glance at him, his eyes are on the minister waiting in the wings.

"Let's begin," President Lattimer says. Everyone on the stage shifts into position, standing across from their intended spouse, Bishop and me in the center where everyone in the audience can watch. Bishop takes my other hand in his, our hands joined across the small space between us.

I want to shout out that this is wrong. That I don't know this boy across from me. Have never had a single conversation with him in my entire life. He doesn't know that my favorite color is purple or that I still miss the mother I don't remember or that I am terrified. I shoot a panicked glance out to the audience but see only smiling faces reflected back at me. Somehow, that makes it even worse, the way everyone goes along with this charade. How no one ever cries out or tries to stop their child from marrying a stranger.

Our compliance is the strongest weapon President Lattimer has in his arsenal.

And, in the end, I'm just as bad as the rest of them. I open my mouth when everyone else does, repeat the words I can't even hear over dozens of louder voices around me. I tell myself that none of it matters. I have to get through this part, and so I do. I slide the plain gold band that was my father's onto Bishop's finger and he does the same with mine. The ring feels foreign against my skin, tight and confining even though the sizing is correct.

When the minister pronounces us man and wife, Bishop doesn't try to kiss me, not even on the cheek, and I am thankful. I don't think I could have stood it if he had. It would be like someone on the street grabbing me and planting his mouth on mine. An assault, not affection. But all around us, couples hug and cheer and most of them have no trouble kissing as if they've known each other for much longer than an hour. Will these girls be so happy in a few months when their bellies are heavy with babies and they realize they are stuck forever sleeping next to a boy they barely know?

For them this ceremony is about keeping the peace, about honoring a tradition that has worked to stabilize a society for more than two generations. But unlike them, I know how fragile that peace is, how it hangs by only a few slender threads that are even now being snipped. I am different from all these other girls surrounding me because marrying Bishop Lattimer has not fulfilled my destiny. My mission is not to make him happy and bear his children and be his wife.

My mission is to kill him.

Discover more page-turning books from Entangled Teen

Lux Beginnings, Collector's Edition

Featuring Obsidian *and* Onyx *by Jennifer L. Armentrout*

Obsidian

There's an alien next door. And with his looming height and eerie green eyes, he's hot...until he opens his mouth. He's infuriating. Arrogant. Stab-worthy. But when a stranger attacks me and Daemon literally freezes time with a wave of his hand, he lights me up with a big fat bulls-eye. Turns out he has a galaxy of enemies wanting to steal his abilities and the only way I'm getting out of this alive is by sticking close to him until my alien mojo fades. If I don't kill him first, that is.

Onyx

Daemon's determined to prove what he feels for me is more than a product of our bizarro alien connection. So I've sworn him off, even though he's running more hot than cold these days. But we've got bigger problems. I've seen someone who shouldn't be alive. And I have to tell Daemon, even though I know he's never going to stop searching until he gets the truth. What happened to his brother? Who betrayed him? And what does the DOD want from them—from me?

Lux Consequences, Collector's Edition
Featuring Opal and Origin by Jennifer L. Armentrout

Opal

After everything, I'm no longer the same Katy. I'm different... And I'm not sure what that will mean in the end. When each step we take in discovering the truth puts us in the path of the secret organization responsible for torturing and testing alien hybrids, the more I realize there is no end to what I'm capable. The death of someone close still lingers, help comes from the most unlikely source, and friends will become the deadliest of enemies, but we won't turn back. Even if the outcome will shatter our worlds forever.

Origin

Daemon will do anything to get Katy back. After the successful but disastrous raid on Mount Weather, he's facing the impossible. Katy is gone. Taken. Everything becomes about finding her. But the most dangerous foe has been there all along, and when the truths are exposed and the lies come crumbling down, which side will Daemon and Katy be standing on? And will they even be together?

Mirror X

By Karri Thomspon

At the age of seventeen, I was put into a cryogenic tube and frozen. Now, more than a thousand years later, I've finally been awakened to a more serene and peaceful future. Or have I? Everyone is young. Everyone is banded and tracked. And everyone is keeping secrets. Not even Michael Bennett, the cute geneticist in the hospital, is being honest with me. When I'm told only I can save the human race from extinction, it's clear my freeze didn't avoid a dreadful fate. It only delayed the horror...

Gravity

By Melissa West

In the future, only one rule will matter: Don't. Ever. Peek. Ari Alexander just broke that rule and saw the last person she expected hovering above her bed — arrogant Jackson Locke. Jackson issues a challenge: help him, or everyone on Earth will die. Giving Jackson the information he needs will betray her father and her country, but keeping silent will start a war.